MORGANTOWN

DIFFICULTY AT THE BEGINNING
BOOK TWO

Keith Maillard

BRINDLE
& GLASS

Library and Archives Canada Cataloguing in Publication
Maillard, Keith, 1942-
Difficulty at the beginning / Keith Maillard.

Contents: bk. 1. Running — bk. 2. Morgantown —
bk. 3. Lyndon Johnson and the majorettes — bk. 4. Looking good.
ISBN 1-897142-06-4 (bk. 1).—ISBN 1-897142-07-2 (bk. 2).—
ISBN 1-897142-08-0 (bk. 3).—ISBN 1-897142-09-9 (bk. 4)

I. Title.

PS8576.A49D54 2005   C813/.54   C2005-903472-6

Cover photography: Mary Maillard; Model: Tessa Maria Maud Schick
Author photo: Mary Maillard

Acknowledgements: The story that Natalie reads to John (p. 67) is Frank R. Stockton's *The
Griffin and the Minor Canon* (1885). The opening line is quoted.

Canada Council   Conseil des Arts
for the Arts   du Canada

Brindle & Glass Publishing acknowledges the support of the Canada Council for the Arts
and the Alberta Foundation for the Arts for our publishing program.

Brindle & Glass Publishing
www.brindleandglass.com

1   2   3   4   5   09   08   07   06

PRINTED AND BOUND IN CANADA

ABOVE *The Abysmal, Water*

BELOW *The Arousing, Thunder*

Difficulty at the Beginning
works supreme success.

Morgantown
1962–1963

Part One

1.

THESE ROADS—back-tracking, ass-kissing, built in Depression years when water runoff was more important than high-speed travel so that many of the curves were banked backwards and others so sharp they'd become landmarks in themselves—these insane mountain roads, I thought, must be the very geography of hell for someone from someplace flat, and all of them, according to the map in the West Virginia University Catalogue, lead to Morgantown. "There's your mold, Dupre," Revington said as we shot over the crest of the final hill in the blue evening, as we saw the lights laid out below us in that characteristic smoky haze of the city which could be either heartbreakingly beautiful—evanescent greys and slates, ambers and duns—or the very personification of melancholy. "The mold," Revington said again, chewing the word as though he enjoyed the weight of it in his mouth, "the Morgantown mold."

"It always excites me when I see it for the first time," I said, "when we come around that last curve and there it is . . . the city, the river . . . laid out like that. It always touches me. I think it's the only time I love the place."

"No," Revington said, "it's not this dumb little town you love, it's the road. You wouldn't give a shit where you were going as long as you were moving."

He wasn't entirely right, but he was right enough, and if he knew me really well, I knew him just as well; for years I had watched this absurdly handsome scion of our hometown's aristocracy try out one role after another in the continuing drama that always starred himself: the madcap class fool, the menacing fifties hood, the urbane man of the world, and now—with hair falling over his dark face and three days' growth on his lean jaws—the bleakly ironic survivor of darkest despair. He checked his watch. "Did it," he said dryly—that is, he'd just driven from Raysburg to Morgantown faster than he'd ever done it before. "For what it's worth," he said. He relaxed visibly, slumped, stretched his forearms, pressed his hands against the wheel.

"Yeah, I love moving," I told him, "but it's more than that. It's something I feel about specific places. It's . . . I don't know. It's the site of the suffering, the battle. It's like that thing Hemingway talks about, that finally all that will be left will be the bare record, the location and the date. And I feel it too, that eventually I'll be able to write, 'Morgantown, West Virginia, November, 1962,' and that will say everything."

"So it excites you to return to the site of your suffering? Yeah," sighing, "but only as a movie. But when you're in it . . . Fuck, John, it's just dull, stupid, banal, boring," and then he glanced at me with a quick flash of smile, a signal that he'd caught something. "What it comes down to," he said, his voice no longer flat, now resonant, "do you enjoy finding new places to hang your toothbrush?"

"Oh, you guys," Cohen said from the backseat.

"Another party heard from," Revington said.

"The delegate from Nirvana," I said and turned to look at Cohen who was leaning against the window, his legs drawn up. He was so compact he fit neatly there, at ease in that small space. "In the Northern Mahayana . . ." Cohen began.

"In the Romantic Movement," Revington said, "as in the Bowel Movement . . ."

We all laughed. But Cohen persisted. "In the Northern Mahayana there are awesome hells full of the most hideous demons imaginable. But there are also infinite numbers of compassionate beings waiting to help you. You're surrounded by them on all sides. They're reaching out to you . . . Bodhisattvas. All you have to do is make one step toward them, and they're already at your side . . . angels of infinite light."

"That may be all well and good for John," Revington said. "He claims to live in hell. He could use an angel or two. But for me it's just purgatory. No. Worse than that. Limbo."

"Yeah, angels would be nice," I said, "but demons are more my speed. I keep thinking that one of these days I'm going to meet the devil on the road . . . you know, like in one of those old mountain songs."

"And it'd be a kind of relief, wouldn't it?" Revington said, "to know there's really evil, to see it personified. Yeah, he'd probably turn out to be like Death in *The Seventh Seal*. Completely matter-of-fact, no big deal at all. 'Hi, son, I'm Satan . . . and you're screwed.'"

Revington and I were twenty, Cohen nineteen. We'd just spent Thanksgiving at home in Raysburg. Revington had volunteered to drive me back down to WVU, and it hadn't been hard to talk Cohen into coming with us—taking one of his unofficial leaves from Harvard that never seemed to hurt his grades any. I was in my third year of university, Cohen in his second, and Revington was out of school, either officially withdrawn, temporarily suspended, or irrevocably flunked out of Yale—I'd heard him tell it all three ways. (What he'd told *me* was that he'd found it somewhat difficult to pass courses taught in New Haven when he'd been stoned in New York.)

We pulled up in the alley that led to my basement apartment. "It's weird," I said, "for at least a week after I come back, I'm always happy." And I was particularly happy to see again the narrow concrete passageway outside my door; it was one of my favorite spots. I could stand for hours there, smoking, sheltered from the rain, staring up at that narrow slice of ominous grey Morgantown sky.

"Of course you're happy," Revington said. "It may be a

half-assed school, but at least you're *in* school."

Amazed at my own foresight, I found two quarts of beer in my ancient refrigerator, opened one for Revington and me. Cohen, who never drank alcohol, put a pan of water on the stove to boil.

"You had the right idea, ace," Revington said to me. "I should have said fuck the Ivy League and come down here." He shook himself and stretched. He was too tall for the ceiling, pressed the palms of his hands flat against it. "Jesus," he said, "that drive burned me out."

He slumped back against the wall, slid down it to arrive on the floor. "You know what really pisses me off?" he said. "All that crap we went through at the Academy . . . and it was supposed to prepare us for college. Good God, what horseshit. Do you ever think how pointless our education was? How *monkish*? How absolutely useless for anything in the modern world? Riflery, close-order drill, athletics and cold showers, four years of Latin . . ."

"I wouldn't have minded going to school with girls," I said.

"Right," Cohen said, "and I certainly could have used something that covered the basics of rocketry, deep space navigation, orienteering on alien planets . . ."

"You know, ace," Revington said, assuming the flabbergasted voice of someone who has just made a fabulous new discovery, "you really are out of your fucking mind." This was a standard routine between the two of them. Cohen laughed as he always did.

Cohen never went anywhere without a tea ball and several varieties of tea: the plain green tea you'd get in any Chinese restaurant, the exotic smoky Lapsang Souchong I was sure he'd chosen for the name as well as for the flavor, Earl Grey, because, he said, how could you resist something as startling as bergamot?

He let the water come to a full boil, took the tea out of his knapsack, turned the heat off, allowed the water to cool a specific length of time measured by his Swiss wristwatch, and then slowly filled a mug. It was his personal tea ceremony. The scent of Asia diffused into the room.

I found it hard to describe Bill Cohen. *Wiry* is a word often used for people who are strong but not massive, but it wouldn't work for him. He was the only person I'd ever met who'd developed those distinctive half-moon formations of muscle on either side of the abdomen that the Greeks carved so carefully into their statuary; what he might have done to get them remained a mystery to him. He'd swum and run track at the Academy, had been a dependable back-up man but far from an outstanding athlete. Like me, he was a great walker and climber of hills. It was easy to think of him as small and forget that he could draw a sixty-pound bow to full hunter's nock over and over again without the slightest sign of strain—but it *was* his smallness, compactness, that stayed in my mind—a neat cat quality like a cartoon Felix. His eyes were green, his nose narrow and pointed, his hair a mass of tight black curls. He couldn't sing at all, couldn't begin to carry a tune, but his voice had at times a peculiar chanting inflection as if he were *nearly* singing—in a gentle, chiding tone: "Dupre, Dupre," or "Oh, you guys." He gestured when he talked, great sweeps of the hands. He dressed like a gunslinger in an old western—jeans riding on his hipbones, a broad belt with a Navajo silver buckle, expensive hand-tooled cowboy boots. Not always, but sometimes, he moved through the world with the focused intensity of a mime. He was the only boy I'd ever known I would have called beautiful.

I thought Revington must have fallen asleep slumped against the wall, but now he pushed himself to his feet, poured himself a second glass of beer, and began to pace up and down my living room. Given how small it was, he couldn't work up much of a pace. He glanced at the bulletin board where I'd pinned up the last stanza of Rilke's *"Herbsttag"* in the original German and sent me a look that said, "Who do you think you're kidding?"

He tilted toward the wall to survey my picture of the Buddha reclining in Nirvana and the print Cohen had sent me: a Buddhist monk leaning on his staff, watching two cocks fight. He smiled when he read my version of the Buddha's Four Noble Truths:

  1.) All sentient beings suffer.
  2.) Suffering arises from attachment.
  3.) End attachment, end suffering.
  4.) There is a way out of this shit.

He moved on to examine my bookcase and the altar to young girls I'd constructed on top of it—complete with candles and incense. The cinema princesses—Lori Martin, Sue Lyon, Hayley Mills, Eleonora Brown, Valeria Ciangottini—and then my personal princesses, the real ones. "Ah, the jerk-off corner," he said.

"Angels," Cohen said.

"No," Revington said, "just ordinary female *Homo sapiens* of the barely pubescent variety. You know, John, some people shouldn't be allowed to read *Lolita*."

He pointed to a photograph of Natalie Hewitt, my girlfriend from last year. "So what's happened to this mature, sophisticated, and highly articulate young lady?" It was a candid shot, typically Natalie, that I'd taken of her sitting on the front porch at my Allen Street apartment. She was bent over her Spanish guitar, her long lovely hair drawing a line down her cheek. She was wearing a baggy sweatshirt, pedal pushers, and ballerina flats. Natalie was a tall girl, but, with nothing in the picture for comparison, any sense of her height was lost, and she didn't appear to have any more figure than a twelve-year-old. She and Revington had despised each other. "She's at Swarthmore," I said, my annoyance growing by the second.

"And what do we have here? Why, it's the fair Miss Cassandra Markapolous." He raised an eyebrow at me. He still hadn't forgiven me for dating Cassy when she'd been fourteen.

"And I'm glad to see that you're still cultivating your original neurosis." He tapped his index finger against the photograph. "The lovely Miss Linda Edmonds, Homecoming Queen."

He traded in his sardonic, bantering voice for one of weary gloom. "Why can't we ever find one that just stays with us? That goddamned wench." Meaning, of course, Barbara Daniels, his high-school girlfriend; she'd been his first love just as Linda had been mine. "And don't tell me, Cohen, that unrequited love is a contradiction in terms." He paced to the end of the room and back.

"Do you think it would have made any difference," Revington asked me, "if it had worked out for us?"

"Yeah, I think it would," I said. "Everything might have fallen into place."

"That's right," he said. "I might still be in school."

"Oh, you guys," Cohen said.

I couldn't tell if Revington was genuinely annoyed or if it was merely another performance: with a sweeping gesture like that of a villain in a silent movie, he turned toward Cohen as though to cut him off in the small space. "Hey, ace, have you ever even kissed a girl?"

Cohen was fully aware of how odd he must have seemed to us—he'd yet to have his first date—but if he minded being the butt of Revington's humor, he never showed it. "Spin the bottle in grade school," he said, laughing.

"No, you hopeless jerk, I mean really *kissed* a girl."

7

Cohen smiled. "No," he said.

Revington crouched in front of him, grinning. "Now here's the real question. Have you ever wanted to?"

Cohen thought about it. "Last summer at the pool," he said, "there was a girl. She was lying on the next beach towel. She had glorious long blonde Rapunzel hair. She looked as though she'd spent most of her summer in the sun. She was golden. She had on a bikini, and she had a little round tummy. I don't mean she was fat . . . just a little round tummy. And I wanted to kiss her . . . on her little round tummy."

"Listen to that, will you?" Revington said—Ben Gant's line from *Look Homeward Angel* that he'd been quoting ever since we'd read it in one of our English classes at the Academy. He arranged himself decoratively against the wall in a languid slouch. "Do you think he's conning us?"

"No," I said.

"You sound like my father," Cohen said and fell into a New York accent: "Bill, have you noticed how God created the human race? They come in two kinds, male and female . . . You *have* noticed? Don't get me wrong. I know you're a pretty bright kid. I just thought I'd point it out in case it slipped by you."

"A perceptive man, your father," Revington said. "Now here's another question. Have you been blessed with a sex drive? Yeah, how about *screwing?* Do you ever want to screw someone?" He pronounced the word as though singing comic opera, rolling the *r*: *sca-rrrooo.*

"Revington, Revington." Cohen said. He stood up and began pacing too. "No, I don't ever want to *screw* someone. Not that way. What's important is what happens between people . . . so if I get to know a girl, get close enough to her, sex will happen of its own accord . . . because we'll want to get closer, and then it will be the perfect thing to do." He smiled. "Of course I feel

8

desire too . . . on one level. On another level it just doesn't matter. And it doesn't matter what you say about it."

"You bastard," Revington said with affection, "either you *are* a saint, or you're the world's biggest asshole."

Only a few minutes earlier I'd been happy, but now I felt myself sinking into the old familiar pit. I didn't like to think about it, but I was just as much of a virgin as Bill Cohen. Sometimes I imagined us as the only two boys left in all of America who'd never been laid. But Cohen didn't seem to mind talking about it, didn't seem to mind who knew it, didn't even seem to mind being kidded about it, and I couldn't understand how he could be so cool, so unconcerned. I was ashamed of my own virginity, would never have admitted it to Revington, or to anyone else for that matter—not even Cohen—and I felt like a hypocrite. And, yes, here I was *back in Morgantown*—the site of my suffering—and, no, nothing was going to change. All I had to look forward to was more of the same old shit. "Hey," I said, "let's get out of here."

THE OWNER of The Seventh Circle had known enough Dante to come up with the name for the place but not enough to decorate it accurately—not evoking terrifying iciness, the absence of heat or light, but rather the most banal, man-in-the-street conception of hell: cartoon flames, demons with pitchforks. A grinning Satan with horns and tail presided over the bar; he looked more like a Budweiser Beer commercial (and indeed he was raising a tankard of something to his lips) than the Prince of Darkness. But the Circle had, in some obscure and disgusting way, become a kind of hell for me, one totally lacking in grandeur, a perfect *Morgantown* hell. It's where I'd sit by the jukebox night after night, pumping in my quarters to hear "Mule Skinner Blues" or "Everyday," drinking quart after quart of weak

9

West Virginia beer until I was running to the can every five minutes, watching the beautiful young coeds on the dance floor circle by with the fraternity boys. It's where I'd stumble, so drunk I'd be exploding with unused talk, through the circle of tiny interlocking rooms (all painted red, of course) looking for somebody, anybody, no matter how stupid or boring, to share a beer with—where I would see, reflected in a mirror across a press of people, Carol pass by with her wretched Englishman. And it's where I and a few of my cronies would sit till closing time constructing conversation like a madman's scaffolding hastily into the upper air—existentialism, pacifism, theosophy, Jung, alchemy, the Cabala, Sartre, Camus, Heidegger, Jaspers, Husserl, Wittgenstein, Rilke, Kerouac, Ginsberg, Snyder, Henry Miller, T. E. Lawrence, D. T. Suzuki, Zen, the *I Ching*, the *Tao Te Ching*, the Steppenwolf, the Outsider—to have collapsed as always for me the next morning, my hangover screwed tight as a watch spring ticking away my wasted time, debris littering a barren plane, my metaphors mixed and me late for class, and then all of it, all of my tricks and disguises, would seem in that awful morning light the shoddiest of effects, a fucked-up sleight of hand attempted by an incompetent charlatan. Revington was staring into the ruddy gloom with his eyes narrowed to slits. "Christ," he said, "it's crowded."

"Everybody getting their last drunk in before classes start," I said. I loved the Circle most on weekday nights near exam time when it would be nearly empty except for me and those few other diehard souses who really *needed* a drink.

"Gentlemen, good evening." A woman's voice behind us. We turned, and there was Marge Levine who must have come in just after us. "Hey, John," she said, giving me her brief flick of a smile. She'd met Cohen and Revington when they'd come down to visit me last spring. "Bill," she said to Cohen, "great to see you." Then

10

she deliberately turned to Revington, smiled and said, in an amused voice heavily weighted with subtext, "Revington."

"Levine," he said, inclining toward her from his picturesque height. "Here's looking at *you*, kid." Their hands touched briefly, a brushing of fingers, his pale and bare, hers black and gloved.

Marge had drawn emphatic Nefertiti lines around her eyes as she usually did; that evening she'd also painted her eyelids a virulent green. In the dim red gloom of the bar, her face looked mask-like, an effect that both pleased and distressed me. She'd undone the toggles of her unremarkable car coat, revealing beneath a black wool dress so unadorned and matronly it would have been ugly on anyone else; her hip bones showed through the skirt like knife points. She was startling as always, in black nylons (no one else on campus wore black nylons out to a bar), and pulled to one side of her head, so unlike her that it had to be a deliberate joke, a velvet beret. Oh, I thought, remembering, it's Carol's. "Hey, buddy," she said to me, "when did you get back?"

"Just now."

"Maybe we can find a table." She pushed through a knot of students, her body a lean tension balanced on high heels, and I trailed after her, saw her give Revington another thin smile. I loved the noise and press of the crowd, loved seeing girls all around me—but even as I felt a surge of elation, I knew how treacherous it was. I didn't care. I was going to get pissed.

Jammed into a corner, knocking back my first beer, I told Cohen, "My God, Bill, sometimes the world sizzles like a frying pan. It's incredible how the days can pass like bland beads on a string, with a deadness so total you forget completely there's anything else, and then . . . WHAM . . . it hits you again. The power. Like that drunk old man in the bar in South Raysburg told me . . . that Bodhisattva: 'Son, you're never late.' I keep forgetting it, keep thinking there's somewhere else I have to be, and then I miss it.

The power turns off. But when it's moving . . . the clarity . . ."

"Yes, clarity, that's it," he said. "Mornings when I walk through the Yard and see, really *see*, the branches of the trees, outlined so clearly, so sharply . . ."

"Yes, *yes*. Even the power lines right outside my apartment . . . just to be able to *see* them. As though the quality of light . . . I don't know . . ."

"As though the light's *alive*."

"That's right. That's exactly right. But why can't we stay there all the time?"

"If it's going to happen, it'll happen," he said. "It's something given to you."

"What do you do when it goes away?"

"You wait."

And Marge was asking Revington, "How long will you be staying?"

"Long enough," he said. Right, I thought. He's here for a while, but *I* won't see much of him.

Speaking quietly so no one else would hear, I asked Cohen, "Do you ever get tired of waiting?"

"On one level, no. But on another level . . . of course I do."

"All right, let's look at that bottom level . . . that ordinary, everyday level. How do you feel there?"

He smiled. "Stupid, clumsy, and slow."

Suddenly, Carol, with her Englishman, was leaning over the table, bestowing her graciousness upon all of us. She kissed me on the forehead, marking me with her lipstick, as I wouldn't discover until hours later. Unlike Marge, Carol didn't appear as a sinister masked figure in the dim light of the bar. Looking closely, I saw how cleverly her makeup had been done: in daylight, she'd look garish; here, she looked merely healthy. A goddamned consummate artist, I thought, infuriated by her feminine skills as I wouldn't have been if they'd been used on my behalf, but she was gazing up at that vapid visiting professor who was saying, "Oh, we didn't go anywhere, actually." *Actually?* Tweedy bastard.

Conservative Carol in an exquisitely tailored suit. Sexy Carol with her generous breasts and tiny waist. Helpful Carol pushing a chair to the Englishman. And suddenly angry Carol saying to Marge, "Oh. You're wearing my beret." Marge raised a finger, touched it to one eyebrow, and flicked it away, an abbreviated salute: Yes, I am. So what?

The blood rising into Carol's cheeks, igniting her face, over-whelming her makeup; the involuntary toss of her head, swing of her glossy black pageboy; the flash of outrage in her eyes; the quick inhalation of her breath— A fresh round of beer had, thank God, arrived at the table. "Knock it back?" I said to Revington.

He nodded in reply. I hoisted that beautifully chilled quart; we clinked bottles and drank. I watched him. He was watching me. Neither of us stopped until we hit bottom. I slammed my empty bottle down first, my throat burning from the effort. Far away, behind the nasty, rising murmur in my ears, behind the yattering voices all around me, I heard him say, "Ah, Dupre, you're still the fastest drunk in the West," as I let myself sink, flop into the plastic red padded seat of the booth, thought: here we are again, everything known, mapped, pre-drawn, laid out, predictable, and expected him to say: nada, nada, and yet more nada, or some such—just as he was already saying, leaning across the table to me like a conspirator, "See that old fucker over there in the corner, that campus cop? All by himself, right? Probably came in to get loaded so he could sleep . . . Yeah, and that's how I'm going to end up if I don't watch it. Some dead end like that. Campus cop, night watchman, hotel clerk on the night shift . . ." and let it trail off. On the tabletop, his hand was resting on Marge's. Carol was talking to her Englishman.

"*Déjà vu,*" I said to Cohen, but I meant stale, flat, pointless repetition—to watch Revington light a cigarette and stare at nothing, to light a cigarette myself, burp the fizz up, inhale smoke, hear that damnable visiting professor say, "the underpinning of the mythic structure . . . ," see Carol's doe eyes gazing up at him, rapt and attentive, hear myself launch in dizzily, losing control: "Oh, it's the mythic structure, is it? The underpinning structure. The mythic overpinning. The structuring mytho-pin. The mythic structuro-pin." I was imitating his accent. "That bloody book is the most over-rated major work of the twentieth century," I said in my own voice.

"*Ulysses?*" he said, our Oxford straight man, "Indeed?"

"Indeed," I mocked him. I wanted to stop the spill of my words, but I didn't know how. I was being obnoxious and hated myself for it. "Oh yes, the bloody subtext. But what's the point? What's the use? Where's the icy outline of things in themselves? Where's the fiery transforming numina of lived experience?"

My God, I was pontificating like an owl. "All those guys," I went on. "Symbolists. Cross-references. Word games. Anacrostics. It's pointless, pointless, pointless." Washing away, I looked to Cohen as an anchor, said to him *sotto voce,* "Out of the cradle, endlessly talking."

"I'm not sure I understand you." The Englishman was bending over me like an earnest gargoyle. "If it's that icy outline you want, then surely the opening in the lighthouse . . . the clarity of the prose . . . the clean, brilliant sea light . . ."

"John's our resident outsider," Carol said.

"That's right. Explain me away."

"Are you all right?" she asked me, and now I had what I must have wanted—her attention, her concern, her splendid eyes turned to me.

Cohen was looking at me too. The beautiful Jews, I thought, seeing them together. "Let's walk," I said to him.

Out on the street we were met by the first snowfall of the season, stopped by it. The sky was thick with the motion of the fat wet flakes; they quieted the campus as though someone had said, "Shhh." Cohen smiled—not one of his elusive, enigmatic smiles but a little kid's broad delighted grin—and gestured to me: look.

BILL COHEN and I hadn't become friends until after I'd graduated from the Academy. I'd known who he was, of course—the top student in the class one year behind me—but the military structure of our school didn't encourage fraternization with younger cadets, and it wasn't until my freshman year at WVU that I got to know him. I'd been at home at Christmas; Cohen had turned up at a hootenanny at David Anderson's. Cohen didn't sing or play anything, but he loved the music. I sang "Whoa Back Buck," and he came up to me afterward to tell me I'd killed him. We started talking and couldn't stop.

We talked at David's until they threw us out. I drove down to the Pines where I used to go with Lyle; we sat in that dark back room surrounded by evocative pools of guttering candle light and ate kielbasa sandwiches. I drank whiskey and water; Cohen drank root beer. We talked until two in the morning; then I drove over to the Island and we sat on the pilings under the bridge, watched the reflections of the city lights in the river, and talked until four. Cohen had some things at home he wanted to show me, so we drove out there, crept in quietly, closed ourselves into his bedroom, and talked until dawn. Eventually the rest of his family got up, and his mother made us breakfast. After that, we were quite literally inseparable for the last few days of the Christmas break. Whatever I was doing, I brought him along—even to visit Cassandra. He slept at my house or I at his. I don't think either of us planned it that way, but we just couldn't stop talking.

What did we talk about? Every damned thing under the sun. Folk music got us going, and then we moved on to science fiction—which used to be my passion and was still his. We'd read many of the same classic authors: Asimov, Heinlein, Arthur C. Clarke, Ray Bradbury, Frederik Pohl, Clifford Simac. Neither of us got too excited by the space-ships-and-robots variety of Sci-Fi; no, we wanted something stranger—time travel, alternate realities, weird worlds that would bend our minds. We agreed that *Galaxy* was a better magazine than *Fantasy & Science Fiction*, but *F & SF* certainly had some wonderful stories from time to time—for instance, I said, there was Manly Wade Wellman. "Oh, my God, yes," Cohen said, *"Manly Wade Wellman!"*

But he'd read a lot more than merely science fiction; Cohen had read everything—a million Westerns, all of Sherlock Holmes, the American school of hard-boiled detective novels, even Agatha Christie. (He was the only other boy I'd ever met who would admit to having read *Little Women*.) He'd read, and memorized, yards of poetry. He'd also read all that stuff we would have called "literature"—everything from Dickens to Kerouac, from *Moby Dick* to *The Catcher in the Rye*. He read so compulsively he saw it as a flaw in his character. He would read *anything*—any book or magazine that someone had momentarily laid down, junk that came in the mail, the cereal box on the breakfast table, the newspapers his mother spread on the floor under the kitty box. He said he was afraid to open the dictionary because he could get lost in it for hours. Like a jackdaw collecting bits of glitter, Cohen collected words; he'd forget how rare some of them were and use them in his ordinary conversation—to the consternation of his listeners, including me—words like *anacreontic, katabatic, viverrine, quillet, sequacity, epilimnion, anacoluthon.*

His bedroom astonished me. The walls, of course, were lined with bookshelves, and the shelves, of course, were crammed with books, but that's not what drew my attention. His American long bow rested in the corner next to his six-foot African spear. A quiver of target arrows hung on the wall next to his samurai sword. In another corner stood his fencing foils and his rifle. Arranged on top of the bookcase were his Bowie knife, his collection of throwing knives, his coiled bullwhip, and his BB-guns—not toys, but exquisitely made replicas of real guns. High on one wall, in a place of honor, hanging in a leather holster, was his Ruger Single-Six twenty-two caliber revolver. Looking out from his bulletin board at all these instruments of mayhem was a little girl of about twelve. Her hair, bound by a white ribbon, was a dark honey blonde with red highlights; she wore a black velvet dress with a white collar. She wasn't smiling. Her face was both wise and innocent—a face with a luminous, nearly other-worldly beauty.

I'd never met another boy who shared my fascination with young girls—as Cohen obviously did—but I would never have pinned up a girl *that* young. For me the magical age was still fourteen, just on the edge of womanhood, and I knew perfectly well how my pictures might look to other people (for instance, to a relentlessly cynical William Revington), but I didn't see the girls on my altar as *erotic*—rather, for want of a better word, as *religious*. Like Rilke's "already lost beloved," they were my icons, my muses. So I was dying of curiosity to know how Cohen felt about his little blonde. She wasn't anybody he knew, he said. He'd cut her picture out of a catalogue and put it up in his room because, "She killed me."

Cohen would talk about anything—that is, he seemed capable of being genuinely interested in anything—and there were no taboo subjects. I could ask him any question, no matter how personal, and he would try to answer it—often at great length, because, for him, the world was "infinitely complex" and his experience of it came "on many levels." Being "killed" by something—the word was Holden Caulfield's, and you could be killed by all kinds of things: a folk song, a girl, a crystalline morning, a line of poetry—but the word was just a shorthand, he had to admit; the experience itself was what mattered; as he described it (and he really didn't want to be pinned down by words, trapped by them, but he was doing his best to communicate), being killed was an aesthetic, nearly mystical, utterly heart-stopping moment of pure bliss. "OK," I said, "but that particular little girl in the picture . . . how do you *feel* about her?"

He had to think about it. His first reaction was that his feelings were too complex to describe. Finally he said, "I probably feel about her the way Holden Caulfield did about his little sister, Phoebe."

How he felt about guns, knives, swords, bows, spears, and bullwhips was also infinitely complex and required several days' worth of elucidation even to begin to plumb the depths. He loved the old American myth of the lone man standing up to all the forces of evil; he'd seen *High Noon* over a dozen times. The skill and the speed of the Western gunman—both in legend and reality—fascinated him. In grade school, he'd begun practicing the quick draw with BB-guns. He'd bought that Ruger only in the last year. Of course he couldn't fire it within the city limits, but if I wanted to ride out of town with him to a spot he knew, he'd show me what he was talking about—because it was a topic you could talk about forever and not get to the heart of it, but if you *saw it*, you might get a better feeling for it. "I'd love to," I said.

Cohen brought along a bag full of tin cans. He lined them up on an old fence, then turned and paced off a *High Noon*'s worth of distance and stood, regarding the fence. As he always did when he wasn't in school, he was wearing jeans and cowboy boots. He'd told me that when he'd first bought the Ruger, he'd worked over it for weeks—smoothed and polished the moving parts, fitted it with Fitz Gun Fighter Grips and Flaig's Ace Trigger Shoe, lightened the trigger pull to little more than two pounds. He wore the Ruger high to the rear of his right hip, in a holster canted oddly forward.

Cohen simply stood there awhile, his face altogether devoid of expression. He didn't make the slightest motion to give away his intention, but suddenly I heard a sharp spitting sound followed instantly by the metallic ping of the first can being swatted off into the woods; then he was again at rest, crouched slightly forward. He'd already drawn and fired. It had happened so quickly that the motion had to be reconstructed in memory— the high rising elbow, hand back to the hip and then thrust out, smooth as a cat's jump, the gun itself an unintelligible blur, like a hummingbird's wing. He was smiling, very slightly. He settled the gun back into the holster. Doc Holliday's cavalry draw, Cohen had told me, was the fastest method of drawing and firing a single-action; it was also the most difficult. He'd never been able to figure out a way to time himself, so I'd brought along my stopwatch. "Now!" The best I could tell, he could draw and fire that Ruger in less than half a second.

Cohen didn't demonstrate his gunplay to very many people, said he didn't like to show off, so I think I might have been the only other person who ever got to see the whole show. He demonstrated in his basement at home, used a BB-pistol, not the Ruger, and gave me an exhaustive account of the evolution of the handgun as a weapon. He showed me the cavalry draw, the border shift, the FBI draw, the ankle draw, the shoulder draw, the inside-the-pants draw, the unorthodox across-the-body draw perfected by the Ringo Kid. He showed me "drop the dollar" too;

with that BB-pistol and a fifty-cent piece, he hit the coin eight tries out of ten.

I could have called Revington, simply, one of my best friends, but I was never sure what to say about Bill Cohen. I knew that he'd gradually come to fill the void in my life that Lyle had left, so Cohen was a friend, certainly, but something more. Even when we first met, my regard for him bordered on awe—but there's one more twist to the story. He won a full scholarship to Harvard. His family was so delighted with him that they wanted to give him something special—what did he want? He wanted to travel, he said. That was easy enough. In the spring after he graduated from the Academy, he went to New York, stayed with his Uncle Syd, came back talking ecstatically about the paintings in the Met and the Guggenheim, about hearing Lightning Hopkins at the Ethical Culture Society, about the wonderful foreign flicks. Then, later in the summer, he went to visit his Uncle Harry who owned a hotel in Miami Beach, and when he came back from Florida, he'd been *enlightened*. We'd both been reading about Buddhism, but he'd been the one to have the experience, and it had been just the way Watts and Suzuki described it: mind-shattering and utterly beyond words—although, God knows, he tried to tell me about it over and over again.

I kept studying him to see what difference it might have made. For one thing, he now spoke occasionally in flat declarative sentences, as though he *knew*. (It was what Revington came to call, "Cohen speaking *ex cathedra*.") Some of his dicta were: "What's important is what happens between people," and "Despair is evil," and "Words are no damned good." And for another thing, there seemed to be—and here was where I had trouble finding the right way to put it—an enigmatic sweetness growing in him. It was more than kindness (although he *was* kind); it was as though he had acquired the ability to hold anyone he met in a nearly infinite regard.

He never claimed to have achieved *the big one*—perfect incomparable enlightenment like the Buddha's; he didn't mind the word the Zen masters used for an enlightenment experience, *satori,* but the way he referred to it was "my awakening." It was like a rock inside of him, he said; it was eternal. In an instant, everything he'd ever thought about himself in the world had been changed.

"Was it like when you used to say, 'It killed me,' only more so?" I asked him.

"No."

"Did you lose consciousness?"

"No."

"Was it like an incredible insight?"

"No."

"Do you remember what you were thinking?"

"Thought had nothing to do with it."

Florida in the summer is hotter than hell, he said, and he'd loved it. He felt as though he'd been born to live in the tropics. He'd been having a great time, running on the beach, swimming in the ocean. His uncle had taken him fishing, and he'd caught a marlin. One night he couldn't sleep because he was so filled with joy. He got up and walked on the beach. Just as the sky was turning the intense lucent blue that comes just before dawn in the tropics, he stopped walking and looked out to sea. He didn't remember what he was thinking. And that's when it happened.

It's August two summers ago. We're sitting in his kitchen, and he's been trying to tell me *again* how it happened, what it *was* that happened. He keeps trying—pouring out more and more of those words he doesn't trust, those words that he says are "no damned good." He's just cooked cheeseburgers for us, gigantic ones with nearly a pound of meat in each. Bright sunlight, broken at the windows, patterns the room; we're glowing with it. The West Virginia dog days, hot and humid, pulse with the locusts in the trees—that ancient, monotonous drone that says to me, as it has since I turned six: almost school time, almost school time. The cheeseburgers drip grease and mayonnaise onto our plates, small pools giving back sun; the plates are glowing, the pickles are glowing—light through the pickle jar, light on the bubbles in the sink full of dishes, light on our faces. We're sweating, the kitchen vivid with heat, the sun everywhere. Cohen, brown from Florida, is wearing only swimming trunks. Black curly hair on his chest and legs, his bare feet wrapped around the rungs of the kitchen stool, his eyes on my face, and I've been asking him over and over, "But what was it *like*? Tell me what it was *like*," until finally he reaches out to me, seizes both my hands in his, and squeezes, hard, until I can feel the heat of his flesh, the tightening of his muscles, even the bones underneath. His smile is so fierce it's beyond any term as mundane as *joy*; his eyes are blazing. "John," he says, "you're alive."

COHEN HAD stopped walking to look up at the snow falling through the brilliance of a streetlight. He hadn't said a word since we'd left the Circle; trying to match his mood, neither had I, yet I couldn't stop my mind from nattering—still coming up with trenchant lines to stun Carol's Englishman (although we'd left him behind a long time ago), still writing descriptions of the obsidian luminosity of Carol's eyes as seen in the dim red light of that phony hell. But Carol was not here; *I* was here, and looking to where Cohen was looking, I finally caught up to where we'd arrived, hoped that I could see what he was seeing—simply the snow falling in flakes fat as cotton balls, white in the street light, grey beyond in drifting curtains that enveloped us like a blessing.

Even though the curfew was still a half hour away, already girls were hurrying up the hill toward the Women's Dorm, some paired with dates, some in all-female clusters. I heard their voices all around us, but the snow hid their images.

Once again I had the sense of intense quieting, of the snow smoothing out sound. The feeling of staleness that had been oppressing me in the Circle dropped suddenly away. I could, I knew, if I kept on walking, shed my drunkenness like stepping out of an inept disguise. This was new, as though I'd awakened to catch Cohen and myself *in medias res*; I didn't know what drama we were enacting, but wherever he was going, I'd gladly go with him. He was grinning at me like the Cheshire Cat. I hadn't felt either of us choose a direction, but we were leaving behind the center of the campus—the focal point of the library—to follow out white blankness toward the curve of the stadium, to climb the hill, to look down on the empty circle of the track where we would find no one.

"You know, John," he said, "this student business . . . On the maintenance level, it's getting harder and harder to pull off."

I laughed. "Oh, yeah, it sure is." But I was surprised. It was the first time I'd ever heard him say anything like that. I'd always imagined him having no trouble at all with school.

"I've got a paper due on the Amaravati stupa slab," he said. "It's not hard. I just have to go through image by image, identify each one, say what it represents . . . Here the Buddha's hand is open, welcoming all who come to him, and here the Buddha's hand is pointing downward to the earth, representing his vow to sit beneath the Bo tree until he achieves perfect incomparable enlightenment . . . But I keep thinking that if I were a pilgrim coming to Amaravati, I wouldn't be cataloguing the images. I'd be coming to *experience* them."

"Right."

"Of course, on another level, none of that matters. I might as well be at Harvard as not be at Harvard. But I'm glad to be here with you, right now, in the snow, in Morgantown, and not in Cambridge getting ready for my classes tomorrow."

From our viewpoint on top of that hill, WVU looked ghostly, unreal; the snow obscured even the nearest buildings. "I thought you liked Harvard," I said.

"Oh, I do. On one level. On that level I wouldn't be anywhere else . . ."

"But how about the other levels?"

"On another level, I keep wondering how much use any of it is."

"I know what you mean," I said. "I had all these illusions. I don't know what I thought it would be down here . . . some kind of medieval university maybe, or a continual Socratic dialogue. But no, you've got to fill *this* requirement, *that* requirement . . . sit through another boring lecture. Maybe we were just incredibly naïve to think that going to school has anything to do with learning."

"Oh, I'm sure we could do a hell of a lot better job educating ourselves," Cohen said, "but there's . . ."

"What?"

"OK, let's imagine it as a kind of science-fiction story. You're being tested for a mission into deep space, a very important mission. But they don't tell you what the mission is, and they don't even tell you that you're being tested. Part of the test, one of the most crucial parts, is to see if you can figure out that it *is* a test."

I didn't know why I should find Cohen's metaphor so thoroughly unpleasant. "That's not science fiction," I said, "that's Kafka."

"Ah, but it could be any day now," Cohen said. "It could be the buildings-and-grounds guy. It could be one of my professors.

It could be the secretary in the Registrar's office. She gives me a significant look. I wonder how I could have ever missed the purposeful steely glint in her eye, but this time I pick up on it instantly. I don't need any explanation. Without a word, I follow her out into the middle of the Yard, well away from the bugging devices. 'Cohen,' she says, 'we've been watching you for years. And now we see that you're *ready*.'"

"Revington's right," I said, laughing, "you really are nuts."

We looked down from our elevation toward the blurry shapes of the buildings obscured by the scrim of snow. I lit a cigarette. I'd been waiting for the chance to talk to him alone, to tell him about Carol without having Revington around to drop his funny cynical lines into the conversation; I'd had several opportunities in Raysburg, but I hadn't taken advantage of them. Now might be a good time, but no, it still didn't feel right. We began to walk back the way we had come. We continued to talk—about courses, papers, professors—the mundane miseries of student life. It was one of our meandering conversations that could last forever, go anywhere.

At first we could see our own boot prints leading up the way we had come, but the snow was falling so thickly that soon the sidewalks stretching before us were blanked out to the untouched whiteness of typewriter paper. Then I saw that someone else was out there sharing the snow with us: a single set of small footprints, obviously a girl's. The length of her stride was less than half of ours. The weight at the balls of her feet had left delicate marks in the shape of valentine hearts; her heel prints were so tiny they could have been covered by dimes. She couldn't have been very far ahead of us or the snow would have hidden her tracks. I looked at my watch, saw that it was after midnight and felt a rush of sympathy for her—poor kid, whoever she was, caught out in high heels in the snow after curfew.

To overtake her, all we had to do was continue to follow her footprints. I didn't tell Cohen what I was doing, but I began to walk faster. I felt that the ordinary lines of the world had fallen away, leaving things chancy and unpredictable. Then I could see her at the end of the block: a blurred and elusive image, a hazy pale silhouette—slender and hooded. I was startled to have caught up with her so quickly without having first heard the tap of her heels; the snow must have muffled the sound. She seemed to turn and look back at us.

I stopped walking. With an outstretched hand, I stopped Cohen. "What are we doing?" he said. "Don't you want her to see us?" I hadn't known until then that he'd seen her footprints too.

"I don't want to frighten her," I said.

"Then we should behave absolutely normally." He started walking again; I fell into step with him.

For a moment I'd been looking at him. Now, looking back to where the girl had been, I saw nothing but snow. "You did see her, didn't you?" I asked him.

"Of course I saw her."

I pointed down. Her footprints were still there. We followed them downhill toward the center of campus. Eventually they led us into that curious cul-de-sac behind Woodburn Hall. "Oh, she must be lost," I said. "This goes nowhere."

I saw her again—or at least I think I did—an even more elusive image than before, a slender wavering line drawn momentarily into the snow and then gone. "Excuse me." I called out. "Are you lost?" There was no answer.

"The way in's the only way out," I said to Cohen, and, walking fast, led him into the cul-de-sac. Halfway in, I couldn't see her footprints any more. I stopped, confused.

Cohen sank into a crouch, and, with one bare hand, began to brush snow from the sidewalk. I sank down next to him. He'd uncovered one of her prints. As we watched, it filled with snow. We walked to the end of the cul-de-sac, then back. There was no sign of the girl. As we retraced our steps, I saw no footprints but our own.

IT WASN'T until we were back inside my apartment doing maintenance things—washing away the interesting green slime I'd been cultivating on the dishes I'd left in my sink over Thanksgiving break, emptying ashtrays, collecting the empty beer bottles, boiling water for Cohen's tea—that I realized just how disquieting it had been to track that elusive girl across campus in the snow. It had been like finding a fascinating piece of a jigsaw puzzle that, unfortunately, didn't happen to belong to the puzzle I was working on.

Cohen was standing against the wall in front of my bulletin board. He'd propped an empty carton against the opposite wall, and, with relaxed deft flicks of his wrist, was throwing knives into it. In a leather pouch in his knapsack he always kept five of them: thin slivers of forged steel small enough to be hidden in the palm of his hand, the cutting edge at the points (as he'd showed me) sharp enough, with a bit of spit as a lubricant, to shave the hair on his arm. "Half turn," he said, "I've almost got it." I didn't know why he bothered with the "almost"—he hadn't missed yet. The knives struck the cardboard with a neat thwack and stuck up to the hilt. Soon the carton would be ripped to shreds and he'd have to find another one.

"Cohen," I said, "what the hell happened?"

"You mean the girl who wasn't there?"

"Of course that's what I mean. What else would I mean?"

"Funny . . . my watch has stopped too."

I could see that he was in one of his playful moods—kittenish and a bit silly—that could drive me absolutely nuts. "Look,"

I said, "let's just get the facts straight, OK? Did you see her?"

"Yes," he said, laughing, "I saw her."

"How about in the cul-de-sac? Did you see her in there?"

"I think I did, but I'm not sure."

"Yeah. I'm not sure either. But her footprints led in there, didn't they?"

"Oh, yeah."

"OK, so where the hell was she?"

"John, there's a simple, perfectly logical explanation for this. When she saw that we were getting too close to her . . . she flew away."

"Oh, for Christ's sake!"

I went back to drying my dishes. I could see that I wasn't going to get anywhere with him on that topic, but maybe I could get somewhere on another one. "Cohen," I said, "there's something I've been wanting to talk to you about . . . You know Carol?"

"That little raven-haired beauty who came in with the British guy?"

"Yeah. Exactly. Well, I know what you say. Unrequited love is a contradiction in terms. But I think I'm in love with her, and I can't stand it this time. It just hurts too much."

The motion of his arm on the next throw was not small and deft but a broad powerful sweep. The knife shot past me, through the archway to the kitchen, and stuck, quivering, in the wall above the stove. The sound it had made, striking, had been loud and vicious as a whip crack. "Turn and a half," he said.

I must have jumped a foot. Adrenaline was charging through me; my entire body felt licked with electricity. All I could do was laugh. "You're a goddamned ham," I said. "You're as bad as me or Revington."

He had to use both hands to pry the knife from the wall.

"That was stupid of me. I'll get some plaster tomorrow and fix the hole." But he couldn't help grinning; he looked as pleased with himself as a little boy.

I filled his teacup, poured myself a beer, sat down at the table, gestured for him to join me. "I really want to talk about this stuff," I said, "I want to ask you something. I want to use words. I want you to *try*, OK? No more silence or dramatic Zen gestures . . . just some good old-fashioned words, OK?"

"All right, I'll babble like a brook." He put his knives back in their pouch and sat down.

I pointed to the picture of Linda. "I keep thinking that she's the key to everything. She was the first girl I was ever in love with, and I fucked it up, and somehow that means I'm doomed to fuck up again, forever and ever."

"So love's like a gun with one bullet?" Cohen said. "If you miss, you never get another shot?"

"Boy, is that a sexual image."

"Yeah, I guess it is, isn't it? I didn't even think of it . . . All right, how's this? Love's like a . . ." He began laughing. "Is it bigger than a bread box? Oh damn it, John, words are so damn silly . . . OK, is it like diving off a high cliff into a pool with rocks all around it? You only get one jump because you either hit the water or you break your neck?"

"Hey, that's not bad. And if you've ever done it once, you know you can do it again. Yeah, that's close to how I feel about it, but . . . I don't know why I'm even thinking about Linda. Cassandra means more to me than Linda Edmonds ever did, but Cassy and I . . . Well, we were never exactly boyfriend and girlfriend . . ."

I found it difficult to talk about Cassandra. She'd always refused to play by the rules, and she still maintained her old distinction between *love* and *in love*. By her definition, we'd never been in love with each other—although I wasn't sure of that. If she was the only girl I would have called one of my best friends, she was also the only one of my best friends who made out with me from time to time. Sometimes we made out like fiends. "I love her," I said. "I know she loves me, but she's like a sister . . ."

Cohen was smiling at me. I could guess what he was thinking: what's wrong with that?

"OK," I said, "and then there's Natalie," and I tried to tell him how I felt about *her*. I'd never been sure if I'd loved Natalie—or, to stay on topic, if I'd ever been *in love* with her—because on some elusive level I certainly had *loved* her— Well, maybe what I'd loved hadn't been Natalie herself but simply the convenience of having a steady girlfriend. It had made things so damn easy—not having to wonder what you were going to do on weekends or in the evenings. And, as I kept on talking, listening to myself backtracking, revising, editing—stopping to erase everything I'd said so far to launch in again with yet another elaboration of something else that would probably turn out to be wrong, I thought, Christ, I haven't got a clue how I felt about Natalie. "We were so different," I said.

He kept on smiling. He was right. Sometimes you did hit a point where words were no damned good. "I miss her like crazy," I said. That was true enough.

"Oh, hell," I said. "I know how pathetic I must sound . . . like Romeo in Act I, but . . . OK, and now there's Carol. And she just drives me fucking nuts. And she's completely infatuated with that goddamned stupid Englishman. And I've managed to convince her I'm her friend . . . you know, her good buddy."

He couldn't help himself. I could see how it had been building up in him, and now all he could do was laugh. But it was absurd for me to expect any kind of useful advice from him; he'd never even had a girlfriend. "Go ahead," he said, "just love them."

"'For God's sake hold your tongue, and let me love,'" I quoted for him.

"Yes. That's exactly right. On one level, love is just love. But on another level . . . I think love's like something you have to practice. The more you practice, the better you get." Then, seemingly as an afterthought, he added, "It helps to look into their eyes."

It took a moment for it to sink in. *"It helps to look into their eyes!"* I said. "What did you just say, Cohen? Did I just hear you admit that you feel desire?"

"You guys talk about me as though I'm not human."

He'd sounded genuinely pained, and I thought, oh, Christ, now I've hurt his feelings, but he was saying, "Come on, John, I'm just as human as you are . . . Of course you have to overlook the odd greenish iridescence that reflects back from my skin in certain lights and the pale white nictitating membrane that appears over my eyes when I get overly tired, but other than that . . ."

"Cohen. Shut up. What do you mean, it helps to look in their eyes?"

"To stop attachment . . . You never stop it completely . . . because we *are* human. But you look into a girl's eyes and remind yourself that she's a coming Buddha."

"You've really done that?"

"Yes."

"And it works?"

He smiled. "Sometimes."

Looking at him now, I saw how his own face was beginning to show precisely that quality that had moved him to clip a girl's picture and put it on his wall—not merely beauty but something more elusive, something remote, mysterious, and self-contained.

"Have I told you about Musashi?" he said, pointing at the

painting he'd sent me: the monk leaning on his staff, watching the cocks fight.

"Yeah, you wrote me a long letter."

"What did I say?"

"You said it was painted in something-or-other style . . . that's very demanding. You have to be really fast. You can't make a single mistake."

"That's right. *Sumi*."

"You said the painter, Miyamoto Musashi, was Japan's greatest swordsman, and he died in bed. The caption on the painting says, 'There is no slayer, and there is no slain.'"

"Sounds like I wrote you a pretty good letter . . . But did I tell you what he said? When someone asked him how to be a good swordsman?"

"No, I don't think so."

"He said, 'Arouse the mind without fixing it anywhere.' OK? And I've been thinking about that a lot. If you fix the mind somewhere, that's attachment, and attachment slows you down."

He must have seen that I wasn't getting it. "Look," he said, and all of his playfulness had dropped away. "If you're standing there thinking, oh, my God, I could be killed any second, then you're attached. If you're thinking about *anything* other than the motion of the blade, then you're attached . . . You must know what I'm talking about. Playing the guitar must be like that."

I was getting it finally. "Oh, right. The times when the music plays itself because you don't get in the way."

"Yes, yes, yes. That's it exactly."

There were moments, such as this one, when I expected everything to be revealed. "So what is this thing with girls?" I said. "What the hell were you talking about?"

"As long as you're attached to *any* outcome, you won't see the human being in front of you. You'll only see your own mind stuff.

Attachment makes us stupid, clumsy, and slow. So if you can look into a girl's eyes and *see her* . . . as equally empty, equally awake, equally a coming Buddha . . ."

"God, that's impossible."

"No, it's not. Hard, but not impossible."

"And if you're *not* attached . . ."

"You're fast. You're unbelievably fast. You're the absolute master of now."

2.

WHEN VIEWED from the vantage point of my already fairly miserable junior year, my first two years at WVU hadn't been bad at all. I'd lived with Joe Kruszka and Eddie Caldwell, classmates from the Academy, in a first-floor apartment on Allen Street not far from campus. Whenever our parents bothered to drive down to visit us, they always told us our place was a dump; we thought it had character. The sagging front porch might have been threatening to drop off the house, but at least we had a front porch— and we even had an old squeaky glider, the perfect spot to sit on warm fall or spring evenings, drinking beer and watching the world go by. Freed from home and the Raysburg Military Academy, I'd set out to do exactly what I damn well pleased—but that had turned out to be nothing more daring than hosting a series of loud drunken parties. I'd made it to most of my classes. Without half trying, I'd got straight A's.

Tucked away in a pocket of the Monongahela River valley, sleeping in an obscure corner of an impoverished state, West Virginia University dreamed on under the old myth of the Golden College Years. JFK might have been in the White House, generating, as Revington liked to say, the winds of change, but Morgantown felt scarcely a breeze and looked firmly backward with a countenance as bland as Eisenhower's smile. The most significant activity at WVU was football, with basketball running it a close second; the Greek letter societies dominated the social life. The boys wore buzz cuts and madras shirts; the girls looked as though they bought their clothes from last year's Sears Roebuck catalogue.

I wore nothing but jeans, a Levi jacket, and cowboy boots, grew sideburns as long as a riverboat gambler's, knotted a railroader's bandana around my neck, and smoked thin black cigars not so much for pleasure as for the image. I was a pioneer of a style that would eventually become a youth uniform, but in Morgantown in those days, I couldn't have had any higher visibility if I'd been wearing a wizard's pointed hat decorated with stars and moons. When I strode across campus with my guitar case in hand, the few other rebels, loonies, and fuck-ups could see me coming for five blocks and know me for a brother. I was stopped on the street, invited to parties. I fingerpicked my steel-strung Martin and tried to sing like a lower pitched version of Dock Boggs or Clarence Ashley—or, if I really wanted to snow them, in an incomprehensible black dialect painfully memorized from Library of Congress records. The word went around that my style was "authentic" and "ethnic." I was a success with the out crowd.

There were *girls* in the out crowd, of course. The first one I met was Marge Levine. She was a year ahead of me, one of a handful of student radicals known on campus simply as "the Commies." She was the president of the SPU—the Student Peace Union—which I joined, largely because they had a hootenanny once a month. We met in Strider Hall in the basement of Trinity Episcopal Church, sat on wooden folding chairs, drank coffee out of paper cups, and talked about what a hopelessly benighted asshole of the universe WVU was. On a hootenanny night, there might be a dozen students, even an occasional professor; on ordinary meeting nights, six was a good turnout. We never did much of anything but talk—although once we picketed the ROTC building. I dutifully walked up and down with my sign reading, GROW UP, GENTLEMEN, WAR IS OBSOLETE, even though I was *in* ROTC, as, indeed, I had to be if I wanted to graduate from WVU.

Marge was also the editor of a small five-cent newsletter, mimeographed in dirty purple ink and erratically stapled together, that told us what would happen to Morgantown if a nuclear bomb hit Pittsburgh and listed the restaurants in town that wouldn't serve Negroes—which was most of them. She played the autoharp, picked it nicely in Sara Carter style. She taught me old labor songs like "We Shall Not Be Moved" and the one about marching to Blair Mountain; I taught her old-timey tunes like "Reuben" and "Bonaparte's Retreat." She lent me C. Wright Mills; I lent her D. T. Suzuki. Marge was fascinated by the bloody coal wars in southern West Virginia. "We had the most radical labor movement in America right here in this state," she would say, and she was always telling me, "John, we've got to know our own history." In some cases, that would mean discovering it and writing it herself—which is exactly what she went on to do.

Marge was a short, plain, skinny girl who, in my memory, always appears as tall, lean, intimidating, and eerily beautiful. She had presence; that's what filled space and dominated it, left behind an illusory afterimage of size and power. Her flat, dry, ironic voice (she was the first girl I'd ever met who could use the word "fuck" like a boy—as a throwaway effect) demanded to be heard by its very quietness, an understated intensity. Visually she was neither quiet nor understated. Her dark brown hair twisted itself naturally into a mass of curls tight as ringlets; she wore it long and untamed halfway down her back—and huge loop ear-rings, thick black lines around her eyes, and eyelids painted the most wildly artificial colors, the blues and greens of a peacock's tail. There was nothing of the coed about her, never sweaters or cute pleated skirts, but severe dresses in blacks and greys, worn with dance tights or black nylons and, inevitably, high heels. Her sense of style—and, of course, her political opinions—were an insult to every decent, right-thinking, rosy-cheeked American student on that conservative campus. I didn't know where she got the guts to pull it off. I admired her.

I even took her out a couple times. Whatever mysterious

quality I was seeking in a girl, she didn't have an ounce of it. She didn't feel merely a year older than I; she felt a millennium older. We both sensed it at once, and the one and only time I tried to kiss her (not out of any great desire; I thought it was required of me as a male), she even said it: "What are you *doing*, John? Don't be silly. There's no spark between us whatsoever." I felt both crushed and curiously relieved. I couldn't do anything but laugh and agree with her. After that, we settled down to being friends.

T H E   O N L Y   thing I took seriously was folk music. I'd long ago outgrown the Kingston Trio and hadn't bothered to bring their records to Morgantown; even Joan Baez was beginning to sound too sweet. I still listened to Pete Seeger, Burl Ives, Theodore Bikel, and the Clancy Brothers, but I loved Leadbelly, the New Lost City Ramblers, Jimmie Rodgers, the Carter Family, Bill Monroe, Flatt and Scruggs—and anything that had been collected out in the legendary hills from the true folk. The stuff that really killed me was in the magnificent *Folkways Anthology of American Folk Music.*

Thousands of kids like me were singing folk songs; every time I walked into a record store, there'd be a new LP from somebody I'd never heard of, and I dutifully bought some of them; most were unmemorable, or memorable for the wrong reasons, like the duo called "The Little Sisters" I bought for their name. I've never heard of them since, have long ago lost their record, but still in my mind, years later, I can hear their breathy little-girl voices singing "the Cuckoo." And one day I bought, simply because I liked the jacket, an LP by a guy named Bob Dylan. He wasn't an old crock who'd recorded in 1929; he was *one of us*, yet he had a raw, authentic, old-time voice that was exactly what I'd been waiting to hear without knowing I'd been waiting. I can remember taking his record everywhere I went, saying, "Hey, you've got to hear this guy." For a while, until the word went around and people got to know him, I could crack up any party by singing Dylan's version of "Fenario."

Of course it would be folk music that would lead me to my first serious girlfriend in Morgantown. I picked up Natalie by playing the authentic ethnic folk singer—although "picked up" is probably not a good description for what happened. I'd spent the entire summer between my freshman and sophomore years trying to sing like Roscoe Holcomb an octave lower. I'd worked out my own version of "The Rising Sun" that was, I thought, not bad at all, and I was ready to show it off at the first SPU hootenanny in September. Because it was the beginning of the new academic year, we had more people than usual that night, all of our regular members and a few visitors.

As we always did, we tuned to Marge's autoharp, and we'd just about finished when I saw a scruffy nondescript teenage boy step into the hall, carrying a guitar case. He was wearing a grey sweatshirt with a hood—like something left over from track practice. Marge, always eager to recruit new members, walked directly over to him and said something. I saw him reply. He followed her in, and I was just realizing that there was something quite odd about him when he pushed back the hood and shook out a great torrent of lovely brown hair. Oh, my God, I thought, it's a girl—although, for one bewildering moment, I wasn't absolutely sure. But only a girl could have had hair that long: dead straight and almost to her waist, cool brown hair with not a hint of auburn in it.

She looked as though every item of her clothing had been discarded by a bigger older brother: under that old sweatshirt an equally old flannel shirt, plaid and worn out at the elbows, baggy jeans rolled up at the bottom, and badly scuffed oxfords—the kind of ugly sensible shoes that mothers in those days often made their children, girls as well as boys, wear to grade school. "This is Natalie," Marge said, and we went around the circle, telling her our names.

When her turn came, she lifted a classical guitar out of its case; as soon as I heard the first chord—a sound rich as baker's chocolate—I knew it was a superb instrument. I was sitting on the opposite side of the circle from her, about ten feet away, and even at that distance I could see that she was so nervous her hands were shaking. Her guitar playing wasn't much, but her voice was clear, strong, and accurate. She didn't look outward but sang with her eyes focused on a spot on the floor about three feet in front of her, her hair partially obscuring her face.

> Don't sing love songs. You'll wake my mother.
> She's sleeping here right by my side.
> In her hand a silver dagger.
> She's says that I can't be your bride.

She'd obviously been listening to Joan Baez as much as I'd been listening to Roscoe Holcomb. Folk music, especially an old ballad like that, has a way of prying open a singer: you can imitate someone else all you want, but in the end you're going to have to sing the song yourself. Baez is Baez; her "Silver Dagger" is magic—shimmery, silvery, sinister—and no kid singing in the basement of an Episcopal Church in Morgantown, West Virginia, was about to match it. And Natalie didn't. But she had something that was almost better. Baez had been singing about a girl in a song; Natalie *was* the girl in the song. She killed me.

We gave her a good round of applause, asked her to sing another one, but no, she said, that's all she wanted to do. She hadn't been playing that long. She didn't know that many songs. I volunteered to go next.

I took "The Rising Sun" a hair faster than Holcomb did but tried to reproduce his unbelievably long bent notes. I didn't start out with the intention of impressing Natalie, but after the first verse, I knew that's exactly what I was trying to do. I saw her watching me, so I sang directly to her, saw her sit up straighter in her chair as though drawn upward by an invisible wire. Our eyes met. I thought she would look away, but she didn't. I sent the last lines straight to her:

> Look up, look down that lonesome road,
> Hang down your head and cry.
> If you loved me as I love you,
> You'd go with me or die.

Then, picking up the tempo, I kicked into "Spike Driver's Blues," played it through as an instrumental three times, driving it hard, stomping out the beat with my left foot, and ended it laughing. I was getting the kind of applause I loved: excitement, whistles, Marge yelling: "Hey, buddy, all right!"

We ran through our usual repertoire for the rest of the evening, ending, as always, singing along with Marge's labor songs. Every time I glanced over at Natalie, I caught her watching me. At the end of the night I walked straight over to her without pretending I was doing anything else. "Hi, I'm John Dupre," I said in case she'd missed my name.

"Natalie," she said and offered her hand. I took it, and she shook with me like a boy.

"You have a lovely voice," I told her.

She didn't say, "Thank you." She simply stood there and looked at me long enough to make me uncomfortable. It was impossible for me to guess her age. She had a very young face, almost a child's. "You're really good," she said. "You should make a record."

I was flattered and heard myself laughing nervously. "Oh, I'm not that good."

I was wearing cowboy boots as I always did, and our eyes were perfectly level; she was exactly my height. (With our shoes off, as I would find out later, she was a good inch taller.) She was looking directly at me with watchful eyes that were a pale brown so translucent I could see the blue behind it. No makeup whatsoever but a lovely ivory skin with a rosy glow, an ovular unmarked face—wide across the jaws and narrow at the chin—a strong nose (but not too strong), fantastically long eyelashes, and a mouth that could have been too thin but somehow wasn't. It had taken me a while to get there, but I finally realized how lovely she was. She had a face like one of those you sometimes see in a Daguerreotype, a face that radiates a beauty impossibly lost in time, not our contemporary idea of beauty at all, but a beauty nonetheless and one that stops your heart. Why, I wondered, was such a stunning girl working so hard to make herself look so damned unattractive?

"Are you a freshman?" I asked her.

"No," she said, "I'm still in high school."

I felt that like a fist in the solar plexus. "I'm a senior," she added so quickly that she must have really wanted me to know. "You're at the university?"

"Yeah. I'm a sophomore." Again, as they had the entire evening, our eyes locked; I didn't know how I knew it or what it could mean, but I thought *this girl is special.* Unlike what had happened with Linda or Cassandra, it didn't feel fated or inevitable. It was certainly not love at first sight. I knew it was something that was mine to choose, one way or the other. "Can I walk you home?" I said.

"Yes." That's what she said. Not "Sure," or "OK," or "Why not?" or "That'd be nice," but "Yes."

Walking was nearly a religion with me, and I hated to have

anything in my hands when I did it, so I carried my guitar stuffed into a knapsack on my back. I offered to carry hers. "It's OK," she said. "We're not that far away." She led me down Spruce Street and over the Pleasant Street Bridge. She was one of the few girls I'd met who could keep up with me.

"I bet you're a professor's brat," I said, trying for a light humorous tone.

"Yeah, I am," she said in a flat voice. "My dad teaches economics."

"You going to go to WVU?"

"I don't think so. I'll probably go to Goucher or Swarthmore or Smith."

Oh, I thought, so that's the way it is, huh? "Those are good schools," I said.

We walked the rest of the way in silence. She lived in a stately old house on Grand Street. We walked up onto her porch; by then, I was sure I'd made a grotesque mistake. I was about to murmur goodnight and take off when she set her guitar down, turned back, and kissed me.

She did it deliberately as though she'd been thinking about it all the time we'd been walking. She wrapped the fingers of one hand around the back of my neck, caught me with the other— the palm of her hand on my cheekbone and her fingers over my ear—and held me a moment, looking into my eyes, then pressed her lips against mine. I opened my mouth and so did she. However awkward it had been trying to talk to her, there was nothing awkward about kissing her. She led me away from her front door to a dark side of the porch. I shed my knapsack and pressed her against the wall. I'd never before held a girl as tall as she was, and I was surprised at how good it felt. There was no sense that we were strangers; it was as though we could read each other's minds. On one level, nothing else mattered but kissing her; on another level, I was sick with apprehension: I didn't know her, didn't know her parents, didn't know the rules of the game. "Don't you have to go in?" I said.

She looked at her watch. "No."

We were out on that porch for a hell of a long time. I couldn't believe how intense it was. It didn't make the least bit of sense: a scruffy high-school girl I'd never met before in my life, a girl wearing baggy jeans and those *goddamn awful brown Oxfords*? She checked her watch again. "I have to go in now."

"Can I see you tomorrow?"

"Yes."

"Do you want to do something . . . go to a movie . . . or out to dinner?" I didn't know why I was being so extravagant with the invitation. She probably wasn't old enough to go to a bar, but it would have been enough to ask her out for a Coke.

"Yes."

"Well, what? Dinner?"

"Call me."

I pulled a pen from my pocket, began pawing around to try to locate a scrap of paper. She took the pen from me and, with the same deliberation with which she'd first kissed me, took my hand, turned it over, palm down, and wrote her phone number onto the back of my arm.

I NEVER got enough sleep; most Saturdays I wouldn't have emerged from bed before noon or even one, but that morning I found myself wide awake at seven-thirty, asking myself just what the hell I thought I was doing. Natalie might not be fourteen, but she was *exactly the same age as Linda Edmonds*, and that, I realized, could not possibly be a coincidence. If I'd been playing it cool, I would have waited till afternoon, but I needed something like a confirmation that there was a real person out there in the world who existed independently of whatever I might be thinking about her. I called her around ten. On the phone, her voice was flat and noncommittal. Sure, dinner was fine with her, she said. I said I'd see her at six. By late afternoon I was absurdly nervous. I shaved, took a shower, changed into clean jeans, and then had a second thought: I would almost certainly be meeting her parents. (Damn it, this really was like high school!) I changed again—into a white shirt, dress slacks, and a pair of shoes left over from the Academy. I showed up at her house at six on the dot.

Natalie met me at the door, opened it so quickly that she must have been waiting for me. I saw at once that I'd made the right decision: she was wearing a grey wool sheath with a black sweater under it, nylons, ballerina flats, and even pink lipstick. The night before, when she'd been engulfed in her grotesque clothes, I hadn't been able to form any impression of her figure. I'd expected her to be thin, and she certainly was, but not the kind of thin that gets called "willowy." She was a big strong girl, flat-chested and narrow at the hips, who looked as though she'd be great at sports—as indeed she was. "Hi," I said, or something like it. She didn't say anything but took my hand and led me into the living room.

I was expecting her to introduce me to her parents; there they were, her father leaping out of his recliner to greet me, her mother on the couch turning to stare at me, but Natalie merely led me in and stopped in the middle of the room, clinging fiercely to my hand, and said nothing as though it was enough simply to bring me in and display me. I was nonplussed, then made (I thought) a brilliant recovery, stepping forward, offering my hand: "Hello, I'm John Dupre."

Her father dwarfed me as he approached. Like Natalie, he looked lean and powerful; I couldn't get any sense of the eyes behind the flaring light reflecting back from thick bifocals; he had a huge shock of silver hair, a tense grin, and a strong grip. "Frank Hewitt. Pleased to meet you, John." (That was the first I'd heard Natalie's last name. Later, I looked up her father in the university catalogue, discovered that he was Doctor Hewitt, an associate professor.) "This is my wife, Emily."

I stepped toward Mrs. Hewitt who was still aiming her lined, white, haggard, moonlike face at me; she looked older than her husband, too old to be Natalie's mother. Her mouth was working oddly as though chewing something. Before I could say a word, she nodded to me and turned abruptly to stare into the fireplace. "Lilly tells me that you're at the university," I heard Dr. Hewitt saying.

"Yes, sir," I boomed back at him, "I'm a sophomore."

Even after I became familiar with it, I always found something spooky about Natalie's house, but that first night it was like stepping into The Twilight Zone: a nightmarish combination of dark wood and ancient furniture, a clutter of too many knick-knacks, the smell of dust and old cigarette smoke, pools of amber light pouring out from under elaborate cloth lampshades—but never enough light, most of the room lost in a deep brown soup. The TV was going but with the volume on low; newspapers were strewn about on the couch and the floor. The space in front of the fireplace was dominated by a marble chessboard, far larger than the usual size, with a game in progress. (In my overheated imagination, Death and The Knight from *The Seventh Seal* had just slipped out of the room.) One whole wall was crammed with small inept landscape paintings, each with something wrong with it: clouds that looked like sinister organic forms, a cow with a face that was nearly human, shadows that were cast toward the sun. Dr. Hewitt was asking me what I was doing at WVU, and I was trying to tell him as Mrs. Hewitt stared into the fire and Natalie held my hand.

Words poured out of me like popcorn out of a hot skillet. I managed to convey the fact that I was on the Dean's List. Dr. Hewitt stood rooted to the spot a few feet in front of me, his mouth partially open and his glasses gleaming. Periodically he emitted short meaningless phrases of encouragement: "Oh, that's good . . . Yes, yes . . . Yes, I can see that . . ." Suddenly Mrs. Hewitt leapt to her feet, seized a pack of cigarettes from the mantel, worried one out of the pack and lit it. "You're a handsome young man," she said, interrupting the bizarre conversation I was having with her husband.

"Thank you," I said, astonished.

"Isn't he a handsome young man, Lilly?"

Natalie looked directly into her mother's face and said not a word. Mrs. Hewitt turned away, dragging on her cigarette. "Where are you going?" she said, addressing the fireplace.

Natalie looked at me and rolled her eyes up to the heavens in what, I would discover, was a characteristic gesture, one that went perfectly with what she sometimes said when she did it: "Oh, brother!"

"To a dinner and a movie," Natalie said. "I told you that, Mom."

Mrs. Hewitt flicked her ashes into a large ashtray made of bottle-green glass. I was dry-mouthed, sweating, dying for a smoke. What the hell, I thought. "Do you mind?" I said, extracting my cigarettes from my shirt pocket.

Dr. Hewitt answered: "Oh, no, go right ahead." I pounded one out of the pack and so did he; he was offering me one of his, but I'd already got mine pressed into my mouth. He gave me an embarrassed, apologetic grin and said, "We're very pleased to meet you, John."

"Oh, yes," Mrs. Hewitt said. "We're certainly pleased. Very pleased. Yes, indeed."

My God, I thought, what weird gauche people. It was as though they'd learned how to behave by reading about it in an Estonian tourist's guide to the United States.

"Would you like to take the car, Lilly?" her dad said.

"Sure."

He jerked the keys out of his baggy tweed pants and winged them in her general direction; she snagged them easily out of midair although she had to dart to the side like a tennis player to do it.

Mrs. Hewitt followed us to the door. "No later than midnight, Lilly."

"Yes, Mom."

Mrs. Hewitt picked a bit of lint from her daughter's dress; Natalie backed away from her. "That doesn't mean five after or ten after or even one after."

"I know, Mom."

Mrs. Hewitt looked at me with distressed eyes—the kind of look you might get from someone found wandering away from an automobile wreck—and I caught the familiar scent of whiskey. Years of experience with my dad had taught me how to catch that scent and gauge it. Everything finally added up: Natalie's mom was drunk as a lord.

Their car was a station wagon, the kind with the wood panels. Natalie didn't give me a chance to open the door for her but jumped into the driver's seat. I got into the other side. She put the key in the ignition but then sat there a moment, her hands on the wheel, staring straight ahead. Took a deep breath and exhaled: a long sigh—*whew!* Turned to look at me, gave me a small conspiratorial grin as though we were both in on the same joke. I hadn't been sure of her before, but that grin made me like her enormously. "Where did you want to go?" she said.

I'd been planning to take her to a Greek place, a student

hangout that was barely a cut above Johnny's, but now that didn't seem right. "I didn't know we'd have a car," I said.

"Do you like Italian food?" she said, taking over the date.

She drove us to a part of Morgantown where I'd never been; it wasn't the world's classiest restaurant but several cuts above the places where I usually ate, and I thought, oh, my God, this kid's going to be expensive.

I'd been expecting her to be hard to talk to, but she wasn't. She immediately began asking me a series of questions. Where was I from? What was my major? How long had I been playing the guitar? How had I learned to play it? Who did I like to listen to? After each of my answers, she volunteered information about herself to match what I'd just told her. The Hewitts were from Wisconsin; they'd moved to Morgantown when Natalie was ten. She thought she'd probably go into science. Maybe physics. Everybody kept telling her that girls shouldn't go into science, but she didn't care what people thought. She'd only been playing the guitar a few months. There was a guy in her class who was really good; he'd showed her the chords to "Silver Dagger." He wasn't anywhere near as good as I was, though (giving me a shy smile); would I show her some stuff? She loved Joan Baez and Carolyn Hester. She hadn't heard of a lot of the people I liked, would I play them for her?

While we were talking, she did something I found quite disconcerting: reached across the table, took my hands, and then I didn't know what she was doing with them—not merely holding them, it was almost as though she was examining them. She stroked each of my fingers, massaged my palms. Her own hands were nearly as big as mine but thinner. She let go of my hands only when I lit a cigarette. She smoked one too. It wasn't an affectation; she obviously enjoyed smoking.

She wouldn't let me pay for her dinner. She picked up the

bill, calculated the tip and added it in, divided the total in half, announced the figure right down to the penny—all of this done in her head in less than a second. "I don't believe in boys paying for everything," she said. "It's not fair."

I took her back to my place. It was Saturday night; Eddie was off with his girlfriend, and Joe was exactly where I would have been if I hadn't had a date: in The Seventh Circle getting loaded. If it made Natalie nervous to be in a boy's apartment, she didn't show it. I taught her the basic two-finger Travis pick; my steel strings hurt her fingers, but she got the idea fairly quickly. I thought that the first date was a little too soon to invite her into my bedroom, so we made out on the couch. She really did love kissing. At the end of the evening, I said, "Do you want to do something tomorrow?"

"Yes."

"What?"

"I don't care. What time do you get up?"

"Around eleven."

"I'll come over."

It never seemed to have occurred to her that there was anything unusual about starting a date at eleven in the morning.

AS A possible philosophy major, I kept trying to read Wittgenstein. He was demoniacally difficult, but I kept coming back to him because I had the feeling that he held the key to something that was of vital importance to me if only I could figure out what it was. "If a Lion could talk, we could not understand him," Wittgenstein wrote, and I knew him well enough to know that what he was saying was *not* something as simple, and trivial, as "a lion's language would require translation." No, I was sure that he was referring to encountering something utterly alien, a mode of being incomprehensible at its very root. As I was getting to know her, I began to think of Natalie as Wittgenstein's lion.

We never discussed how we felt about each other, but, immediately after our first date, she seemed to assume that we would spend most of our time together. While we were making out, I told her that her skin was like alabaster and rose petals. She laughed. "Oh, brother! You don't have to snow me, you know." But a moment later she startled me by adding, "I'm already snowed." That was the closest she ever came to telling me that she liked me. I think in her mind it was something she didn't have to *tell* me.

Confronted with people she didn't know, Natalie didn't speak at all, couldn't manage even the most basic of *hi, how are you?* conversations—but with me, and, after she got to know them, with my roommates, she talked a lot. A standard conversational gambit for her was to say something like, "Do you know about the Purkinje shift?" and, if you didn't, she would tell you all about it. She could be counted on to know the phase of the moon at night and the dew point in the day, the species of the tree you were standing under or of the bug that had just landed on your coat, and not only the name of the cloud above your head, but its elevation. For Natalie, nothing could be more beautiful than the periodic table of the elements: "Oh, it's just so neat!" A true child of Sputnik, she followed the space program the way a teenage boy might follow baseball. Her mind was stuffed with a million mathematical formulae and scientific facts. Yet she could not recognize a line of even the most well-known poetry. One night I told her that I had "miles to go before I sleep."

"Oh?" she said, obviously surprised, "where are you going?"

I played chess with Natalie only once. We used the big marble board in her living room and played three games. "You play white," she told me when we started. Oh, I thought, the poor kid must feel more comfortable on defense where all she has to do is respond. I opened with the standard old-fashioned knight's game. Several moves in, I saw that she'd left a bishop uncovered. "Did you mean to do that?" I said. "Sure," she said. I took the bishop, and she mated me five moves later. Stung, I played the second game by the book. She opened with a fast slashing center game—lots of exchanges—and mated me in less than ten minutes. Back to playing white, I confronted her with my sneaky Russian opening—closed front and fianchettoed bishops—and all I succeeded in doing was slowing things down; it took her all of twenty minutes to win that one. "Hey, that was fun," she said, "you really made me think." To show me how hard I'd made her think, she replayed that last game. She remembered every move of it—apparently without any effort at all. Watching her show me the crucial moments, a stunning array of possibilities of how it might have gone, I realized not merely that she was a far better chess player than I was but that, in her ability to manipulate abstract patterns, she was in another universe altogether.

But Natalie's world was an oddly literal one. I read her some of my poetry, and she said, "I don't get it." When we talked about it, I could see that she really didn't. She had trouble with metaphor, couldn't understand how something might mean not one thing but several, how words might be put together for their strange resonance, their ability to open up unexpected paths in the mind. She had, to use a term Cohen loved, absolutely no "contradiction tolerance." She wouldn't sing religious folk songs because "I don't believe in all that crap." She wouldn't even sing the Carter Family's "Keep on the Sunny Side" because of the line that says "trust in our Savior always." When I sang the song, I could make "our Savior" a metaphor for anything I wanted—a general God principle in the universe or even the Buddha himself—but for Natalie "our Savior" could only mean the stupid

Jesus who'd annoyed her in Sunday school. She didn't want to hear about Zen Buddhism. "There's no scientific basis for religion whatsoever," she said. "When you die, it's lights out."

When we went out together, she never wore a dress again until her grad parties in the spring. She did make an effort though, retired the ratty outfit she'd worn to the SPU hootenanny, and usually wore neatly pressed blouses, nice sweaters, and sleek jeans—not as tight as I would have liked but tight enough to show off the lovely lines of her adolescent figure. (This was in an era when girls most emphatically did not wear jeans all the time, and on the WVU campus she stood out as much as I did.) She never wore makeup, not even, as most girls did, a once-over lightly with lipstick. Her only feminine vanity seemed to be her magnificent long hair. She never braided it or put it in a ponytail, simply brushed it straight back Alice-style and let it hang, or, if she wanted to get it out of her way, held it with a hairband. She washed it often and brushed it one hundred strokes every day. (I watched her do it, and then, later on, did it for her.) Girls' clothes, she said, were "really stupid." Especially nylons. "Who could have invented the damn things? Can you imagine anything dumber? They don't keep you warm, don't do *anything*. You wear them once and they get runs in them. You've got to attach them to some ridiculous contraption, and then they never stay up anyway."

Natalie wanted the world to be "fair" and was constantly either saddened or infuriated when she found out yet again that it wasn't. It wasn't fair what we had done to the Indians. It wasn't fair that Negroes couldn't go to school or eat in restaurants with us. It wasn't fair that there were different rules for boys and girls. "I believe in girls and boys being equal," she told me.

"So do I," I said.

"Good," she said. "I thought that's what you'd think."

52

She never played games with sex, was always absolutely clear on what she would and wouldn't do. Yes, she would go in my bedroom and shut the door and lie down with me on my bed. No, she wouldn't take her clothes off. When I tried to touch her between the legs, she said, "Don't do that, please," and so I didn't. I could, I discovered, touch her anywhere else. It was obvious that she understood what a male orgasm was; when I was getting close—dryfucking as we always did, our legs intertwined—she knew exactly what to do to help me to get there. I was so naïve in those days that I thought only married women had orgasms (I thought women had to be *penetrated* to have orgasms!), but, looking back on it, I'm pretty sure that Natalie had a few herself lying with me on that narrow bed in my Allen Street apartment.

I'D BEEN imagining her as a weird eccentric loner, but it turned out that she did have friends. Tom and Dave were both, like Natalie, seniors and members of the science club (Natalie was president); the boys had girlfriends, Janet and Sharon. From my lofty pain-in-the-ass vantage point as a university student, they seemed to be strangely old-fashioned teenagers like something out of *Our Miss Brooks*, but they were perfectly nice kids, and I probably would have liked them if I'd taken the trouble to get to know them. Now that Natalie had a boyfriend—this appeared to be the general assumption—we could all do something *together*.

But I wasn't sure I wanted to be Natalie's boyfriend. I felt as though I'd lost control of things almost as soon as I'd met her; I felt, as a matter of fact, somewhat invaded. I couldn't imagine having much of a future with a girl whose mind seemed so profoundly different from mine, a girl who wasn't interested in poetry or Zen, a girl who hated wearing dresses and nylons. I certainly didn't want to be her boyfriend in a way that would be defined by the mores of Morgantown High, and I didn't want to hang out with a bunch of high-school kids, especially kids whose idea of a good time was to go bowling at the Mountainlair. I'd turned down a couple invitations to do something with "the gang" (what era were they living in? I wondered), but I knew I was running out of options.

In January, shortly after Christmas break, we had a bitter cold snap, one that set records. I came over to Natalie's house expecting us to go out to dinner and then back to my place to play our guitars and make out. "We're going ice skating," she said.

I'd never been on any kind of skates in my life and said so.

"It doesn't matter," she said. "It's easy. I'll show you. It's lots of fun. We do it every year if it gets cold enough. You can probably wear my skates. How big are your feet?" We were sitting on the couch in the living room. She lifted one bare foot, offering it for comparison. I pulled off a boot and held up a foot next to hers. As implausible as it seemed, our feet were almost the same size; mine was slightly shorter and slightly wider.

She had two pairs of ice skates, she said. Her old pair was a little too small for her, but she could still wear them if she wore thin socks. The new pair she'd got for Christmas would probably fit me. She handed me the box. I opened it and found a pair of girls' figure skates—brand new, immaculate, white. I took one out of the box. I'd never realized it before, but there's something quite sexy about girls' white figure skates. "I don't know," I said.

Our eyes met. My discomfort must have shown on my face. "We're going to be out in the woods," she said. "Who's going to care?"

The gang came over, and we piled into the Hewitts' station wagon. Natalie drove us out of town. I was too apprehensive to pay much attention to where we were going. We ended up rattling over a narrow, badly rutted dirt road that ended at what they called "the pond": a blank, flat, dully reflective area that emerged suddenly out of the dark trees. It looked to me big enough to call a lake. The first order of business was making a fire. I wasn't much help. The girls and I gathered twigs and branches while Natalie and the boys constructed a tidy scaffolding that looked like something out of a Boy Scout manual. The night was lit only by a thin slice of moon and so cold it was painful. For a while we stood around the fire warming up, passing around the beer the boys had brought, and then they began to put on their skates.

I sat on the back seat of the car, stuck my feet out the open door, and laced on Natalie's skates. I couldn't imagine how I'd got myself into this preposterous situation. Whatever cool I had—as an older boy, university student, and authentic ethnic folk singer—would very likely not survive my appearance as a clumsy inept clown in girlish white skates falling methodically on his ass.

Natalie was already shooting off onto the pond. "Be careful, Nat," they yelled after her. I was astonished at how fast she was moving; she vanished into the darkness, then reappeared, bent forward with her hands behind her back, skating directly at us. At the last possible moment she cut to a stop, spraying ice. "Show-off," Janet yelled at her.

"Come on, you guys," Natalie said, "it's solid as a rock. The temperature at noon hasn't been above freezing for eight days."

I didn't know that you could walk in ice skates, but Natalie walked up to me (I was still glued to the car seat) and took my hand. "It's easy, John. Just try standing up on them. Get used to having the blade under your feet. OK, now just walk around."

I wobbled down to the fire. The kids didn't know me well enough to tease me, but they teased Natalie: "Oh, what tiny little feet you must have, Nat."

"Yeah, you must be a real Cinderella."

"Barges," Natalie said wryly, "tugboats."

She and Tom helped me out onto the ice. I wrapped my arms around them, and they showed me how to push off and glide. I'd spent hours teaching Natalie chords, picking styles, and tunes; she seemed to enjoy turning the tables on me, becoming the teacher. "Simple," she said, "just one thing at a time."

After a few minutes Tom skated away, and I was left with Natalie. She held my hands and skated backward as I skated forward. "I won't let you fall," she said, and I believed her. I was surprised that my body was getting the hang of it in spite of myself. "See how easy it is," she said. "Now let's really *skate*."

She didn't give me even a few seconds to worry about it but shot deftly backward until she was side by side with me, wrapped her right arm around my waist and caught my left hand in hers. "Don't lean on me," she said. "Find your own balance. Just do exactly what I do. Now I'm going to push off on my right foot and glide on my left." I knew that if I hesitated, we were doomed; when she pushed off and glided, so did I.

I stared down at our radiantly white feet. Side by side, we skated slowly forward. "Don't fight me," she said, "or you'll pull us both over." When we played music together, I was always in charge—firmly—but now she was leading. Could I allow myself to go with her? "You're doing great," she said. "You want to go faster?"

"I don't know," I said, but she was already increasing our tempo. At first I was so focused on doing exactly what she was doing that I couldn't look at anything but our feet, but then I realized that it *was* like music, that we were stating a rhythm as steady as a guitar strum—I could *hear* it—so I allowed myself to look up. We were so far out in the woods, away from city lights, that every speck of light counted—even that thin smile of a crescent moon—and our skates shone, white against black, moon against night, as our breath made fluttering feathers of steam, momentarily, to be swept away into a cold so intense I swear I could feel the air contracting. The sound of our blades was like that of an organ pipe meeting its first bite of air, that initial cut, the chiff before there's a note, then a metallic sheen: chiff with the push, and shhh of the glide, a rhythm that wouldn't let me down just so long as I could hold it.

But could I hold it? I was afraid that if she went any faster, I wouldn't be able to think through the motion of each foot, and if I couldn't think through it, I wouldn't be able to do it, and then we'd both go careening onto our asses on the ice. But she was already going faster, and I was already going with her, and then it was as though I had skated through a barrier in my mind: I didn't *need* to think through each motion any more than I needed to think, "now thumb, now index finger," when I was picking my guitar. I felt my mind open, stared upward at the stars, an infinity more than we could have seen in town—brilliant pin points, prickles of light, ice shards—and saw that they were not merely brilliant dots, but some were dusted, some were smeared, as we rode on the bite and glide of our skates.

The pond was opening out, becoming larger, unfolding itself as magically flat in West Virginia where nothing is flat: edged with black silhouettes of winter-stripped trees, a sense of being in cupped hands, and the curve of moon low to the horizon, a sideways smile, the last of the cat, his whiskers encircling us long past any fear of falling. So far away now that the other kids were tiny black figures backlit by a child's fire on the bank, receding, opening in the mind to a hugeness, vastness, an open blank, a cold emptiness, crystalline. Shiver light, chiff and shhh, the motion like heartbeat, held. "You OK?" Natalie said.

"Oh, yeah." I wondered how far she was taking me. Like waking from an imagined story to the immediacy of a story in motion, a meditation, not the least bit elusive, but everything packed into right now. For all the rebel nonconformist I thought myself to be, how often had I limited myself, protected myself, inside known and safe routines? Even my endless walks through the geography of Morgantown had become predictable, a reconfirmation of what I thought I already knew. I felt my ordinary life as false and limited, blinkered, and it struck me finally how completely I must have trusted Natalie to allow her to take me on this journey; it was magic, it was fabulous, the distant fire unraveling smoky sparks into the sky, the distant skaters emblematic images of an ancient American pageantry, a Currier and Ives print. But we were leaving all that behind, leaving a crucial message behind, cut into the ice in an illegible script; the Natalie with her arm around me and the Natalie in my mind were in motion, were converging, had become a single magnificent girl, aiming us out into a black open blankness where I would not understand myself when I got there, and, if we ever came back, I would not understand where I had been.

But the pond did not go on forever. It did have an edge, and we followed it back. Breathing hard, holding hands, we stepped off the ice and walked up to the fire. Natalie was laughing, and so was I. One of the girls handed me a beer. The kids were roasting hot dogs. "You were terrific," Natalie said and kissed me. I looked into her flushed, vivid face, her happy fire-lit eyes, and thought: I'll be your boyfriend, Natalie.

WE WENT together less than ten months, but in memory it feels far longer because after Christmas we were hardly ever separated. She walked to my place every day after school; I had a key made for her so she could let herself in. She really did hate wearing skirts; she always changed into jeans. She ate dinner with us so often that Joe asked her to contribute to the food bill; she thought that was only fair. She even took her turn cooking, but she wouldn't help clean up: "I'm not picking up after you pigs." She did her homework sitting on my bed. For days at a time she only went home to sleep, and most nights she didn't go home till midnight. Joe and Eddie thought I was screwing her, and I didn't disabuse them of that notion.

At first we tried to spend some time at her place; it must have been the bare minimum she estimated would keep the peace with her parents. One night, as we were sitting in the Hewitts' spooky living room watching television, we heard her mother come lurching down the stairs. "Don't say anything," Natalie told me. "Anything you say just makes things worse."

Natalie's mother, wearing an old flannel dressing gown, shuffled into the living room and stopped, extended one hand to support herself against the wall. She was smoking; she flicked her ashes onto the floor. She stared directly at me and said, "You're a very clever young man."

Even if Natalie hadn't warned me to keep my mouth shut, I couldn't have found a response to that. "Who do you think you are?" Mrs. Hewitt said. "Insinuating yourself into our good graces. Taking advantage of us like this." She was obviously a seasoned, experienced, dyed-in-the-wool drunk: even though she was so loaded she could barely stand upright, she was slurring only slightly; her voice was loud and cutting: "Do you think we're idiots? Do you think we can't see what's going on around here?"

Dr. Hewitt, in robe and pajamas, was hurrying down the stairs. "Emily," he said. "Please, Emily, come back to bed."

She turned to her husband, her face pulsing with rage. "It's obvious what's going on around here. Any idiot could see what's going on around here. Well, what are you going to do about it, Frank? Nothing? Is that right? Nothing? Oh, I know you. You'll do what you always do. Nothing, nothing, and yet more nothing."

Dr. Hewitt sent us a sickly look of apology. "Emily, please."

He gently pried the cigarette out of his wife's fingers and butted it out in an ashtray. Then he began herding her back toward the stairs. She sagged and nearly fell. Dr. Hewitt wrapped one of her limp arms around his shoulders, grabbed her by the waist, and began hoisting her up, step by step. Her feet, as though on their own, tried their best to help him. We heard them shuffle and thump back to their bedroom, heard the door shut. Then Mrs. Hewitt emitted one last shriek that came through to us loud and clear: "She's not your little girl any *more*, Frank!"

Natalie, staring straight ahead, had frozen into absolute immobility. I knew that this time she wasn't going to give me any small conspiratorial grin.

"My dad's a drunk too," I said.

"As bad as that?"

"Oh, yeah. Every bit as bad as that."

She turned and looked directly into my eyes. She didn't say a word, but an essential communication passed between us nonetheless. "Let's go back to your place," she said.

OVER SPRING break I took Natalie home to Raysburg. If her parents had any objections, I didn't hear about them. I kept worrying about her parents—and told her so. "I'm a straight-A student," she said. "I got spectacular Board scores and somebody's going to give me a scholarship. I've never come home drunk in my life, and I'm not going to get pregnant. They've got nothing to complain about."

If she could be that blunt, I thought, so could I. "How do they know you're not going to get pregnant?"

"I told them," she said as though that had taken care of everything.

I loved showing Natalie around my hometown. We drank beer in the Cat's Eye, hit the Polish bars with some of the guys I knew from the Academy, walked across the Suspension Bridge, sat on the riverbank. I showed her the Jamboree Shop where I bought my cowboy boots, and she said she'd been wanting cowboy boots. She wasn't the least bit attracted to the girlish white ones I pointed out; instead, she bought a pair like mine. Intentionally dressing her up like a boy (I didn't tell her what I was doing, but I'm sure she knew it), I lent her one of my shirts to complete the outfit and photographed her leaning against a tree at Waverly Park.

Of course I had to take her to the Markapolous household to watch Cassandra turn green with jealousy. What I told myself was that I wanted all of my friends to know each other, but, looking back on it, I suspect that I was getting even with Cassy for starting to date high-school boys. "She's a pretty enough girl *in her way*," Cassandra said. "Does she ever talk?" My father tried his flirtatious bullshit with Natalie, but the moment she smelled alcohol on his breath, she closed up like a clam, and, much to my amusement, he got precisely nowhere. My mother, just before we left, took me aside to say, "She's a nice girl, John, but she's much too kiddy for you." I couldn't figure out what she'd meant. She hadn't said anything like that about Cassandra even when Cassandra had been fourteen.

For a long time I thought that Natalie, unlike every other girl I'd ever met, simply didn't care about clothes. When she found the stack of *Vogues* and *Seventeens* by my bed, she said, "You're more of a girl than I am." Girls' magazines, she said, had always bored her silly. She never talked about clothes, but it became apparent that she did think about them. After we came back to Morgantown, she wore her cowboy boots all the time—with jeans and boys' shirts. When Joe first saw her walking up Allen Street to our place, he said, "Hey, Dupre, here comes your little brother." Her friends started calling us "the twins."

Natalie and I spent a lot of our time together playing music. We played in public every chance we got, at parties and hootenannies with both Natalie's friends and mine; dressed the way we were, we must have looked like a fledgling Country and Western duo. I fingerpicked a steel filigree behind her strummed guitar chords while she sang the melancholy old ballads she loved. She delivered some of her lines with such intensity that it was impossible not to believe she was going to do exactly what she said:

> I'll venture through England, through France,
> and through Spain.
> I'll venture through England, through France,
> and through Spain.
> My life I will venture on the watery main.

Much to my surprise, she also adored Irish drinking songs. We learned a half dozen of them—which made us welcome anywhere we went. We sang them in unison, took them in a good rollicking tempo (my Martin drowned out her Spanish guitar, but it didn't seem to matter), and belted them out for all we were worth, usually with everybody in the room joining us:

> It's NO! . . . NAY! . . . NEVER!
> No nay never no more.
> Will I play the wild rover,
> No never no more.

A year later, I would buy Ian and Sylvia's first record and be killed by "The Pride of Petrovar." That sound was exactly where Natalie and I had been headed; if we'd stayed together, we might even have got there.

I COULD never decide how I felt about Natalie. My close friendships had always been based upon intense, personal, even confessional dialogues, and Natalie did talk to me—sometimes non-stop and at great length—but the confessional was definitely not her mode. We never discussed how we felt about each other or where we were going as a couple—*if* we were going anywhere, *if* we were a couple. Sometimes I loved the childlike quality about her that could make her seem as gloriously pure and naïve as Joan of Arc; at other times I thought that she was, to use my mother's bizarre word, "kiddy."

Just as I had been my whole life, I still loved all the outward trappings of femininity—the nylons and petticoats and high heels and lipstick that Natalie didn't wear—and I'd always been attracted to ultra-feminine girls. Even Cassandra, for all of her boyishness, had a feminine side. But the only thing overtly feminine about Natalie was her long hair. When I'd photographed her in the park, I'd encouraged her (and none too subtly at that) to look like a boy, so I supposed I deserved exactly what I got when she started dressing like my twin. Sometimes she really did look like a pretty boy, and on one level I liked it. (Was I the same guy who'd sent Linda back to her room to put a skirt on?) On another level, I was embarrassed by it. And then came the final demonic complication: I was embarrassed that I liked it.

I was relieved when the weather got hot and Natalie switched from jeans and cowboy boots to pedal pushers and ballerina flats. I'd never thought much about pedal pushers, but now I came to appreciate them. They were feminine *and* boyish; they showed off her cute, lean-hipped figure even better than jeans did—and I couldn't imagine any garment better designed for dryfucking. "I love you in pedal pushers," I told her.

"That's good," she said; "they're comfortable."

We were sitting out on the porch one afternoon; I ran my

hand up her bare calf, felt the prickles. "Hey, buddy, you need a shave."

"You're the one who cares," she said. "You do it."

We went into the bathroom, and then the girl who had never allowed me to remove a single article of her clothing simply unzipped her pedal pushers and pulled them off. Just as I'd guessed, she wore plain white cotton panties. She sat on the sink counter, and I shaved her legs. "Boys respond to visual stimuli more than girls do," she told me.

Natalie in her pedal pushers was, I thought, like a distant echo of a girlish boy from another era—a Blue Boy or a Little Lord Fauntleroy. To bring that image alive, I bought her a pair of black patent flats. "You're like a crow," she said. "You like shiny things."

ONE WEEKEND in May Natalie's parents decided to drive back to Wisconsin to see Natalie's grandparents; they wanted her to come along, but she refused. She didn't want to waste the time, she told them; she had a project due, some tests coming up. They had several spectacular fights about it, but Natalie got her way as she usually did. As soon as they were gone, she said, "Do you want to stay with me?"

"You could stay at my place."

"No, I can't. They'll call to check up on me."

I wasn't absolutely certain what the invitation to "stay with me" meant, maybe nothing at all, but then again, maybe something quite significant. There was, of course, more than one way not to get pregnant. I wasn't planning anything, but, on the other hand, I thought that a man should always be ready, so I bought a package of rubbers from the dispenser in the men's room at the Circle.

By the time we walked over to Natalie's place that Friday

night, I was so apprehensive I had to keep gulping down waves of nausea. In case any of the neighbors just happened to be looking out their windows, Natalie was going to walk straight up the sidewalk and in through the front door; I was to sneak up the alley in the dark, and she'd let me in through the kitchen door. That was just dandy, I thought, but how was I supposed to get out again tomorrow in the daylight?

The alley was one long inky black shadow. Feeling as though I'd just been cast into a role in one of Cohen's spy stories, I slipped off my boots and ghosted quickly into the darkness. She met me at the kitchen door; my heart was beating like a pile driver. She locked us in, closed all the drapes, and lit the lamps in the living room. The damned place seemed more than ever like a setting for a horror movie: all that ancient dark brown wood, a few patches of dirty yellowish light, and long reaches of crepuscular blackness in which, I imagined, there could be anything—maybe even Mrs. Hewitt herself who hadn't gone off to Wisconsin after all but was waiting, drunk and drooling and primed to start howling the moment she saw us. Natalie sat down on the couch, motioned me to sit down next to her. "You want to watch TV? They'll call a little after midnight. Mom will be out of it, so Dad will make the call, but she'll be standing right next to him."

A little after twelve the phone rang. She gave me a smile that said, "See, I told you," and answered it. She was a superb liar, talked to her father with exactly that thin edge of sullen teenage impatience she would have used if everything she'd been saying had been absolutely true: "Hi, Daddy . . . Oh, about half an hour . . . Over at Dave's house . . . just played music, you know . . . Yeah, John walked me home. Yeah, I locked all the doors. Everything's fine . . . Say hi to Gram and Gramps . . . Love you too."

She hung up and sat for a moment holding the phone on her lap. She was staring at all those weird little paintings on the wall. "My mom did those." She sighed. "She was nice when I was little . . . Come on, let's go to bed."

Upstairs, she showed me where the bathroom was. In her bedroom, where, of course, I'd never been, she pulled open a dresser drawer. "You probably don't want pink, do you?" she said, giggling, and handed me a pair of baby-blue flannel pajamas. I went into the bathroom and put them on. They fit me just fine. I came back and found her in an identical pair in baby pink. I was too nervous to be able take in much of her room, but it seemed to be a friendly clutter, and, like Natalie herself, not particularly girlish. We got into her bed, and she turned out the light.

I'd been trying to convince myself that everything was all right, but no, things were not all right. A traitorous panic was taking over my entire body—a vise screwed to the back of my neck, a cold sweat, a weight on my chest, a dull pounding from my heart; worst of all, I couldn't think straight. I was terrified that she'd find out how frightened I was. Could I tell her I was sick?

"What's the matter?"

Having to pretend was making things worse. "I'm scared."

"What are you scared of?"

"I don't know."

She turned on the light. "Hey," she said and took my hands. I didn't know what that single syllable had meant, but it had sounded comforting.

I hated myself. If I hadn't clenched my jaws, my teeth would have been chattering. My entire body was shaking. Holding my hands, she could obviously feel it. "I forget how creepy this house is," she said. "I guess I'm used to it."

She studied me as though I were a complex mathematical problem; all I could see on her face was concern. "Oh," she said, "listen. Do you hear that?" I heard a distant, sinister, watery gurgle. "That's the refrigerator."

I couldn't believe it: she knew exactly how the refrigerator worked. She explained to me how each stage of the coolant cycle made a different sound. Then she told me about how changes in the temperature and humidity affected the wood in the house. "It just happened a few seconds ago. It'll happen again. Listen." I listened. Eventually I heard a tactful creaking—stealthy, purposeful. "When I was little," she said, "I thought that was somebody sneaking up the stairs, but it's just the wood contracting."

I was starting to feel a little better, but I still couldn't speak. "Hey," she said again, squeezing my hands. Now she looked truly worried. I wanted to help her, try to bring myself back to something like normal, but I didn't know how.

She let go of my hands, jumped out of bed, pulled a book from a shelf, came back and slid under the covers. "This was my favorite book when I was little," she said, and, much to my amazement, settled back onto her pillow and began to read it to me: "Over the great door of an old, old church which stood in a quiet town of a faraway land there was carved in stone the figure of a large griffin . . ."

In spite of myself, I was drawn into the story. The real griffin flies into the town to see his own image carved over the church door; everyone is terrified of him, but he becomes friends with a young priest. More interesting to me than the story itself was trying to figure out why Natalie would have liked it. I would never have guessed that she would have been drawn to a book with a priest and a church in it. I decided that she'd probably loved the griffin, that outlandish beast who turns out to be, not kind, but something, from her point of view, better than kind—*fair*. Yes, I thought, Natalie as a child would have liked that.

She finished the book and closed it. "You OK now?"

I looked into her pale brown eyes and knew that there was no one anywhere any more trustworthy than she was. "Yeah, I'm OK."

"I get scared too when I don't know where I am. It's natural. You know, the 'fight or flight' response. We still get it even though we're not in a state of nature anymore. It feels awful doesn't it? When there's nothing to fight and you can't run away?"

"Yeah, it sure does." I loved her for being so profoundly different from me.

"If you get scared again, wake me up. I won't mind."

My fear was gone, and I also knew that nothing sexual was going to happen between us that night. I was exhausted, but I was afraid I wouldn't be able to sleep. When I'd been little, my best friends had all been girls, and boys didn't go to pajama parties with girls, so I'd grown up without ever sleeping in the same bed with anyone else. As I was worrying that I was going to stay awake the entire night, Natalie fell asleep; I could hear it in her breathing. And then sleep must have sandbagged me too; the next thing I knew, daylight was streaming into the room. It was sweet and very strange to wake up to find that I was in bed with a sleeping girl.

The way Natalie got me out of the house without anyone seeing me was simplicity itself. Dave turned up in his dad's car, drove it into the Hewitts' empty garage. Natalie got into the front seat, and I got into the back and lay on the floor. Dave dropped us at my place.

We had one more night to play house. By then, I knew that we weren't going to have sex, not even the kind we usually had. Again I listened to Natalie lying to her dad on the phone; we watched TV and then went upstairs and changed into our pajamas. I was relaxed enough that second night to walk around her room and look at everything. Girls' rooms always fascinated me. Natalie's reminded me of Lyle's; she too had a rock and fossil collection, a telescope and a microscope. There were stuffed animals but no dolls. "I guess you didn't play with dolls," I said.

"No, did you?"

"Yeah, I did."

"Yeah, that figures," she said, laughing, but I could see that she didn't mean anything by it. She'd merely been teasing me.

I was delighted to find all of her Girl Scout badges displayed on a bulletin board. "I can't believe it," I said. "I'm going out with a Girl Scout."

She pushed me hard with both hands, sent me staggering backward a few steps. It was one of her kid-at-recess gestures that always took me by surprise; she didn't know her own strength. "You shut up about the Girl Scouts," she said.

"I bet you looked cute in your uniform."

"Oh, brother."

We got into bed, and she said in all seriousness, "Scouting helped make me into the person I am today." I knew enough not to laugh at her.

That second night we talked until four in the morning. She was still far from confessional, but she told me things I knew were close to her heart. She talked about camping with her dad when she'd been little, about Scouting. She told me about all the things she loved—hiking and fishing, horseback riding, and, not just ice skating but skiing and even snowshoeing. (My God, I thought, what an active girl!) She'd cried when they'd left Wisconsin, but she'd grown to like West Virginia because there was so much to explore. Caves, for instance. She described beautiful underground rooms gleaming with stalagmites and stalactites like something out of a fairy tale; she told me how sweet bats looked sleeping with their wings folded up. And trout fishing. "It's as hard as chess," she said. "You've got to think like a fish."

"This is really fun," she said. "It's so nice having you here. It's stupid that we couldn't just live together . . . if we wanted to. Most rules are stupid. That's why people break them. We haven't done anything bad, but Mom would never believe that."

ONE AFTERNOON that spring I stumbled home, exhausted, fell over onto my bed, and was out like a light. It was during the last big push of the school year when Natalie and I were both writing exams, and I'd been running on hardly any sleep. The first I knew that she was in the room with me was when I heard the door close. I opened my eyes just in time to see her climbing onto my bed. I was lying on my back. "What are you doing sleeping in the afternoon?" she said. With a wicked little smile, she sat on me. Then she caught my wrists and pinned me down.

I tried to get up, push her off, and got absolutely nowhere. Most of her weight was resting on my pelvis. My arms were stretched out to either side; she had a vise grip on my wrists and was leaning down with the full strength of her arms and shoulders. "Come on, Natalie," I said.

Grinning, she shook her head no. I thrashed from side to side, certain that I could dislodge her, but I couldn't. It was this simple: unless she let me up, I couldn't get up. I suppose it was just a silly game to her, but I felt myself slipping into a blind panic like the one that had damned near murdered me the first night I'd stayed at her house. For a minute or two I fought back stupidly, flapping like a landed fish. Laughing, she held me down. The small part of my mind that was still capable of rational thought was telling me that what I was feeling was ridiculously out of proportion to what was happening, that if I could calm myself down enough to say something like, "Natalie, you're scaring the hell out of me," she'd let me go, but I didn't want to admit it. "You're not going anywhere," she said, bent forward and kissed me.

At first I didn't want to be kissed, and resisted her, but then, as I felt her tongue in my mouth, I stopped resisting. It was a lovely kiss, Natalie at her best, and I felt the painful knot in my stomach melting away. "Let your hair hang down, Natalie," I whispered to her, "let it hang down on me."

"I know that song," she said—as well she should: I'd given her the *Folkways Anthology of American Folk Music* for her eighteenth birthday.

The thought of trying to push her off was ridiculous now; all I wanted was for her to go on kissing me. She was no longer a bratty kid goofing off, and wherever I'd gone, she was already there with me. She let go of my wrists, and I wrapped my arms around her. She rolled partially to the side, freeing me, slid one of her long legs between mine, and then, I swear, we were each other's breath and heartbeat. I didn't know I was crying out until she said, "Shhh," giggling, and pressed her fingers against my lips. Returned to the world, I could hear, through my closed bedroom door, voices, the hi-fi. Someone was playing that country-pop tune "Tennessee."

Natalie let herself sink onto the bed next to me, her head next to mine on the pillow. I looked into her pale brown eyes and said the only thing that made any sense: "I love you." It was the only time I ever said it to her.

"Oh, brother," she said, but she smiled. Later we sat on the swing on the front porch and chatted with Joe and Eddie and some other guys—I don't remember who else was there. It was a glorious spring evening, warm, full of the smell of flowers. We drank beer and smoked and played our guitars. Natalie sat close to me. She couldn't stop touching me, taking my hands.

AS NATALIE'S senior year drifted toward its end, we began to get invited to semi-formal parties. Assisted by her pals, Janet and Sharon, she bought a black cocktail dress. "Thanks for the shoes," she said to me and wore the patent flats with it—and even lipstick and mascara. "I feel like I'm going to a Halloween party," she said, but I thought she looked great and told her so.

She wanted to surprise me, she said, so wouldn't tell me anything about her prom gown, only that I should send a white corsage. I thought I was ready for anything, but she did surprise me. She'd been to a hairdresser who'd put her lovely hair into an elaborate French roll. She wore shoulder-length gloves. Her gown was a genuine Cinderella, baby pink with a full bell skirt all the way to the floor. "I thought you'd like it," she said.

At the Prom, the boys in "the gang" (which I supposed now included me) danced with each other's girlfriends. While I was dancing with Janet, she told me how happy everyone had been when I'd started going out with Natalie. "You were her first boyfriend, you know." Good God, I thought, how could she have learned to kiss the way she had that first night on her front porch? And then I answered my own question: she must have learned it by imagining it.

Of course I went to Natalie's graduation and sat with her parents. Natalie had known that she was going to get the science prize and the math prize, but she hadn't expected the citizenship award and didn't know what she might have done to deserve it. "Maybe it's because I was always nice to the younger kids." And then she was no longer a high-school girl. She walked me away from her friends and her parents, hugged me and cried silently for a few seconds. I knew exactly how she felt.

To be with Natalie as long as I could, I stayed in Morgantown until the end of June. I felt torn. Waiting for me in Raysburg were Cohen, Revington, and, of course, Cassandra. Natalie came to the bus station to say goodbye to me; as we were waiting, she began to leak tears. "Don't cry," I said, panicking, "we'll see each other again."

"Oh, I know we will. But it'll never be the same as it was."

Surprised at myself, I started to cry too. We sat on a bench, holding hands, quietly crying together, until it was time for me to go. I sat by myself at the back of the bus and cried all the way to Raysburg.

3.

MY JUNIOR year should have been a breeze. I had everything going for me. I'd become a well-known campus character with a small but dependable circle of lunatic pals and drinking buddies. I'd completed all those damnable university requirements—aced two terms of Rat Psych for my science, plodded through four terms of German for my language, got my two years of ROTC out of the way. I'd chosen English over Philosophy for my major, and that had been the right decision; English courses were easy for me. I liked most of my professors, and they liked me. I was still on the Dean's List. Even my feelings for Morgantown had grown to be curiously affectionate and proprietorial. I was proud of the insanely steep streets, the months of pearly grey rain. I liked the slate-colored buildings, the somber hills that surrounded the town, the little bridge over Deckers Creek I crossed every day on my way to campus. I liked the Monongahela River—a good stand-in for the Ohio. I liked my cheap rattrap apartment. Whenever I stepped outside my door, I liked the view—a slice of bleak sky criss-crossed with black power lines, an image from Edward Hopper. I kept trying to convince myself that I liked living alone. I hadn't been prepared for how much I was going to miss Natalie.

I'd talked to her a few times over the summer, but Natalie wasn't good on the phone. I'd ended every conversation by telling her that any day now I'd be down for a visit, but I hadn't been able to pry myself loose from my friends—from the agreeably useless rut of the high fat summer of Raysburg—and by the time I got back to Morgantown, Natalie had already left. Alone again and plunged back into the familiar grind of student life, I finally had to admit that I'd treated her, exactly as my mother would have put it, "shabbily." Then, as the year wore on, I realized that

I might have treated myself shabbily too. Nothing could have changed the fact that she was going to Swarthmore and I was going to WVU, but why, I kept asking myself, hadn't I come back a few days early? It wouldn't have killed me. Boyfriends and girlfriends were separated all the time and somehow still managed to stay together. They looked forward to vacations, wrote letters to each other, talked on the phone, planned their future. Maybe Natalie could have given me what I'd always wanted from a girl: a reason to get out of bed in the morning.

The worst time of day for me was that period of nothingness stretching out interminably between my last class and my solitary dinner. That was the time when Natalie would have been arriving at my Allen Street apartment. We would have made out and had a beer with Joe and Eddie and cooked something. Now I came home to nobody, jumped straight into bed, jerked off, fell asleep, and woke, disoriented, to the night.

I called Natalie's dad for her address at Swarthmore and wrote to her. I didn't say much of anything except, "I miss you." I got a letter back from her so quickly she must have mailed it the same day she'd received mine. She wrote exactly the way she talked, listing everything she'd be doing without saying how she felt about it. Because of her College Board score, they'd put her into a small advanced math class, and it was, I gathered, taking up most of her time. She ended with: "I miss you too. I'll never forget you and all the fun we had together." I read her letter over and over again. The subtext beneath her last line seemed to be: "It's over if you want it to be."

SEPTEMBER, 1962. Morgantown, West Virginia. My junior year at WVU.

I have a free hour before my class in The Romantic Movement. I sit in the Mountainlair and watch the girls. I drink

75

coffee. I open my notebook, and I write: "It rained a lot that autumn, and I walked in the rain. The mist flattened the buildings of the campus into distant layers as though they were the cardboard cutouts of a movie set. It was the season of shiny raincoats, of penny loafers and knee socks, of plaid skirts with demure coed kick-pleats, of smoky colors—green, dun, ochre, orange, and scarlet—and the girls were dimly beautiful like the falling leaves. I heard their bright voices, indistinct in the distance, and I watched them from my remoteness, so drawn back that I could do nothing with my desire for them. The mist, the girls, the autumn, and my own preoccupation with my growing isolation blended to form an ambience I can recreate now by closing my eyes and thinking myself back to that corner table in the Mountainlair where I sat between classes, smoking, drinking coffee, writing about the rain."

I am writing as though I had left Morgantown years ago, writing as though I were an old man looking back, understanding everything. I'm twenty, but I feel old. My body aches from too little sleep; my eyes are gritty. I desperately wish I could understand everything, see it through the eyes of an old man.

I write, "It rained a lot that autumn," but it *is* that autumn; it is raining *right now*. The Mountainlair is filled with a sodden sheeplike smell: moist wool. The rain gets into everything; people create puddles where they sit, water dripping from coats and umbrellas. The windows are steamed, voices muted, meetings uneasy. I write: "The girls were dimly beautiful like the falling leaves," but they're dimly beautiful *right now*.

I've drunk my first cup of coffee. I stand and carry the empty cup across the room. I hear a girl's voice: "I don't know what I'm going to *do!* I'm so used to having *a boyfriend* . . . with his own *car* and *apartment*."

Oh, what a little pain in the ass that one must be, I think, and I turn to look. My body sees her. My chest goes as hollow as my coffee cup, hangs emptied, then fills again in a rush, slamming the base of my throat. The girl is talking to Marge Levine. Marge gives me a wave as they pass.

Like a somnambulist, I refill my coffee cup and walk back to my table. They're sitting not too far from me; I open my notebook and pretend to write. Marge settles back in her chair, composed, smiling faintly. The girl leans toward her, gesturing; I can't hear the girl's voice, but I can feel the bright energy of it. The way she's sitting, the way she's looking at Marge, the way she's punctuating her words with her hands—every inch of her is saying, *"Listen to me!"*

The girl has draped her raincoat over the back of a chair; beads of water catch glints of light as they run down the shiny red plastic and onto the floor. What has been revealed by the shedding of the raincoat is an outfit so tasteful, so carefully constructed, that she could have stepped out of an issue of *Seventeen* devoted to "going away to college"—forest-green sweater, Stewart tartan skirt, penny loafers the color of brandy. Almost any other girl would be wearing knee socks, but she's wearing nylons. A small girl. (If I were ever to kiss her, I would have to bend my knees or she would have to stand on tiptoe.) The kind of old-fashioned hourglass figure that would always say, even from across a vast rainy distance, *woman*. Hair not merely a dark brunette, not an *almost* black, but a true black, worn in a deliciously archaic pageboy with perfectly straight bangs cut halfway down her forehead. Huge shining dark eyes, full ripe lips emphasized with plum-colored lipstick. A face easily one of the most beautiful I've ever seen in my life. And that day I missed my class on the Romantics.

THE KEY to my mystery girl was Marge Levine. I could have waited for the next meeting of the SPU, but I didn't. I knew that if I wandered around campus long enough, I'd run into her, and I did the next day—coming out of the library. We stopped, chatted for a while—until enough time had passed to allow me to ask my burning question: "Who was that girl I saw you with in the Lair?"

She laughed. "You really set me up for this one . . . That was no girl, that was my cousin."

"Your cousin?" I said as though I'd never heard the word.

"Yeah, my cousin. We're sharing an apartment this year. Her name's Carol Rabinowitz. Why? You think she's cute?"

I didn't say anything, but my expression must have said it all.

"What happened to Natalie?" she asked me.

"She's at Swarthmore."

"Oh. That's too bad. Well, if you want me to introduce you, I will, but believe me, buddy, you're barking up the wrong tree."

I'd been imagining my mystery girl as a freshman. She'd certainly been dressed like one, and why else would I never have seen her before that fall? But no, Marge told me, Carol had an honors BA in English from Marshall. Not only was she in her first year of grad school at WVU, she was even a graduate assistant with her own section of freshman English.

The university officially regarded girls as children and itself as a stand-in for their parents. A dress code as strict and arbitrary as anything in any high school prohibited them from wearing pants to class. Girls were forbidden to set foot in a boy's apartment (a rule, as I recall, much honored in the breach). Their night life was cut off by a curfew; after that magic hour, they were locked away inside the Women's Dorm or in other supervised on-campus housing where boys were never permitted beyond the lobby. But a handful of girls were allowed to live off campus. As a senior on the Dean's List, Marge was one of them. As an MA candidate, Marge's cousin Carol was another. "Yeah," Marge said, "we've got a great place. It's on Beechurst. Come over some time."

"Am I allowed to visit you?"

She shrugged. "No, of course not . . . It's around the back and up the stairs. Don't make a spectacle of yourself."

Later in the day, I took her up on her invitation. She met me at the door, called back over her shoulder, "There's a man here," and I heard a single startled yelp.

Looking past Marge, I saw a brief image of Carol. She was wearing a blouse, slip, stockings, and shoes, but no skirt. Then she was gone with a stutter of angry footsteps, her bedroom door slamming behind her. She'd left an ironing board with a skirt on it. Marge obviously found the situation funny. "Do you want a beer?"

"Thanks, yeah . . . Hey, it's really nice," I said about the apartment (wondering if Carol was going to reappear). Rather than scavenged junk like I had in my place, they had real furniture: an easy chair, a couch that was actually comfortable, muslin curtains on the windows, a red and white checked cloth on the kitchen table, a row of neatly labeled spice jars lined up behind the stove, candles in Chianti bottles placed strategically around as though to create the ambience of a homey Italian restaurant. Of course they had a hi-fi and a record rack. A Picasso print hung on one wall, a Modigliani on another. I found out later that most of the effort that had gone into fixing up the place had been Marge's; all Carol did was live there.

At the first meeting of the SPU Marge had suggested that all of us—all six of us—join a new organization called Students for a Democratic Society. She'd handed out mimeographed copies of a paper that SDS had drafted the past summer, and I almost hadn't read it. I was dubious about political manifestos, but the *Port Huron Statement* hit me exactly right. In those days, people like Marge and me were nothing more than a tiny lunatic fringe on college campuses; if anyone had told me that in only a few years thousands of students would have read the *Port Huron Statement* and liked it as much as I did—that SDS, the obscure organization we'd just joined, would be considered so dangerous it would be infiltrated by the FBI—I would have laughed out loud.

To have some excuse for dropping by, I'd brought my copy with me. As with everything I read then, I'd underlined the best passages, written my own marginal notes. "I love this," I said to Marge, reading from the blurry purple mimeographed pages, "'We ourselves are imbued with urgency, yet the message of our society is that there is no viable alternative to the present.' That's wonderful. That could be a line in a poem . . . *no viable alternative to the present.*" Even as I was talking, I couldn't stop myself from glancing over, every few seconds, at Carol's closed door.

"Well, is there one?" Marge asked me.

"I sure as hell don't see one."

I had to broaden my definition of political, Marge told me. Real politics brings people out of their personal alienation and isolation and into community. We had to shed our apathy, change the university so that it reflected our values and aspirations, use the university as a fulcrum to change society. I told her it all sounded good to me, but at a place like WVU, it'd be like tilting at windmills.

In the middle of this, Carol floated into the room in a long shimmery bathrobe. Now I could see what she'd been doing all the time she'd been in her bedroom: her hair and makeup. Marge and I stopped talking and looked at her. With a dazzling smile, Carol walked straight to me and offered her hand. I rose to my feet and took it. "Hello," she said, "I'm Carol Rabinowitz. I'm afraid you're not seeing me at my best."

"Oh, I'll bet John's seen a girl with a robe on before," Marge said.

I think I said, "Howdy" (the authentic ethnic folksinger), but

I was so overwhelmed that it might have been anything. I couldn't even manage to tell her my name, so Marge did it for me.

Carol asked us what we were talking about. Marge told her. "Oh," she said, "is John one of your *comrades*?"

"Yes," Marge said, "that's exactly what he is." I saw a look pass between the two of them. I couldn't read it.

"Carol thinks politics is boring," Marge said.

"No," Carol said, "not boring. It's just something that's never interested me very much. My father's been telling me my whole life, 'Carol, you should take an interest,' and I suppose I should, but you only have so much time." She shrugged, gave me another delightful smile. Then she went back to the ironing board to finish her skirt.

With Carol in the room, the conversation gravitated toward things that she *was* interested in. Dante, Petrarch, and the Troubadour poets, she said. Their effect on the English lyric had been simply enormous. About those guys, I knew not very much. She said that she'd recently become interested in Yeats. I'd read a lot of Yeats; I loved him for "mad abstract dark" and said so. Carol gave me a cool assessing look that I translated as: oh, this guy's not quite the fool I thought he was.

She carried her ironed skirt into her bedroom and returned wearing it. The skirt was burgundy and so were her three-inch heels. She had precisely the kind of figure that the tight straight skirts of those days were designed to show off—a very girlish rearview—and she really did have the smallest waistline I'd ever seen on someone who wasn't a corseted actress in a movie. "Is my slip showing?" she asked Marge.

"Not a scintilla," Marge said.

A few minutes later Carol's date arrived—Andrew Forbes, the English Department's visiting professor from Merrie Olde Englande. I saw him as an enormous cliché: a lean, knobby scaffolding of bones, easily six feet tall, draped in a tweed jacket, who spoke with an impossibly plummy accent and had the kind of mature, weathered face that, if one is being kind, one calls "craggy." Carol turned her full, brilliant-eyed attention on him in a way that made me sick with envy. As though speaking by rote, she told me how nice it was to have met me, and then they were gone.

Sighing, Marge unplugged Carol's hot iron and set it on the sink counter to cool, folded the ironing board and put it away in the hall closet. "He's the reason she's developed an interest in Yeats," she said.

"My God," I said, "she's really incredible."

"John," Marge said, "don't you have something better to do with your time?"

I'D FALLEN in love at first sight yet once again, and yet once again it had happened exactly the way Lyle and I had envisioned it back in high school—as an unpredictable event that simply occurred, certainly nothing to do with *choice*—so I was relieved that Cupid hadn't presented me with the latest in a series of girls who were too young for me. Maybe I was growing up, I thought. Carol was two years older than I was. Carol was a real woman.

Pretending that I was coming over to see Marge, I dropped in unannounced as often as I thought I could get away with it. Marge was out a lot of the time; Carol, who was what was called in the campus slang of those days "a big booker," usually stayed home. I showed up prepared to impress her with my intellect. I didn't have an extra year of my life to read Dante, Petrarch, and the Troubadour poets, but I could certainly read bits and pieces of them, and I could certainly read, or skim, quite a lot of what had been written *about* them. When we talked about poetry, I was pleased to see her response to me shift from condescending to collegial. But I discovered soon enough that what Carol really wanted to talk about wasn't poetry, but herself.

She obviously needed someone who would hang on her every word with rapt attention, and if there was ever a guy who could do that, I was the one. Then I discovered that if I told her a personal story about myself, she would respond with an even more personal story about herself. Soon we were swapping increasingly intimate details of our lives. I heard about her childhood, her parents, her two older brothers, her high-school days, her undergraduate career at Marshall. The only thing she seemed reluctant to talk about was Stephen, her former boyfriend, the one "with his own *car* and *apartment*." She did mention his name, but that was about it, so of course I was curious.

I told her that when I'd first seen her, I'd thought she was a freshman. I'd meant it as a compliment, but it made her surprisingly angry. "People always think I'm younger than I am. It must be because I'm so small. It drives me crazy." When she taught her section of freshmen, she always wore a suit and heels so they'd take her seriously. She was an armchair Freudian and often professed an inability to understand her own unconscious motivations, and here, I thought, was a perfect example. It never seemed to have occurred to her that if she really wanted to look older, she should retire her tartan skirts and grade-school pageboy.

She'd known Marge her whole life—since they'd "been in diapers together"—and she thought of her more as a sister than as a cousin, but if she could talk the way she did about "a sister," I would have hated to hear what she might have said about someone she genuinely disliked. "Boy, does she have a reputation on this campus. She thinks she's daring and modern, but I just think she's sick." Carol thought Marge had appalling taste. "I can't believe some of her outfits. She looks like a tramp."

"I think Marge has a wonderful sense of style," I said.

"Oh, you would! Your fetishes are so obvious. If she didn't wear high heels all the time, you wouldn't look at her twice." That was unfair, I thought, and not entirely true—but true enough to make me uncomfortable.

I couldn't imagine how anyone with a waistline as small as Carol's could think of herself as overweight, but she did. She was always either on a diet or planning her next one, either stuffing herself on chocolate or living on cottage cheese. "Only three pounds," she kept saying all the time I knew her. "That's all I ask." There were also, I gathered, many other things wrong with her that needed fixing—bad habits and "complexes." She worried that she would never be "mature" enough or "adjusted" enough.

Carol saw Marge's radicalism as "sophomoric" and professed a complete disinterest in politics, but, if pressed, would admit to being "conservative." I'm fairly certain she didn't mean that she agreed with Barry Goldwater. More to the point, she called herself "an old-fashioned girl": her goal in life was marriage and babies. But not just yet, she said. Sometime later, after she had "matured," and, of course, had found the right man. She had a very clear idea of what she wanted. He would have to be "manly" and have morals just as strict and old-fashioned as hers. "I wouldn't marry a man who'd marry a girl who'd slept around," she said. He would have to be much older than she was—confident, self-assured, well established in his career—and she would be his helpmate. "Nothing would make me happier than ironing my husband's shirts."

All the time when I'd been with Natalie, I'd been imagining a phantom future girlfriend, and I'd told myself that the next one was going to have to be really feminine. There was no doubt about Carol being feminine. I never saw her in pants, and, for all I know, she might not have owned a pair. She set her hair every day, and, after a while, stopped being embarrassed when I caught her in rollers. With her tartan skirts—she seemed to have an infinite supply of them—she always wore nylons, never socks, because "*children* wear socks." She wore demurely clear nail polish because "colored polish looks cheap on girls my age." She always wore gloves, even when the weather wasn't particularly cold. She curled her eyelashes. She was always redoing her lipstick. She never left the apartment without putting dots of perfume behind her ears and on the veins of her wrists.

But, however immaculate Carol might have been about her person, she created a howling chaos all around her: face powder, hair rollers, bobby pins, open containers of makeup, combs and brushes blasted out from her like debris from an explosion. I was never invited into Carol's bedroom, but I could see through the open door that she flung her clothes everywhere. When Carol was working on a paper, she took over the entire apartment: books, note cards, various drafts left on the couch, on the floor, on the bookshelves, on the kitchen counters. Before she went anywhere, Carol always had to go through a frantic hunt for something; her gloves, purses, loafers, scarves, and lipsticks turned up in obscure corners, on bookshelves and windowsills, under chairs and under the couch. There was a drying rack in the bathroom, and she draped every rung of it and then kept on going, draped the towel racks, the top of the shower, every usable surface, with nylons, cashmere sweaters, bras and girdles, waist cinchers, garter belts, and panties—which I couldn't help seeing whenever I had to go in there. Sometimes one of her intimate objects—some naughty bit of black lace and boning—would stop me dead, and I'd get stuck, standing there staring at it, thinking, oh, my God, what would it be like to wear something like *that?*

Carol was playing a game with her British professor Andrew similar to the one I was playing with her. When they went out together, they talked about Yeats. If he had any romantic interest in her, he had yet to show it. "What do I have to do, lie down at his feet?" she said.

He had the nasty habit of pointing out beautiful girls on campus. They were usually sorority girls and had *a look* that Carol thought was appalling but one that obviously turned Andrew's crank. "What kind of look?" I said.

"They wear their skirts too tight and their heels too high. And they do something with their eyes . . . They look like negative raccoons, this little white mask . . ."

"Oh," I said. "I know what you're talking about. Wide eyes, lots of white eye shadow, lots of mascara, and pale lipstick. You could do that. You have gorgeous lips anyway. You don't need to focus so much attention on your lips. Why don't you try it? It's a more up-to-date look anyway."

"How would you know?"

"It's in all the magazines."

"What magazines?"

I'd obviously slipped. I was embarrassed, but I tried to sound utterly nonchalant. "Oh, you know, the fashion mags . . . like *Seventeen* . . . *Vogue*."

"Oh, do you read *Seventeen* and *Vogue*?"

"Yeah, I ah . . . look through them sometimes."

"That's charming. I've never met a boy who reads girls' magazines."

Carol began advising *me* how to dress. "You should wear something besides jeans for a change. You always look like such a thug, and it doesn't suit you. I'd love to see you in a madras shirt and a nice pair of pants . . . and loafers instead of those utterly absurd cowboy boots." But that was too much; not even for love at first sight was I about to change my public persona.

She called me "the brightest boy she'd ever met"—and "a

Holden Caulfield," a "Huck Finn," and "a Jacksonian democrat."
I didn't know whether to be annoyed or flattered by any of those
comparisons. "Every girl needs a friend like you," she said one
night when we were alone in her apartment. That statement had
an ominous ring to me, and I said nothing. We were drinking
wine, and Carol was more than a little tipsy; it made her giggly
and confessional. "Like me how?" I asked her.

"I never thought it was possible to have a friend who was a
boy. You know, a real friend." I felt a spiraling sensation of things
going hopelessly wrong. "Most boys, after you get to know them,
are just trying to make you all the time." She gave me her most
exquisite smile. "With you, it's like having another brother."

INSTRUCTIONS FOR anyone who might wish to approxi-
mate the exquisite tension of the state I was in that fall. You don't
choose your lady; she happens to you as suddenly and irrevocably as an arrow from the hills. Then you must see her often,
become her friend and confidant. When you're away from her,
you must carry her image in your mind like an icon. You must
imagine making love to her in obsessive detail, undressing her
layer by layer down to the bare skin you've never seen. You must
make small talk with her while she prepares for dates with
another man; you should advise her what to wear and help her
with small attentions—fastening her pearls or zipping her dresses.
You must, it goes without saying, never have made love with a
woman, and you must never tell this particular woman what you
are thinking or touch her—not even a brushing of the fingertips.
If you follow these simple rules, I guarantee that you will come
to understand Dante, Petrarch, and the Troubadour poets better
than if you were to take a dozen university courses.

It's early in November, just a week before Thanksgiving.
Even though Carol's been telling me that I'm her best friend at

WVU, she's never been in my apartment before, and I can see her discomfort by the way she holds herself—her weight high in her body, letting nothing relax, her lower back tense. She's wearing a forest-green suit with a matching beret. The jacket's tailored tightly to the lines of her body, a dramatic indentation at the waist; she hasn't unbuttoned it, hasn't taken off her gloves either. There's a silk scarf the color of turned earth at her throat. I love her attention to detail. Circling my apartment, she pauses to look at the pictures on my walls, the notes on my bulletin board. "What's this?" she says.

"Rilke."

"Yes? Rilke. What's it say?"

"It's poetry. You can't translate poetry."

"Oh, John, don't give me that. I'm certainly aware of what can and can't be translated in poetry."

I know by now that she thinks of herself as infinitely more mature than I am—and certainly far better educated. If she's begun to call me her brother, I'm sure it's a kid brother she means. "OK, do you want a literal translation?"

The German of the poem is so simple I never bother to turn it into English in my mind. I work through it slowly for her: "'Whoever doesn't have a house by now isn't going to be building one . . . ever. Whoever is alone now is going to be alone for a long time . . . will wake, read, write long letters, and restlessly wander the streets here and there . . . while the leaves are falling.' Well, *driven* is better than *falling*."

"Oh, what a cheery German poem."

"It's lovely in the original."

"I'm sure it is. I try to be open-minded, but I can't really appreciate *German* poetry . . . My God, it's cold in here. How do you stand it?"

I kneel at the gas heater and light the burners; the flame is sodium yellow and copper blue. Her glossy black hair catches glints of light and throws them back; her eyes seem all pupil, her painted lips full and pouting. She brushes my alternate pair of jeans to the floor and sits down carefully on the only chair, still holding herself tightly reined as though she might break at the waist. She takes off her gloves. They're so tight she has to tug at each finger. I walk across the room as though I have some place to go and let my hand lightly brush her shoulder. It is an extremely daring gesture for me. I feel her sudden withdrawal.

A thin point of anger between my eyes. I open the bottle of red wine and pour us each a glass. *"Noli me tangere,* for Caesar's I am . . ."

For that line of antique poetry, she rewards me with a smile. The glitter of the glass in her hand, the ruby clarity of the wine, obediently point up her lips. "I'm not *that* untouchable. It's just that . . . I suppose it makes me nervous being alone here with you."

This is a tiny victory: her first admission that a sexual tension between us is even possible. "Haven't you ever been alone with a man in his apartment before?"

"Yes, of course I have, but . . ." an exasperated toss of the head. "Give me a cigarette." She's an occasional smoker, buys herself a pack every few days, keeps it on her vanity table: ladies don't smoke in public. When she's with me, she bums mine. "It's just that he was . . . well, sort of my fiancé."

I light the cigarette for her. "Sort of?"

"We never announced it or anything. It was just understood. Until it wasn't." Oblique gaze, tightening of the lips. "I was tame enough with him."

"Stephen?"

"That's right."

"Did you make love with him?"

"You don't ask girls things like that," but she decides to laugh. "No, of course I didn't. You know me well enough to know that."

I withdraw, sit on the floor opposite her. I'm beginning to feel an obscure knotting of cross-purposes. "Did you make love to *her*?" she asks me.

"Who?"

She points. "Your little high-school girl." She has, after all, noticed my altar to young girls.

"No."

"That's Natalie, isn't it?"

"Yes, that's Natalie."

"She looks so young."

The wine tastes metallic, unpleasant in my mouth. We look at each other across the space of the room. The gas heater hisses. I can't tell what she's thinking. The only way I can possibly approach her is with a conceit so elliptical that she can deflect it immediately if she chooses: "I feel like Actaeon."

"I thought *I* was supposed to be the deer. And are you sure you're not one of the hounds?" I remind myself that she teaches this stuff; if I try to keep the game going too long, she'll beat me at it—but maybe one more move. I search for the next possible twist of metaphor, but before I can find it, she says, "You've never made love with anyone, have you?"

I have to consider it before I tell her the truth: "No."

"We both belong to Artemis then. I didn't think it was possible for a boy to be twenty years old and still a virgin."

"Well, you're looking at one."

"Don't be angry."

"I'm not angry."

"I don't believe you. You sound angry . . . John, I didn't mean anything . . ."

I was only mildly angry before, but now I'm furious. She must sense it: "Come on, let's get out of here, please. Walk me home. I'm really uncomfortable."

But she doesn't move. Neither do I.

"Tell me about Stephen," I say. I've already told her plenty about the girls in my life.

"Oh, hell."

"I just want to understand what happened."

She stamps the words out separately, "Well. So. Do. I."

"You don't?"

"Oh, I'm beginning to. It takes so damn long to get any insight into yourself . . . and by the time you do, it's always too late."

I wait. "He was a strong person," she says eventually. "He knew exactly what he wanted, where he was going."

"What was he in?"

"Electrical engineering."

"What on earth did you talk about?"

"He wasn't exactly your dumb engineer type . . . I used to think that he just didn't appreciate how good I could be for him, how much help and support I could be, but . . . Oh hell, give me another cigarette."

I stand and carry it across to her. "See what you're doing to me? Now I'm chain smoking." But she doesn't inhale: angry puffs of blue smoke blown out as soon as they're drawn in. "He was right. He saw how weak I was. I wouldn't have . . . Oh damn it, John, I was such a bitch."

"What's that mean?"

She laughs, an unpleasant sound. "Surely you've heard the word before. Oh, I was horrid. You have no idea now horrid I can be." She's drunk her wine, holds up the glass. I refill it.

I cross to the far side of the room and lean against the wall.

I want her to feel that there's enough space between us. As though admitting to herself that she's going to stay a while, she unbuttons her jacket, reveals that her tartan skirt is part of a jumper fitted tightly at the waist. "I went over to his place one time," she says in a low, intent voice. "I didn't call or anything, just went over. Midterms were coming up, and he had a fantastic amount of work to cover. He didn't seem very glad to see me, and I was disappointed . . . just like a child. He went back to his books, and I tried to read, but . . . I kept asking him things, interrupting him. I was really in a bitchy mood. I knew I should let him alone, but I just couldn't. He was getting more and more annoyed. Finally he just stood up, walked over, and slapped me."

I'm profoundly shocked. "For real?"

"Sure. He wasn't kidding. He really hit me."

"What did you do?"

"Nothing. You know that Emily Dickinson line: 'zero at the bone'? That's how I felt. Just this whoosh, a kind of emptying. A little voice in my head said: 'Carol, that's exactly what you deserved.' He went back to his chair, picked up his book, and started reading, and I just sat there and waited. I was absolutely quiet. I didn't make a sound. And after about an hour, he looked up and said, 'I'm not going to apologize.' I told him that *I* was sorry, that it was my fault."

"He hit you, and you apologized?"

Now she's obviously as annoyed and uncomfortable with me as I was with her a few minutes earlier. "When you put it like that, it sounds so . . . *neurotic*. But you don't understand."

"I guess I don't."

"I didn't have any right to . . . expect anything. I got what I deserved."

It does indeed sound neurotic to me; I can't make any sense out of it. "What happened then?"

"Nothing."

"Something must have happened. Did you go home or what?"

"No, I made dinner. He finished his work, and we had a lovely evening."

"What's that mean? A lovely evening?"

"What do you mean?"

"What did you do? Go to a show? Walk along the riverbank? Play chess?"

"We *petted,*" she snaps back at me. Her choice of words feels archaic, a throwback to grade school.

She rises slowly to her feet, stretches as though to unknot herself, takes a deep slow breath. The heater's finally cut the worst of the dank chill off the room. Deliberately she slips out of her jacket and offers it to me. Time is arrested; in a dreamy, viscous trance, I stand, walk to her, and take the jacket. Her face is flushed. I bend to her with a lightly brushing kiss. She catches me behind the neck, rises onto her toes, and draws me into her open mouth, thrusts her tongue against mine. A welding torch lit: first the hiss of gas, then the sudden resonant statement of flame, burning immediately white hot, with the sound of a huge banner cracked, once, violently, in a high wind. She pulls back smiling. "Well now, that's not very brotherly."

"You're the one who decided I was your brother, not me."

She pulls me down to kiss her again. She may be a virgin, but she must have trained with Stephen to an absolute mastery of dryfucking; her hips move with the calculated expertise of the virtuoso. "Baby, we've got to stop this," she says.

Her wool skirt has ridden up; I slide my hand over the top of one sleek stocking, but she pushes me away. "Now, John," she says, "I'm not one of your little schoolgirls." I tense and draw back, but she's after me immediately, her teeth on my earlobe.

Her voice is thick. "This isn't good for me. We've really got to stop this."

We've somehow taken two steps forward so that I've got her pressed against the wall. I can feel under the waistline of her jumper a ring of hard, geometrically precise boning. I can see, in vividly glowing colors, a vision of myself stripping the clothes from her, freeing her arching little body from its layers of confinement.

The first distant seismographic warnings of orgasm are beginning in me. Dazzling, emptying, I will be left stunned—I know that—to drop away from her, singed like a moth. I'm driving her into the wall: nothing else but this, to finish this—to vanish into the target of her huge, black eyes. Dimly, from a vast distance, I hear her voice. "Damn it. No! Stop it."

We're fighting, two violent bodies with their brains off somewhere else, tabled for the moment. She twists away from me. We're panting like dogs. "John, stop it right now!"

She's pulled free. I hate her. The controller forces itself down. She has been talking, is talking now, the words slap-dashing out of her: "I just can't take it. Oh, John! All last spring. This is what I did all last spring. With Stephen. And it was just terrible. I couldn't stand it again. I just couldn't stand it. I couldn't get any work done. I couldn't get to sleep at night. All I could think about was him." I'm sickened, nauseated.

I walk into the bathroom and shut the door. I bend double, press my sweaty forehead into the cold, unyielding porcelain of the sink. There's a pain like a thick stave shoved up me. Time doesn't mean a thing; it could be five minutes or half an hour. I straighten up, light a cigarette.

She's standing exactly where I left her, still breathing hard, her shoulders shaking just perceptibly. Her color is vivid, cheeks as bright as if she's just come in out of a high winter wind. Her

94

perfect pageboy is not so perfect anymore. She looks at me searchingly; her dark eyes reflect back light like obsidian. One part of me could cheerfully beat her to death where she stands; another part tells me that I have never in my life seen a girl as beautiful.

"Some brother you turned out to be," she says, her voice deliberate.

I sit down on the floor in a corner of the room, my back against the wall. "I love you, Carol."

"Oh Christ, John, you do not. You just want to make love to me."

"That's not true."

"Oh damn. I never should have come here."

We stare at each other. "You have lipstick all over you," she says.

"Yeah, I suppose I do . . . Goddamn it, I love you. I've loved you since I met you."

She has two voices. The cultivated one is precise, ladylike, and slightly British. This is her real one: "Just shut up, OK? I don't want to hear that crap."

"What the hell were you doing kissing me like that?" I yell at her.

She stiffens. She says in an icy whisper, "You're too young for me."

She opens her purse, takes out a brush and a tube of lipstick. She strides into my tiny bathroom, banging the heels of her loafers down hard on the floor. She doesn't bother to shut the door. I watch her restore her hair, redo her lips. She's quick and efficient.

She puts her lipstick and brush back in her purse, picks up her jacket from where it has fallen and holds it out to me. I help her slip into it. She buttons it up, draws on her gloves. She shakes her head—a gesture of infinite superiority—and smiles. "Come on, walk me home."

I simply stand up, look at her.

"All right, I'll go home by myself."

I grab my jacket. We're out of the apartment and walking quickly toward campus. "Carol, I don't understand you."

"You think *I* understand me?"

"I love you. I want you to know that."

She stops dead, turns to look into my eyes. "John, never never *never* say that to me again."

Not another word until we get to her door. She gives me a sisterly peck on the cheek. "Call me tomorrow, OK?"

When I called her the next day, she talked as though nothing unusual had happened the night before.

4.

I WOKE as suddenly as if a curtain had been drawn back, returning the world like the next act of a play. I never got enough sleep at night, always took a nap after my last class, always woke to a state of bleak clarity—and there I was again, at the same zero point I had been the day before and the day before that, at the same zero point where I would be tomorrow. I didn't open my eyes, but I knew the location of everything in my room nonetheless, felt the solidity of every object; that knowledge was appalling. I jumped out of bed, pulled on jeans and boots, grabbed my jacket, and ran outside. The alley, stretching between the ugly backsides of buildings trellised with fire escapes, opened to a gap to the sky where I knew I must look. Above was a thick roiling grey from which the rain was falling steadily. If I left here, I thought, it would be just as though I had never been here at all.

I was fully aware of starring in my own melodrama, fully aware of how absurd I would look to anybody with any sense, but I also knew that something was wrong with me—something far more serious than the usual Morgantown mold and all the ordinary absurdities of being a horny virgin halfway through a university degree. *There's only one thing that troubles my mind,* I thought—a standard line that floats through a dozen old mountain tunes—and I would have loved to be able to say what that one thing was, but looking inside myself, all I saw was the usual incomprehensible tangle.

I was obviously fooling everyone. My professors took me for a scholar and always gave me A's, but I was nothing more than an asshole with a big mouth who didn't have a clue what real academic work was, having never done a lick of it in my life. The handful of people on campus who genuinely cared about folk music might find me authentic, but I was a white kid from a seedy middle-class family in an industrial town in the Northern Panhandle, and the closest I'd ever come to the authentic folk had been getting drunk once with a miner in Moundsville. Cohen, kind as he was, probably considered me a fellow Buddhist and seeker after the truth, but did I meditate, study the Sutras, try to practice Right Action? No, of course not. And, by now, I was sure that everybody saw me as a normal male, but whenever I woke again to that clear bleak zero point, I always knew better.

I needed to talk to Cohen. By the time I saw him walking down the alley toward me, it was all I could do not to start blathering the moment he stepped into voice range. His face was shining with an inner radiance. He was carrying a brown paper shopping bag. I ran forward to meet him, took the bag. He rubbed his hands together and blew on them; his knuckles were red with cold. "All the good things of life," he said. "Spanish onions, Mexican tomato paste, Italian spaghetti, Greek olive oil, West Virginia ground beef, and vintage 1962 Morgantown cream soda."

He followed me inside. My mind was still racing, but I was so strangled by my own misery I couldn't find a single clear thing to say. Cooking was something we didn't need to talk about; we just did it. Cohen began cutting up onions; I put my cast-iron Dutch oven on the stove, sloshed in some olive oil, and lit the gas. And already that level Cohen called "maintenance" was trapping me in the mundane, but what other level was I waiting for? A clarity I couldn't simply choose: the power of it would have to enter me from the outside, as it had done with him. But he hadn't been waiting for anything, had expected nothing; I expected everything, posed the problem to myself in a form as mind-cracking as any Zen koan, and each of my schemes drew the same hermetic "No!" from the master inside my head. No, don't try to force it. No, don't try to plan anything. It's got to be like Cohen throwing knives. No tricks. This is the only way: you are one with the target and the knife is gone.

I couldn't hold it back any longer. "Listen, Bill," I said, "there's all this shit going around in my head. I'm trying to make some sense of it. There are times I could call 'gathering points.' Everything leads into them, everything leads out of them. They're hard to see when they're happening, but you look back and say, 'Right. That was it.' And they're the points where everything in your life changes."

His eyes met mine; he scraped the diced onions from the cutting board into the hot oil. I began to crumble in the ground beef. He turned the flame down to medium. "It's like the time that Lyle and I hitchhiked to St. Stevens," I told him. "He didn't say anything different. He just said what he'd always been saying. 'You've got to *train hard*.' But somehow that time was different."

Remembering Lyle, I realized how much I missed that intense all-male world of athletics. We'd seen it as a metaphor even at the time, but it had been a good metaphor. Running was like praying. Heroic effort was the norm—merely something that was expected every day at track practice. It might not have been a Zen monastery, but it was the best we had. Yes, of course, we had to train hard. I saw it now as a ritual of purification.

"That night with Lyle," I said, "oh, that was such a magical night. I'll never forget the guy who picked us up . . . the guy with the Isky Roller Cam in his car, driving like a madman. And wandering around that dumb little town, and checking out the girls, and then walking out of town . . . under a sky just blistering with stars. And it all came together and made a gathering point. We hitchhiked back to Raysburg, and I finally did what Lyle told me. *I trained hard*. And it changed my entire life. I was never the same after that."

Cohen's moment of awakening on the beach in Florida must have been, I thought, just such a gathering point for him—although, of course, a far more significant one, on an entirely different level altogether. "Come on," I said to him, "be straight with me. How'd you do it?"

He knew immediately what I was talking about. The question cracked him up. "John, if I could tell you, I would."

"Let's drop down to the bottom level. Were you doing anything that might have contributed to it? Anything you can think of?"

"I really want to tell you," he said. "I'm not being intentionally obscure."

"I know you're not."

"You knew me then. You know what I was like."

"Yeah, you were the science-fiction kid. You were trying to be the perfect killer."

"No, that was just my personal *mishigas* . . . But I was in good shape. I think that did have something to do with it. The beneficence of the mind-body unity. I was swimming every day, running on the beach . . . I was really light."

I felt a kick of excitement. "That's right. I *know* that's right. I've felt it too. When Lyle and I were running, he used to say, 'You've got to get light. Food just gets in the way.' And I knew exactly what he was talking about. When I'd push myself to the edge, I'd feel it in the guts, a kind of heaviness like a stomach full of broken glass . . ."

"The withness of the body."

"Yes. And this is what I've got to figure out. Simple daily things so I don't get lost in all these mental puzzles."

He handed me the can of tomato paste he'd just opened; I spooned the paste into the meat. He poured in a cup of water. I stirred the sauce, handed him the spoon, and he stirred it. I lit a cigarette. "You're still doing it," I said. "That perfect killer business. The throwing knives. What are you doing it for?"

"That's on another level."

"OK, so on that other level . . . Yeah, I know we've changed topics. But what are you *doing*?"

I knew by his silence that words had now become no damned good, but I had to persist: "Do you think you could ever throw a knife into somebody?"

"I hope to God I never have to."

"Yeah, but you could if you had to. OK, Bill, so the Wild West's long gone. Doesn't that make it kind of an arcane skill?"

"Certain situations still require certain skills," he said, smiling. "Let's say there's a dark night lit with only the faint sliver of a new moon, and I'm drifting like a shadow across the border into Latvia. I know that I have to be hundreds of miles away when the guards discover my black parachute. A dog barks in a distant farm yard, and then another, and then another . . . I freeze . . . and then I hear the faint, dry, tactful sound of a twig snapping. I feel the hair prickle on the back of my neck. I slip a knife into my hand. What's required now is *absolute silence* . . ."

"Cohen. Come on."

"You know the weird thing, John? It *is* something like that. It's just to be ready . . . But that's not right. The words aren't right."

"Ready for what?"

He didn't answer. I was pushing him, and I knew it, could feel his resistance. "Ready for what?" I said again. "Can you imagine any possible situation in which you'd *have* to throw a knife into somebody?"

"The highest skill is to have no skill at all. It takes years of work to have no skill at all . . . on that level."

"You just side-stepped the question."

He gave me his cat-like grin. "Yeah, I did, didn't I?"

"Christ, when you're talking about the color of light on snow, you've got millions of words, but when you're talking about something important, you haven't got any."

He laughed. "That's right."

"Listen, you've got to help me. I can't just keep on wandering around waiting for elusive mental states that absolutely can't be forced . . . or even prepared for."

Yes, words were no damned good; all I had was a *feeling*—a rasp at my mind, an existential itch. I paced to the far side of my apartment and back again. I put on water to boil for his tea. I opened my first beer of the night.

"There's an emptiness," I said, "when everything's simple. It must be what you've been talking about . . . or something like it. Sometimes it happens when I first wake up. Sometimes playing the guitar. And it's pure, but it's not a purity you have to work for. It's like . . . Well, here's the difference. You can decide to go on a fast . . . or you can just not eat for a while because you're doing something else . . ."

There was a tap at my door. I was annoyed. I felt that I'd almost arrived at some elusive but essential point. Cohen must have sensed my frustration. I saw him send me a message with his beautiful green eyes. "There *is* an emptiness," he said, "when everything is simple."

I opened the door quickly, bracing myself to see Carol, but it was only Revington with Marge Levine. "Ciao, Marcello," he said. He was swinging a case of beer which he slapped into my arms. She was carrying her autoharp and a bottle of red wine. She'd outdone herself with the Egyptian makeup, had drawn thick precise black lines around her eyes from tear ducts to lynx-like arches at the outer margins, had painted her eyelids gold and turquoise; that hugely artificial gaze drew the force away

102

from the rest of her face, leaving her skin lemony and Fauvish under the bare hundred-watt bulb in my hallway. She looked as though she should speak in some incomprehensible tongue, but what she said was, "Hey, buddy, how's it going?"

"About half," I said, laughing, pleased to see her, ready to let go of my angst for the moment.

Revington was yelling at me, "Help us out, Marcello. You've got to shed some gloom on this discussion." He flung himself down onto the back seat of an old Chevy I'd scavenged from the dump; he held a cigarette compressed between his lips, his eyes narrowed against the smoke.

"Just what is being discussed?" I asked.

Marge was wearing one of her black dresses, this one in a fabric that seemed to absorb all light. When she took the water tumbler of wine I offered her, I saw that a thin gold snake circled her wrist. She'd come to rest against the wall by the window, obviously posed, though apparently at ease, with one hip cocked, her lean body balanced on her usual stiletto heels. "He's just being an asshole," she said to me.

"Comrade Levine has been explaining how we are all declining and falling," Revington said, "while I have been maintaining that the beauty of the process lies in the decline rather than the ultimate fall . . . that we should not go rushing pell-mell into the arms of those grey bureaucrats whom dear Comrade Levine would wish upon us."

"William," she said, toasting him. Her eyes sent him a message, but coded. "You still haven't got the point. It's possible to have a democratic socialism, one that doesn't look like the Soviet Union's."

"Where is it?" he said, raising his eyebrows in mock surprise. "Cuba? Sweden? Patagonia? Andorra?"

"The trouble with Marxism," I said, "is that it's teleological.

But history is cyclical." I didn't know whether I believed that or not, having just thought of it, but it had a good ring to it that I hoped Revington would appreciate. "When the Confucians were in power," I said, half to Cohen, "the Taoists retired to the mountains."

"That's *your* solution all right," Marge said to me. She laughed and then turned to Revington. "He calls me up, right? Says, 'Hey Marge, you want to go to a flick?' I say, 'How can you think about going to a movie at a time like this?' He says, 'A time like what?' And then I remember who I'm talking to. It's John Dupre . . . I say, 'Haven't you heard about the missiles in Cuba?' He says, 'What missiles in Cuba?'"

Marge and Revington were laughing at me; I joined them. I was nowhere near the Li'l Abner that I sometimes made myself out to be, but sometimes it was just too good a role to pass up. It was true that I'd missed the Cuban Missile Crisis.

"He doesn't have to know anything," Revington said. "He's a poet."

I heard another tap at my door, and there was no doubt this time who it would be. Beads of water were trickling down the gleaming red surface of the raincoat I'd grown to love because it was emblematic of her. She rose on tiptoe to kiss me, not, as I'd expected, on the cheek, but, for the barest fraction of a second, on my lips. "Nothing if not obedient," she said, handing me the lettuce and bread I'd asked her to bring. I hung up her coat for her.

She settled into the only reasonably comfortable chair in my apartment and crossed her ankles like a lady. I brought her a glass of wine. She glanced up at me and smiled. She was wearing one of her outfits that was so demure it could have been a school uniform—a navy jumper with a plain white blouse—and there really was, I thought, something perverse about the way she insisted on dressing like that. She was sitting not three feet from the spot where I'd pressed her against the wall. She'd been wearing a jumper that night too, and I had a sickeningly vivid memory of touching her waist, feeling the rigid boning underneath the tight wool—of her hands pulling on my neck, of her tongue in my mouth, of her leg between mine. And now I was supposed to make polite conversation with her? God help me.

Marge and Revington had barely registered Carol's arrival. They were still going at each other full tilt. "What the hell did you expect him to do?" Revington was saying in his dry flat voice, "Give up? The bastards already had their goddamned missiles down there."

"Ours in Turkey don't count?"

"It's a matter of realpolitik. He couldn't let them get away with it."

"But was it worth blowing up the world over?"

"The world wasn't blown up, and the missiles are leaving Cuba," Revington said. "He won."

"I'll give you ten to one," she answered him, "that our missiles won't be in Turkey a year from now, so it isn't a one-sided victory. And they could have slipped. It was *that* close." She gave him her thin smile over the edge of her wine glass. "Maybe you want to die for the honor of the Kennedy brothers, but I don't."

"Oh, do we have to talk politics tonight?" Carol said.

"I'm terribly sorry," Marge said, "it must be so tedious for you."

"Lay off, sweet coz. I'm not in the mood." Carol had been smiling when she'd said it, but I'd heard the cutting edge in her voice.

"Dupre's got the right idea," Revington said. "There's not one fucking thing that any of us can do that's going to change anything. And isn't there something obscene about a bunch of privileged little brats like us sitting around discussing the fate of the world as though it might mean something? Isn't there something rotten about it? What was it you were saying, Marge, about the poor stiffs on the assembly line? That the only reason we're free to sit around and talk about all this shit . . ."

"Wait a minute," Marge said, "I didn't say *anything* about any poor stiffs on the . . ."

Revington rode right over her: ". . . *free* to sit around and talk about it because there are thousands of poor bastards out there who aren't free? Wasn't that the point you were making? However the hell you said it? Well, that's right," and I could hear the rising resonance as he became increasingly fascinated by the sound of his own voice, "but how many times haven't we envied them . . . those poor bastards who don't have time to think because they've got *something to do* every fucking day of their lives? They don't have to read Sartre or Camus or Karl Marx. It's just off to the plant and then home to the telly, right? Mead can do more than Milton can, right?" and to me, holding up his empty beer bottle, "Landlord, fill the flowing bowl. The bird of time has but a little way to fly . . ."

"William," Marge said, "I don't even think you believe yourself half the time."

"But of course. That's the magnificent irony of it."

I picked up the case of beer from the kitchen counter and set it down in the middle of the floor so he could help himself, handed him the church key. "Magnificent irony, my ass," I said. "Too many movies is more like it."

"Well, isn't that it?" he said. "Too many books and too many movies. How can we ever hope for genuineness with those frozen gestures, that toy box of phrases in our heads?"

I wasn't sure where to aim it, but I was inexplicably angry. "'Corruption never has been compulsory,'" I said, quoting. "'There are left the mountains.'"

"Oh, Jeffers," Carol said with distaste, "he's not even a poet."

"Why not?" I asked her.

Carol shrugged. "I am not going to get drawn into this. You're all just playing around."

"No," Marge said, "we're playing around, but we're not *just* playing around. I really want to know what you think, Carol. Why isn't Jeffers a poet?"

"Lay off, Marge. I really mean it." But she couldn't help adding, "His subject matter is . . . Well, it's simply not timeless. And his language is so pedestrian."

"Oh," Marge said with mock surprise, "pedestrian language. Oh, I see."

"Well, how else should we judge poetry? By the language, of course. Magnificent, beautiful, gorgeous language . . . that's what will last when everything else is gone."

"'Time,'" I said, "'worships language and forgives everyone by whom it lives.'" I didn't believe it for a minute, but I couldn't help rushing to Carol's defense.

Carol gave me a grateful smile. "Yes," she said, "that's it exactly."

"What?" Marge said. "Auden's aestheticism? Poetry makes nothing happen? What kind of escapist crap is that?"

"No," Carol said, looking directly at Marge, "you're not going to draw me into this idiotic conversation. None of you mean what you say anyway."

"Ah, but what if we did?" Revington said. "If each of us turned over the rock of our hearts, what would be crawling beneath?"

"*Some* of us mean what we say," Marge said, giving Revington an exasperated look. "OK, Carol . . . this magnificent language. This language that will last forever. What is there about it that will make it last forever? Why is it still relevant? Why don't you give us a sample?"

"No, I will not give you a sample. Why don't you just lay off me? You've been needling me ever since I walked in here."

"I was teasing you," Marge said, "not needling you. But seriously, kid, I really want to know what you think."

"Come on, Carol," Revington said, "won't you come out and play with us? We're all good company, aren't we? Despite our lousy manners?"

Carol looked at each of us, her reluctance written all over her face. Then I saw something change in her. She smiled and, with a impudent toss of her head, recited—

> Western wind, when will thou blow,
> The small rain down can rain?
> Christ, if my love were in my arms
> And I in my bed again!

We applauded her. Revington yelled, "Bravo!"

"Thank you," Marge said. "Yes, it's lovely . . ."

"Lovely?" Carol snapped back at her. "It's one of the finest lyrics in the English language."

"Oh, all right. I suppose it is. But I can't help thinking, why is that poor son of a bitch out in the rain anyway? He's probably a peasant, and he sure isn't out there in the rain working for his own economic interests." Everyone laughed but Carol. I couldn't understand why Marge wouldn't let it go; then I realized that it must have been an ongoing clash that the girls had brought with them.

"My God," Carol said to Marge, "I can't believe you. You take everything as journalism. Exactly like a newspaper story. The world must look really flat to you. Flat and dead and grey."

"No, honey, I bet my world's just as colorful as yours . . . Look, I didn't say it wasn't pretty, did I? But I guess I want something more than beautiful language."

"Oh, you make me so mad! Why are you doing this to me?" Carol's eyes flooded with tears. She took a deep breath and stared down at her penny loafers.

"I'm sorry," she said after a moment, "I obviously take things too seriously."

I'd been afraid that the evening would turn out to be a disaster for me; now it appeared to be turning into a disaster for everyone. We were trapped inside a moment of deadly silence. Then Cohen stepped into it. He hadn't said a word for the last half hour—hadn't left the kitchen, had appeared to be wholly absorbed in cooking. I didn't know if he'd been the least bit interested in anything we'd been saying. But now, with the sudden grace of a gunslinger, he was in the room with us, offering Carol his handkerchief. "Thank you," she said in a prim little voice.

Cohen was looking directly into her Carol's eyes. "Don't be sorry," he told her, "you said what you meant . . . but more than that, you showed us how much you meant it. What could be more beautiful than that?"

"You sound like a character out of a Dostoevsky novel," Revington said to Cohen.

Cohen was not smiling. "It *is* like a Dostoevsky novel, William. Sometimes you have to take the clumsy stupid slow words and take a chance with them . . . speak straight from the heart. Because what matters is what happens between people. Because that's all we've got."

"Touché," Revington said and saluted him just as though we were back in military school. "Is that *ex cathedra*, Bill?"

"That's *ex cathedra*," Cohen said.

"Yeah, we are a bunch of black-hearted bastards, aren't we?" Revington said, "playing our party games." Then suddenly brightening, "Why don't we do it then? Just like in a Dostoevsky novel? All right, let's each of us say what we really believe when it comes down to the crunch. No bullshit now. Just the truth, plain and simple and silly, right?"

No one spoke. "OK, Comrade Levine," Revington said, "why don't you start?"

"Oh, for Christ's sake, William."

"It was all right to do it to Carol?" he said. "We just forced her, didn't we? She might not have intended to, but she told us what mattered. So now let's all take a turn. Just tell us what you believe in, that's all. Let's see how much of a fool you really are."

"Oh, hell," Marge said. "All right."

She looked off into the corner of the room, frowning. "We're all infinitely precious," she said slowly. "We all have vast, unfulfilled capacities for reason, freedom, and love." She was, I knew, echoing the *Port Huron Statement*. "We have to throw off our alienation, our isolation, create an authentic community. We have to find truly democratic alternatives to the present . . . We *will* find them. When we do, we're going to change America from top to bottom."

"Oh," Revington said, dragging out the words, "God."

She gave him her thin smile. "I know you think I'm absurd, but . . . Don't you understand? You think the ability to hope for even a possibility of change . . . a possibility for anything better . . . You take that as a sign of weakness."

I saw him absorb that, think about it. He nodded to her. "It *is* beautiful," he said. "I'll admit that. Although a bit on the utopian side, wouldn't you say? Is that all?"

"Political credos should be short."

"You see?" he said to Carol. "Isn't that as every bit as absurd as being in love with magnificent language? . . . All right, Dupre, it's your turn."

I'd already been planning what I was going to do. "Can I

sing you a little song, judge?" I picked up my Martin and checked the tuning.

"Are we going to let him get away with this?" Revington said.

"Of course we are," Marge said.

Every guy who's ever called himself a folk singer must have sung "The Cuckoo" at least once. I tried to make my version distinctive—had worked out a pattern of finger-picking to make my guitar sound something like a banjo, and I sang it in my most raw, authentic, old-time voice:

> Oh, the cuckoo, she's a pretty bird.
> She warbles as she flies.
> She brings us glad tidings,
> And she tells us little lies.

> Gonna build me a log cabin
> On the mountain so very high
> Just to see Bodhidharma
> When he comes walking by.

Cohen smiled as I knew he would, but I saw that no one else had got it. I picked out the melody once and ended on a sepulchral chord that had nothing in it but Ds and As.

"All right," Carol said, "I know we're supposed to ask, so I'll do it. Who's Bodhidharma?"

"The First Patriarch of Zen Buddhism," I said. "He walked from India to China. After staring at a wall for nine years, he was instantly enlightened. Then, after his death, he was seen walking back to India with a sandal on his head."

Everyone laughed just as I'd meant them to. "OK, so Dupre's answer is Zen lunacy," Revington said, "the sense of no sense."

"Oh, it makes perfect sense," Carol said with a mischievous

smile. "You just have to subject the text to close reading."

"Well, my dear," Revington said, "would you care to enlighten us?"

"Certainly," she said. "The first image is that of the cuckoo. The narrator admits that she is a pretty bird. She warbles as she flies, bringing us glad tidings, but the narrator also knows that she tells us little lies. Her glad tidings are false . . . just as we should expect from a bird that lays its eggs in other birds' nests . . ."

Her tone was so much like that of a professor in a classroom that we were all laughing. "But the narrator refuses to be taken in by the cuckoo's blandishments and decides to withdraw to a mountain. Could the cuckoo's lies, in this context, represent the corruption of the contemporary world? And the narrator knows that corruption has never been compulsory . . ." With that one, Revington was howling like a maniac; I was feeling a growing dismay.

"Mountains in literature frequently represent a purity and return to nature as opposed to the corruption of the cities," Carol went on, still perfectly imitating the tone of a university lecture; the sparkle in her eyes was saying something like, "See what I can do!"

"The narrator plans to build a cabin on a mountain so very high, and there he will wait for the coming of Bodhidharma. Now what are we to make of this image borrowed from another culture? Whatever significance Bodhidharma might have in his original context, here he clearly represents salvation . . . the countervailing force against the pretty lies of the cuckoo. Now we have reached the heart of the narrative, the key to understanding it. The narrator has no assurance that Bodhidharma will *ever* walk by his cabin . . ."

I didn't know if Carol had finished or not, but Revington yelled, "Good Christ," laughing, pounding on the floor with his fist, "That's wonderful! Waiting for Bodhidharma, huh?" and then directly to me: "What do you say there, Estragon? Nothing to be done, right?"

It was hard for me to keep laughing with the rest of them. I felt stripped bare. I didn't know how Carol had managed to do it, but it was as though she'd seen directly into my heart. Yes, I was always waiting, and waiting for what? That mysterious *something* to enter me from the outside—that force, that clarity, that *emptiness*, as I'd told Cohen—but I had no assurance that it ever would. And also, on another level, I felt that Carol had betrayed me. How could she have done that? Only a few minutes ago I'd been defending her.

"OK," Revington was saying, "time to hear from the delegate from Nirvana."

Smiling, not saying a word, Cohen set salad and bread onto the table, motioned us to come and eat.

"That's supposed to be your answer?" Revington said. "Well, I'm not going to let you off that easy. Try the English language."

"I'll accept that limitation," Cohen said. He stepped quickly into the room with us. "Once upon a time," he said, "there was a man who withdrew to the mountains to wait for Bodhidharma."

They were laughing again, but Cohen paused, smiling. When he'd gathered up everyone's attention, he continued, speaking in a compelling storyteller's voice: "And the man built him a log cabin on a mountain so very high. It was just a rough structure because the man expected Bodhidharma at any moment. But Bodhidharma did not appear, so after a while, the man decided to build the very best cabin he could. He took his time, and eventually he built a wonderful cabin, warm and tight and comfortable. Well, the man had to eat, so he put in a garden, and he hunted the wild game that was abundant on the mountain, and he had a good life there, but he was lonely, and still Bodhidharma did not come.

"Now over on the next mountain was another cabin with a whole family living in it, so the man went to visit them, and he kept going back to visit them because they were really nice people, and he fell in love with the youngest daughter, the one with the golden hair, and he married her and brought her back to his cabin, and they had five children, and still there was no sign of Bodhidharma. And the children grew up, and they married and had children of their own, and they settled throughout all those mountains and valleys. And one day the man was sitting on his porch looking down over the valley, something happened, and he woke as if from a dream, and he realized that Bodhidharma was already there, that he'd been there the entire time."

"Oh, that's beautiful," Carol said.

My eyes were stinging. Surely they must all have felt it: Cohen had been turning the Wheel of the Dharma. "Know, Subhuti," I said, "that from the very beginning every sentient being has already attained perfect incomparable enlightenment."

"Yes," Cohen said.

"Oh, Jesus!" Revington burst out, "I envy you guys. I really do."

"You're the only one left, William," Marge said. "What's at the bottom of your black heart?"

He flopped back against the old Chevy seat, covered his eyes for a moment. Then he sat up. "OK," he said, speaking quickly in a low thick voice, "there's that man in Cohen's story, and he's living with his family, and all his good neighbors are living all around him, and one day . . . purely by chance . . . just as a random event . . . a peddler wanders up into the mountains. And he visits everyone. Nobody knows it, but he's carrying the bubonic plague. So they all get the plague, and most of them die. And who gets spared, and who dies, has nothing to do with the kind of lives they've been living. And their deaths have no meaning . . . just as their lives had no meaning."

He pulled a pen and a scrap of paper out of his pocket. He drew a cross with a loop at the top. "In plague time in the Middle Ages," he said, "this was inscribed on the doors of the afflicted. It meant: God help us. But it wasn't a plea or a prayer. There was no expectation that God would help. It was called the Fear Sign, and it stood for ultimate despair. Do you understand," he said, looking directly at Marge, "that no hope is implied? No hope at all?"

Their eyes met. "I understand," she said.

AFTER REVINGTON'S performance (I had to admit that it had been one of his best) our little party could have sunk easily into a funereal slough, but there appeared to be a collective will not to do that, and, in fact, to do just the opposite. I put Pete Seeger on the stereo because I wanted to hear his twelve-string guitar and "The Bells of Rhymney." We opened more beer. I'd saved a gallon of Paisano Red for just such an occasion, and I brought it out. Cohen had seasoned the spaghetti sauce with oregano, bay leaves, parsley, and garlic powder; it was delicious. We ate and drank and talked about nothing serious. Revington and I even did a few of our moronic comedy routines that went all the way back to the Academy. We'd started by learning "The Arkansas Traveler," but, over the years, we'd compiled a dozen more, some long, some short; either of us could kick one off, and then the other would respond with the required lines. What we hoped to get, and usually got, was not a laugh but a groan. Like this one:

"Hey, Dupre, do you know my friend Art?"

"Art? Art who?"

"Art Tesian."

"Oh, yes, I know Artesian well."

And of course we had to sing. I tuned my guitar to Marge's autoharp. She looked at me expectantly, waiting for me to pick a tune. Revington might be able to get into her pants, I thought, but I knew her heart in a way he never would. When she heard the chords, her face lit up, and we sang together, perfectly timed:

> Every little river must go down to the sea.
> All the slaving miners in our union will be free.
> Gonna march to Blair Mountain,
> Gonna whup the company.
> I don't want you to weep after me.

Everyone sang but Cohen. Like me, Marge tried to sound like someone who'd grown up a few miles back of Mud, West Virginia; Revington had a ringing baritone and Carol a pleasantly girlish soprano. We did more labor songs: "We Shall Not Be Moved" and "Which Side Are You On?" Marge had learned the harmony to "Buddy, Won't You Roll Down the Line," and we sounded, I thought, good enough to perform it at the Mountainlair. Of course we did singalongs: "The Sloop John B" and "The Mermaid." We always had to do at least one of those old lugubrious ballads about murdered girls, usually "The Banks of the Ohio," and at least one Irish tune, usually "The Leaving of Liverpool." To show off my guitar picking and my authentic ethnic voice, I did "See See Rider" and "Red Rocking Chair," and the one about Stewball the racehorse for those lines I loved and could sing with absolute conviction even when I was back in Raysburg:

> Oh, the winds they do whistle,
> And the waters do moan.
> I'm a poor boy in trouble.
> I'm a long way from home.

THE PARTY broke up around ten. The curfew applied to all the girls on campus, even graduate students, and Carol wanted to be home well before curfew—to work on a paper, she said, but knowing her as I did, I guessed that what she really wanted was a long hot bath and bed. Cohen and I offered to walk with her. Marge and Revington volunteered to stay behind and clean up. As we were leaving, he bent to whisper to me: "If you guys could manage to stay away . . . oh, let's say until after midnight . . . I'd be forever in your debt."

"You're forever in my debt as it is, William."

The rain had stopped, but the temperature had fallen; the thick-skied night had the iron smell of impending snow. "This crazy city," Carol said. "You never know what to expect. I'm freezing."

"You'll get warm as you walk," I told her.

"Oh, you're so physical," she said.

Cohen and I were walking on either side of her. He and I were, as always, in jeans and boots. She reached out and took our hands. "How lovely," she said, "to have two such handsome cowboys escorting me home." There was a maidenly coyness in her voice that I'd never heard before; I wanted to smack her. "I've never met anyone from Harvard," she told him.

She asked him what he was studying; he told her about the Amaravati Stupa slab. "That's so exotic," she said. "That must be the advantage of a school like Harvard. You can study things that the rest of us can only dream about."

When we arrived at her apartment, she pushed back the hood of her shiny red raincoat and kissed each of us on the cheek. "Thank you, gentlemen," she said, still using that irritating, maidenly voice, "I had a lovely time."

Cohen and I began walking back along Beechurst. "That raincoat kills me," I said.

"I'll bet it's more than the raincoat," he said.

"Yeah, you're right . . . She was flirting with you, you know."

"I noticed."

"Oh, you did, did you?"

"Of course I noticed. It has happened to me before, believe it or not . . . And I am conversant with the subject . . . from a purely theoretical standpoint. I read a monograph on it just before I left my home planet."

"Oh, for Christ's sake."

"The funny thing is . . . Whenever it happens, it never seems to have much of anything to do with me."

We had a good hour and a half to kill, but it wasn't hard to do. Walking was always good, spinning out those endless words that Cohen didn't trust. "Are you going to see Natalie again?" he asked me.

I was startled. I'd been thinking obsessively about Carol. "I hope so. Do you think I should?"

"It doesn't matter what I think. What do you think?"

That wasn't the first time he'd asked me about Natalie. Well, he'd adored her; that had been obvious. And she'd liked him just as much as he'd liked her. It had even crossed my mind a few times that if she hadn't been my girlfriend, he might have liked her well enough to do something about it—although I couldn't quite imagine Cohen making a pass at Natalie, or at anyone. Not that he was incapable of it; I just couldn't imagine how he would go about it. "She was a sweet girl," I said, and then, after a moment, added, "God, that sounds condescending. She was a hell of a lot more than a sweet girl."

"Yes, she was."

"Christ, Bill, I honest to God don't know how I feel about her."

"Why don't you give yourself a chance to find out?"

WHEN WE got back to my place, Revington was outside waiting for us, lounging against his car, smoking. He glanced at the watch he wasn't wearing and called, "Hurry up, please, gentlemen, it's almost time." Seeing him there—disheveled, lean, magnetic, handsome, dark, and grinning; posed as though for a camera of a New Wave director—I was infuriated. "William," I said, "you look self-satisfied."

"One does not require," he said unctuously, unfolding himself, "that the prisoner does not enjoy his meals."

We got into the car. Revington began to drive; he circled the campus. It was well after curfew by then, and there was not a girl or woman to be seen anywhere, only guys, dumb jerks like us with their pants on, hurrying through the chilly night. They'd dropped their girls off, at the dorm or at a sorority house, and now there was not a trace of femininity to be seen—not a swinging ponytail, clicking pair of high heels, shining raincoat, swishing skirt. It felt as though all the power lines of the world had been cut. Cohen was explaining something to Revington about Kurosawa's *The Seven Samurai*: "It's something you can't forget," he was saying, "like keeping kosher."

"Your family doesn't keep kosher, does it?" Revington asked him.

"Are you kidding? How many cheeseburgers have you seen me eat? But it's *like* keeping kosher . . . or anything else that's always with you so you don't even have to think about it." And he repeated what he'd said a moment before: "A real Samurai wouldn't get that drunk." And there were no girls, no women, on the street.

Revington yawned. "Shit, is that what you're going to do when you get out of Harvard? Hire out as a Samurai?"

Cohen laughed. "That sounds like something my father says . . . So what are you doing, Bill, studying all that Chinese? When you get out of school, are you going to open a laundry?"

"That's a good one," Revington said, and then to me, "Where have you got yourself, ace?"

"Thinking how amazing it is what happens to the campus when they lock up all the women."

"Yeah," he said, "swept clean. Jesus, how medieval can you get? . . . *In loco parentis,* which should be translated: the parents are insane. They'd save themselves of a lot of trouble if they'd just lock all the freshmen girls into chastity belts to be removed only upon graduation . . . Oh, God, this is a dismal place, but I'd give my left nut if they let me in."

"Why the hell don't you try then?" I said.

"You don't know what my transcript looks like . . . Shit, let's talk about something else." He gave me a toothy skull's grin. "That little Carol, for instance, who seems to be giving you such a bad case of the hot pants."

I didn't answer. I couldn't let go of my annoyance. "No?" he asked me.

"No."

"We can always talk about baseball then . . . But no, we can't do that either. The season's over."

"Oh, you guys."

"Get off campus," I said. "Drive along the river."

"Off to Nighttown," Revington said and then muttered, "I saw the best minds of my generation driving aimlessly around Morgantown, West Virginia, at one in the morning."

He hunched over the wheel and began piloting us out of town. "Ah, Margery . . ." He appeared to be addressing the first scattering of snowflakes that were being cleared from the windshield with a slap. "You're some bitch. You're sharp as a goddamn tack."

"Drive over by the tracks," I said, and I could hear the anger in my voice. "There's got to be something over there."

When we found it, our open bar was quite literally a shack, with a flaking sign proclaiming: THE NEW PALACE. Lights shone in the veiled window; we could hear the jukebox. "If that's the new palace," Revington said, "I'd sure as hell hate to see the old one."

"We probably won't get served," I said.

"Maybe they'll have an exotic brand of cream soda I've never seen before," Cohen said. "I keep hoping . . . Maybe at the back of an old shop with a sign on the front that says: WE SELL THIMS . . . Ancient, dusty bottles covered with cobwebs . . . The owner, a bent strange man as ancient as the bottles says, 'Cream soda, eh? Well, look at this. Bottled in 1842. Never thought I'd find anyone who'd appreciate it.' Our eyes meet. We exchange the intensely burning glances of true aficionados. He wipes the dust off, opens the first bottle . . ."

"Shit," Revington said. He banged out of the car and walked away, leaving us to follow.

Above the bar was a crude drawing of a pig with a huge red arrow pointing to its backside just beneath the corkscrew tail. The caption read: CREDIT? We sat in a booth. Instead of walking over to us, the bartender yelled across the room: "What do you want, boys?"

"Three beers," Revington said.

"Sorry, boys, it's after midnight."

The others in the place were all old men; they didn't pay the least bit of attention to us. Everyone was drinking coffee. Revington unwound himself, sauntered over, and slouched languidly on the bar. "I guess we'll have what they're having," he said.

Without saying a word, the bartender slapped three coffee mugs onto the bar, poured a shot of whiskey into each, added coffee, and said, "A buck eighty." Revington paid him, carried the mugs to our table.

"I can't drink this," Cohen said.

"For Christ's sake, don't go up there and buy a cream soda," Revington hissed.

"Why not?" Cohen walked to the bar and bought himself a cream soda.

Revington sighed. "Sweet Jesus," he said to me, "it's hard traveling with a saint."

We stared at each other across the table. Revington toasted me. I was amazed that we were in, accepted, and drinking. I'd been afraid that our night's supply would run out before I'd gotten myself as drunk as I needed to be. "Home free," I said.

Cohen slid into the booth, pointed with his pop bottle. "Look at that poster. It must have been hanging there since the Second World War." A yellowing young lady, reminiscent of Betty Grable, wearing seamed stockings, platform heels, and a tight skirt, was leaning forward to pick up a tray, presenting us with her plump rear end, grinning over one shoulder, inviting us to HAVE A COKE. "Maybe we've gone through a time warp," Cohen said. "No, we're *about* to go through the time warp." He gestured toward the bar. The youngest man looked about fifty. "We'll get lost in conversation. Then we'll look up and see that the poster is no longer faded and yellow. All of the men will be suddenly young . . . "

"Yeah," Revington said, "and then we'll remember that tomorrow morning we're going to have to hit the beach at Normandy." He yawned. "Well, at least they had something to do."

I found myself studying him, once again, as I'd done ever since I'd first met him. Sure, he could have played World War II in a Hollywood version; he had the height, the face, the leanness, the carriage, the arrogance, and it all worked. "Revington," I said, "you're milking the existential despair just a bit much."

"Oh, am I?" he said, his face slackening. "Yes . . . Yes, I suppose I am."

I couldn't be content with that but had to keep going. "Sometimes, just for laughs, you ought to try reminding yourself that you're twenty years old, bright, good-looking, and you've got a rich father."

"Touché, John . . . But shit, don't you think I don't know that? It just makes everything . . . fuck . . . even more ridiculous."

"Isn't it beautiful to be precisely who we are?" Cohen said.

"Listen to that, will you?" Revington said to me. "Sometimes I think he's a saint, and other times I think he's got all the emotional prerequisites of an axe murderer."

Cohen laughed. "You know what, ace?" Revington snapped at him. "Everything's just too fucking easy for you."

I could never understand what Revington thought he had to complain about. I, however, had plenty to complain about, and sometimes things did seem too easy for Cohen. I looked back at that silly Forties Coke ad. The fading little sexpot reminded me of Carol, of course. But time will fade and yellow her like the poster, I thought with a certain gritty satisfaction, will fade and yellow us all—a Renaissance sentiment she'd probably appreciate if she were around to hear it. "William," Cohen was saying, "I'm always aware of how far I am from where I want to be . . . on one level. Just how stupid and clumsy and slow."

Revington was staring into his coffee cup. "Fuck, I'm sorry, Bill. I shouldn't have said that. You guys are the only friends I've got. Everybody else has given up on me. Jesus, I'm losing my fucking mind. The whole fucking world's in school but me."

I felt the old familiar despair descending on me like poured concrete. Maybe I should play the jukebox, I thought, but I couldn't move a muscle. Where the hell were we anyway? I looked up and saw that a woman had just walked into the bar.

She could have been anything between a ruined forty and a preserved sixty-five. She shed a vast overcoat like a seaman's (it hung to her knees), revealing enormous breasts sagging in a man's dirty shirt, huge thighs crammed into a pair of man's tweed pants held up with a length of rope. A monstrous beefy block of a woman, she had grey hair that was unwinding itself from various incongruous pins and clips and barrettes, tiny red and pink plastic bows like those a child might have worn. Her wrinkled face was stretched into a wide, yellow-toothed grin, and her eyes glittered like frost. To my growing alarm, she walked directly to our booth and dropped a gigantic purse onto the table with a crash. "Well, boys, are you getting any?" she shouted.

"I beg your pardon," Revington said in his British colonel voice.

"Are you getting your hammer wet, that's what I want to know. Or are you just going home every night and pulling your puds?"

She rummaged a half-smoked stogie out of her purse, stuffed it into her face, and lit it, shedding sparks of burning tobacco leaf. "Viv's the name, fun's the game," she yelled. "I'm the best-educated drunk you boys will ever meet. Mind if I sit down?" she said, sitting down. "All I want to know is are you getting your dorks dunked?" None of us said anything.

"Aren't you going to offer the lady a drink?" Wearily, Revington pushed the third coffee cup across to her. She poured it swiftly into the saucer and slurped.

"Shit," she yelled in a booming, good-humored voice, "I was out there last night, you know what I mean? And there was this old fellow, and damn if he didn't want to rip it off right there in the field . . . goddamn horny old bugger. And I'd rather be dingled than dangled, if you know what I mean, so I told him to lay to it . . . But shit, he got his pants off and damned if he didn't have a dork hanging most of the way down to his goddamned socks . . . Goddamn biggest hunk of meat I ever saw short of a butcher shop, you know? Jesus, boys, I tell you, what a goddamn wong he had! And still like a noodle, right? And I thought to myself, now Viv, if that tool ever stands up, it's going to look like the whole frigging Washington Monument . . . I mean his hammer was hanging down so far he could have skipped rope with it. You'd never know looking at him, he was such a dried-up little fart of a man. But he was a damn good banger all right. Well, boys, what I want to know is: ARE YOU GETTING ANY?"

Revington was staring blankly at her; Cohen was laughing, convulsed in the corner. I gave her the answer I'd always given my father. "We're getting our share."

"Shit, that's good to hear . . . Now, boys, let me tell you . . . looking at me, you'd never know I studied that goddamn Latin at good old Saint Mary's on the hill, would you? *Carpe diem* and all that other horseshit, right, boys? And it's always come in real useful, just the way the nuns said it would. Never know when you might need a few words of that old Latin, stand you in good stead every time. Yep," she said, laughing, "it's all horseshit. You know that, don't you, boys? Every bit of it. From one end to the other, top to bottom. Horseshit . . . Don't suppose you could pick up something more to warm old Viv's tummy, do you, boys? It's a frigging cold night out there, and I'm here to tell you. Freeze your noogies right off you faster than you could say *ora pro nobis.*"

W H E N   W E got back to my apartment, I heard the phone ringing inside as I was unlocking the door. By the time I rushed in and answered it, the line had gone dead. It didn't feel right to me. I stood in the middle of the room, my coat still on, drunk and caught by an ominous buzzing inside my head. "Who the hell could have been calling at damn near four in the morning?" I said.

"Three forty-seven," Cohen said.

"Goddamned foresighted son-of-a-bitch that I am," Revington was saying, "guess what I managed to hide from us? Come on, Dupre, what's the word?"

"Thunderbird?"

"Right you are." He pulled the bottle out of his knapsack, passed it to me.

"Beautiful," I said.

"Why do they always pick us?" Revington said. We'd been laughing about Viv. We'd bought her half a dozen cups of whiskey-laced coffee while she'd told us endless stories, each one more obscene than the last. "Can they see us coming a mile off? Do we have signs around our necks saying: easy mark?"

"Well, she cheered us up," I said.

"She did that."

"Oh," Cohen said, "but couldn't you see the glory shining around her like a halo?"

"Jesus," Revington said, "you're not merely crazy. You're crazy as a fucking coot."

The phone began to ring again. I jumped to get it. It was my mother. When I hung up, I saw both of them looking at me. I didn't want to see it: the waiting. "My father had a stroke," I told them.

Revington fell onto a kitchen chair as though he'd been punctured. "John," he said, "I'm terribly sorry."

I passed him the bottle. I didn't want to be where I was, drunk and confused, time mixed up and folded in on itself. I couldn't take it in. Cohen was asking me quietly, "How is he?"

"They don't know yet. I have to go back tomorrow."

"This certainly puts things into perspective, doesn't it?" Revington said. "Shit."

I sank to the floor, asked Cohen to make coffee. Revington

and I stared at each other. "Do you get along with him?" he asked me.

"He's been around since I was four. We've got used to each other."

"Yeah," he nodded. "Yeah."

I didn't want to talk about me and my father. I felt a cold edge of panic in my chest—and something in my mind that resembled a prayer: please let him be all right. "Do you get along with your old man?" I asked Revington.

"Not particularly. Shit, when I was in high school," he said, "I hated his fucking guts, but now . . . Jesus, sometimes I wish he'd just tell me to get lost. But no, here I am driving the car he bought me. And I've got his fucking money in my wallet. And he's so goddamn understanding . . . Well, maybe he's trying to make up for lost time, I don't know. But all he says is, 'Don't worry, you'll find out what you want to do.' Christ, what kind of a father is that? If I had me for a son, I'd fucking disown me."

Cohen set the percolator on the flame and then sat down between us. "Do you get along with your old man?" I asked him.

"He's funny," he said, smiling. "He's beautiful."

"Your father told me to take you out and get you laid," Revington said. "Did you know that?"

Cohen laughed. "Yeah, he'd say something like that," and then in his father's accent: "OK, Bill, so you don't want to go to the Temple. I can understand that. There's nobody over there but a bunch of Jews. Not one Chinaman would you find in the whole place. Of course you might meet a nice Jewish girl over there, who could tell? You never know who might turn up. Maybe that little Cindy Stein might be there, who could tell? Like a flower opening, that girl, and bright too . . . Not Chinese of course . . . But don't get me wrong, it's your *mishigas*."

I needed to laugh, and I did. We sat at the kitchen table and drank coffee. I don't know what I thought it was going to do for me. "I'm terribly sorry," Revington said again. "Christ, I get so fucking sick of myself. And then something happens like this . . . If there's anything I can do, John."

"Thanks," I said.

He stood and walked to the window, spoke with his back to us. "I just wish the hell I could be of some use to somebody."

IN THE morning, Revington drove Cohen and me out of town. We'd slept only a couple hours, had risen just before dawn, Cohen waking us by singing in the dark, in that wholly tuneless voice of his: "Wake up, wake up, the dawn is breaking." I'd showered, turning the water colder and colder, until I'd been braced against it and shivering, teeth chattering: antidote to hangover and lack of sleep. Then I'd cooked pancakes and sausages. We'd been on the road just as the horizon had begun to lighten in the east to a dirty stripe of grey. I'd asked Cohen to come to Raysburg with me, but he'd said that his parents would worry about him if they knew he wasn't at Harvard, and he didn't want to lie to them, even indirectly, by passing through town and not calling them.

Revington pulled over at the junction. To the left, the road ran north to Little Washington and then on to Raysburg; to the right, it ran east to Maryland and then, in a way that was mysterious to me—but not, I hoped, to Cohen—northeast through Pennsylvania and on to New York and Boston. "When will we three meet again?" Cohen said.

Revington laughed. "I *knew* you were going to say that." He shut off the engine. We climbed out of the car. It was country, fields on all sides, beginning to show dun-stubble and beige in the spreading grey morning. There was no traffic yet, not much sound but that of an improbable winter bird singing. Our breath steamed. Revington lit a cigarette, looked toward the west where the sky was still black. A scattering of snowflakes had begun to drift down on us.

"Hope the snow doesn't get bad," he said, his voice somber.

"Sure you don't want to keep on going?" I asked him. "You've got your choice of two significant destinations."

"Shit, not back to Raysburg . . . but Boston . . ." He scowled. "Christ, I'm tempted. But no, I'm finally getting my horns knocked off. Can't pass it up."

"All right, ace," I said, "don't burn down my apartment."

He snapped his cigarette away. "Let's not make this into a big production."

Cohen hugged him. "It'll be soon, William."

I took Revington's hand; our eyes met. He was so tall that I had to look up. "The hero sustains himself," I said. He smiled. We stepped into a brief embrace—the first and last that I remember with him. To the touch he was amazingly thin.

"You fucker," he said.

He climbed into his car, started the engine, made a squealing U-turn, leaned out the window to say, "Hey, Dupre, plank Cassy Markapolous for me."

Cohen and I watched until we saw the last of the red tail-lights swinging around and vanishing at a curve in the road. "It's funny how sad I feel," I said. "We'll all be together again at Christmas."

"But it could always be the last time," Cohen said, "and we always know it." His face, with its slight smile, was as composed and beautiful as a cat's. "Would we want it any other way? Anything but the simply human? It wouldn't be anywhere near as beautiful."

We squeezed each other. I thought he'd crack my ribs. "I love you, John."

Back in those days boys did not say things like that to each other, and, for a moment, I was too startled to reply. Then I said the only possible thing I could, the truth: "I love you too."

He walked away to the road branching to the right, set his sign up in front of his knapsack: NEW YORK. I remained where I was, set up my sign: RAYSBURG. We were both stamping our feet against the cold. "Write when you get back," I yelled at him. "Send me a card. I worry about you." His laugh rang clearly through the morning air.

Cohen got the first ride.

5.

WE WALKED with irritating slowness across the soft pad of snow in the hospital parking lot; my mother and I were supporting my grandmother Dupre on either side. At the car, my mother handed me the keys. I was surprised; the air had begun to thicken with snow again, and she'd never trusted my driving. I knew that she must have been sending me one of her obscure messages—a commission, a trust—so I drove carefully, at barely twenty miles an hour, from town to the Island where, just as I turned away from the end of the Suspension Bridge, all of the street lights came on at once as though announcing twilight. We weren't speaking; the only sounds were the slap of the windshield wipers and the soft hiss of the tires. Snow was smearing the landscape into an impressionist haze, the lights of town scattered like amber beads on the other shore, repeated, blurred, in the river; above, the diffuse grey hills and factory chimneys were flat as rice paper against the darkening sky. There it was: my earliest memory of painful beauty, when I'd been just tall enough to stand on tip-toe and wipe the moisture away from the window pane to look out at the river. Although it moved me as always, I couldn't imagine making the effort to describe it again for I was sinking into a melancholy so thorough that I was rapidly losing all of my standard avenues of escape. Not through words, I thought, not through studies or plans or a college degree or poetry or folk music or Zen Buddhism—not through anything. When I pulled up in front of my grandmother's apartment, she said, "It's in the hands of the Lord now."

Ever since I'd decided that I was a writer, I'd planned to be a West Virginia writer—the one to explore, definitively, this location, the intersection of this river with these hills. Now I knew that it was impossible, that I could never assimilate it, that I could barely cope with it, that all I could do—and only if I was lucky—was get out. My mother and I helped my grandmother up the stairs and into her living room. We got back into the car. Neither of us spoke. I drove home.

"Why don't you go visit your friends, John?" my mother said.

"Don't you want to go back to the hospital tonight?"

"I'll take a taxi." I looked at her, trying as I had all of my life to understand the thoughts behind that fine-boned face. I'd always seen her as a beautiful woman: fragile and long-necked with aristocratic cheekbones and large, luminous eyes. She dressed with a care I'd come to think of as "perfect taste." Now, dismayed, I saw that she was a mess. She wasn't wearing make-up, and her skin was white and lined. Her hair was coming down; she pushed it away from her forehead. But it was her hands that chilled me the most: knobby knuckles, veins like wires, and the sad incongruity of pink nail polish. I still couldn't read anything on her face. "It's all right, honey," she said. "It'll be all right." She must be in her late forties, I thought, or early fifties. It bothered me that I didn't know her age, exactly, to the year. "I suppose you didn't need to come up," she said, "and miss all those classes, but . . . "

But she'd thought he was dying. Those were words she would never allow herself to say.

DRIVING AWAY, I felt a guilty relief, as though escaping from a long, justly imposed prison term. The worst thing about seeing my father in the hospital had been his immobility and silence: that garrulous joking man. He hadn't said: "Well, son, are you getting any?" He hadn't said: "What did they do, close all the barber shops in Morgantown?" He hadn't said anything since the stroke. The doctors weren't sure that he would ever be able to say anything. His eyes had been open. "Hi, Dad," I'd said, and nothing had happened on his face. Not a flicker. Nothing. And suddenly I found the words to express the numb wretchedness in me: *Christ, I'm glad I'm young.*

Turning onto the National Road, I was going so fast I fish-tailed across two lanes. Luckily there'd been no one behind me. Fear yanked my stomach tight. I slowed to a crawl. I drove to Cassandra's house.

They never locked their door. I stamped the snow off my cowboy boots, pulled them off and left them outside, walked in and yelled, "Hey, Cassy?" I'd called her as soon as I'd got home. She had a date tonight, but she'd told me to come over anyway.

"I'm up here, John."

Her hair was wound onto rollers, and she was standing in the bathroom with the door open, leaning close to the mirror and plucking at her eyebrows with tweezers. She was wearing a dramatically padded bra, stockings, plain black heels, and a shiny white panty girdle that fit her tightly from her small waist down to the garter tabs a few inches above her knees. "Christ," I said, stepping back from the door.

"No, it's just me." She motioned for me to come in.

Coals to Newcastle, I thought. Cassandra was as slender as a grass stem, and the incongruity of her sixteen-year-old body squeezed into that girdle struck me as both distasteful and disturbingly erotic. "You don't really think you need that thing, do you?" I said.

"Oh, but I do," throwing me a wicked sideways smile. "I'm going out with George." She laughed at my uncomprehending face. "He's not going to get *this* off me."

I felt something puncture inside me; laughter poured through the hole. I sank to the bathroom floor, laughing until tears came to my eyes. "Amazing," I said. "I didn't know girls did it on purpose."

"Of course we do. I just know what he's planning . . . the little jerk. A dinner date, right? And then a movie. And if he's going to blow that much money on me, he's going to have to take me parking to see what he can get. Well, what he's going to get is a surprise." She threw the tweezers into the cupboard above the sink and walked past me, heels clicking, to her bedroom. I followed, hesitated at the door. "Come on in," she said. "There's nobody here but me."

I sat down gingerly on the edge of her bed. "How's your dad?" she said. I looked up, saw her somber eyes.

"I don't know. He's alive but . . . maybe not much more than that. The doctors aren't sure . . ." and then I understood that what she really wanted to know was how *I* was. "I'm all right," I said, "but I don't really want to talk about it. Not right now anyhow."

"OK," she said. She turned away to her dresser and began to wind the rollers out of her hair.

"So why do you go out with this George character anyway?" I asked her.

"I've got to go out with *somebody*, don't I? Just like you and Natalie the Silent." I laughed. She still hadn't quite forgiven me for Natalie. In fact, if I had to admit the truth, something between us hadn't survived Natalie: a breathless headlong quality that, if it hadn't been "in love," had been the next best thing.

"And you're not in high school," she was saying, "so what am I supposed to do? And George is fun. I just don't want to sleep with him." Cassandra was still a virgin, and, like me, she enjoyed pretending she wasn't. Neither of us was fooling the other.

I stood and kissed her on the back of her neck. She turned

134

to me. "Hello, John Dupre." And then we were kissing mouth to open mouth. With me in my socks and Cassandra in heels, she was as tall as I was; I liked that. "You were only gone a week," she said, "and I was already missing you."

"Yeah, I was already missing you too." I felt a twinge of guilt because that wasn't entirely true. She had floated through my mind, of course, but most of the time I'd been brooding about Carol.

She took my hand and drew me over to her bed. I was delighted. There was no predicting her these days. Sometimes she'd make out with me, and sometimes she wouldn't. "They won't be home for at least an hour," she said. We stretched out together. I held her and studied her face: those self-contained grey eyes. "You're so beautiful it hurts me to look at you," I said.

"What? In this outfit?"

"I don't mean the outfit."

"Oh, you mean me, then. This skinny little bow-legged kid with a big nose?"

"Yes."

"You just think I'm beautiful because you like me."

"I more than like you."

"I love you too." I always heard the fine distinction she'd been making ever since we'd first met. Being "in love" meant "all that crap" and so was off limits, but it was all right to say, simply, that we *loved* each other. It was never enough for me. "I'm going to be late for poor old George," she said. "Oh, to hell with him. He can wait." We intertwined our legs and kissed.

She giggled. "I wouldn't have thought you would have touched me with a ten-foot pole. I really look like hell, don't I? Not a bit seductive."

"That's what's seductive," I said. "You look unfinished." Our tongues circled around each other; I ran my hands down the hard lines of her flat stomach under the silk panel, over the smooth nylons. We were rubbing our crotches together until we were both panting. An abstracted and intent expression had come over her face, much like the one that must have come over mine. And finally, looking into her clear eyes, I came in my pants. "Goddamn it," she said, "now I've got to pee again." She jumped up and clicked away into the bathroom.

It didn't seem possible: not much more than an hour ago I'd felt like throwing myself into the river, but now I was sailing high on a giddy euphoria. It didn't seem fair that I could be as happy as I was while my father was laid out in the hospital—but, I told myself, I wouldn't be doing him a damned bit of good by being miserable. I lay back on Cassandra's bed, propped up my head with her pillows, and considered my good fortune. Through the open doors, I could hear the discreet plangent sound of her urine tumbling into the toilet; the sound delighted me. And, in that moment of post-orgasmic clarity, I realized that, on some level, I felt an elusive but crucial connection to her that I didn't feel for anybody else in my life except for Bill Cohen.

"There are links between people," I called to her, trying to put it into words. "I don't mean just friendship, and I don't mean being in love either. It's more like being related . . . but at the level of soul. And I feel that you and I are linked like that."

She came back and began to take the rest of the rollers out of her hair. I suddenly felt the hidden power of the world so savagely it prickled the hair on my arms. "So if I'm linked to you, and I'm linked to Cohen," I said, "that means that you're linked to Cohen too. It means that the links go out in all directions, that we're linked with people we've never met. I seriously believe it, Cassy."

"It's just that we're misfits, John," she said, her attention on the rollers.

"No, it's more than that. Can't you feel it?"

She laughed. "Well, I can't imagine any other boy I'd allow to lie there on my bed and watch while I got dressed."

She gave me a slow-motion wink. I didn't know what it meant, but I received it with an uneasy thrill that passed through my entire body; it stopped me for a moment. But then I went on. "We can all depend on each other, that's the beautiful thing. You know you can depend on me, and that means you can depend on Cohen too."

She threw down the last roller; her hair stood out stiffly around her head like ringlets of chestnut-colored marzipan. "I make my own links," she said and began to brush out those stiff curls. "But I know what you're talking about. It isn't just non-conformity, because you can decide to be a nonconformist. And it isn't something you can decide."

"That's right."

"It's something inside that nobody talks about, an unknown . . . an X. And when two X people meet each other, they recognize each other. That's the link."

"But it's more than that," I said, "it's . . ." Downstairs the door banged. I jumped straight up, my heart jumping with me.

"Relax," Cassy said, "that's just Zoë. She's learned to keep her mouth shut."

Little sister, loud as a pony, was taking the stairs two at a time; she arrived running, her face flushed. When she saw me, she slid to an abrupt stop just inside the bedroom door, poised as though she were about to run away again. She stared at me with concentrated, blue-eyed intensity. "Hi, John, I didn't know you were in town."

"Good grief, Zo," Cassandra said, "what have you been doing?" Zoë's hair was full of snow and hanging in a soaked rat's nest in her face; her blazer was torn, her skirt wildly askew, showing slip; both her knee socks had fallen to her ankles, and her legs were splashed with mud.

"Got in a snowball fight. Mom's going to kill me." Zoë shrugged off the blazer and shook herself like a dog. "Don't you have a date with George?"

Cassandra laughed at her. "Yeah, I have a date with George. John's just dropped in."

Zoë appeared to be thinking about that. "Stay for dinner," she said to me. "Dad will want to see you." And then, as quickly as she'd arrived, she was gone.

"How old is she now?" I'd, for quite some time now, been noticing the budding breasts.

"Thirteen. Unfortunately, she can wear my clothes." Cassy gave me a wicked smile. "Still like little girls, John?"

I didn't answer. Cassy was stepping into a pair of white pettipants, lace at the legs, crisp and shiny as icing. "Another layer for George," she said, and then, jerking her head toward the empty doorway through which her sister had fled: "Take Zoë, for instance. There's not an ounce of X in her. It's not something you can choose to have."

"But you wouldn't choose *not* to have it, would you?"

She wiggled into a petticoat, then a black cocktail dress. "Zip me up," she said. "No, I wouldn't choose not to have it, but it doesn't make you very happy sometimes, does it?"

The front door bell was ringing. "Hey, Zo. Get that, will you?"

From the next room: "Oh, Cassandra!"

"Come on, brat, I do plenty for you." We heard Zoë bound down the stairs; Cassandra put on lipstick.

I was feeling a desperate haste. "Don't go for a minute, Cassy. This is just getting interesting. So you think that the link between us is what . . . recognizing each other?"

"Sure. We see each other, and we know. Oh, you're one too. George wouldn't know. Zoë wouldn't know. But we know . . . And that's personal. That's just between two people."

"But the links extend out in all directions. When we're linked to other people, we have a tremendous power. It's right there, underneath us."

"I don't think so," she said. "X people will never rule the world, but we'll never be ruled by it either." She walked toward the full-length mirror, then away from it. I loved seeing Cassandra in high heels because she was a grown-up tomboy and wearing them didn't come any more naturally to her than it would have to me. She adjusted her petticoat so it didn't show. "Maybe you better go down now," she said.

Reluctantly, I got off her bed. "That's quite a production for old George."

"It's not for George. It's for me . . . to prove that I can do it. We X people are very insecure at heart."

I'd met George Murray before, casually, at parties; we didn't like each other. He'd always appeared to me a standard mindless jerk, as predictable as a character out of *Archie,* precisely the sort I had despised when I'd been in high school, and I imagined that I was just as much of a pain in the ass to him, a college boy and therefore at an unfair advantage with girls like Cassandra. He must have heard me on the stairs; he hadn't had time to rearrange his face before I walked into the living room. I could see him thinking: What was *he* doing upstairs with *her?*

"Hi, George," I said, giving him nothing.

"What do you say, John?" he said, stretching his smile. He was handsome, I had to admit, in the yearbook manner: Ivy League suit, wavy hair parted to one side. But I enjoyed my contrast to him: my wrinkled, plaid shirt I'd worn for a week (and slept in), my jeans, my two days' growth of beard, the hair falling over my ears. I didn't restrain myself from disliking him; I knew even then that he would be successful and I would not—successful in terms of a world from which I could not quite free myself. I said nothing to him. "How's school?" he asked me uneasily.

"It goes," I said in a voice like Revington's.

I was out of Cassy's bedroom just in time; here were her parents, loaded with packages, bumbling through the door. "Come on, son," Doctor Markapolous said, "get off your ass and give me a hand." I slid under a bag of groceries and followed him into the kitchen. "How's your father?"

The question stopped me for a moment. I wished that everybody would stop asking me about my father. "I can't tell." I walked back into the living room.

Cassandra was making her entrance. Upstairs, preparing herself, she'd bounded about with a boyish gracelessness, but now she floated, transforming the few yards from the stairs to the couch into a promenade, stepping well within the demand of her heels, carrying herself as regally erect as if she'd trained for it in a finishing school. She bestowed upon George, who rose to meet her, a measured smile. Even I, who'd watched the effort of construction, was impressed. She wore her cocktail dress as if she'd never worn anything else; she looked far older than sixteen—was the very picture of a cool and sophisticated young lady who would have terrified me if I'd met her at a party. But passing, she shot me the most oblique and skewed of glances, momentarily exaggerated the smallness of her steps. Deep in my lungs, I felt the first tickle of silliness.

Cassandra's mother was obviously delighted with the performance. And so was Zoë, who had just turned up to give her sister a critical, assessing stare. And so, I suppose, was George, although for a moment something passed across his face that looked like plain old fear. He helped her on with her coat.

Leaving, Cassandra gave me once again, along a line invisible to anyone but me, her slow and hooded wink. I rushed into the bathroom, flushed the toilet and ran both taps. When I stopped laughing, I slid along a taut wire of ringing giddiness into the kitchen. On a small blackboard where they wrote shopping lists, I inscribed a bit of Rilke: *"Denk, es erhält sich der Held, selbst der Untergang war ihm nur ein Vorwand, zu sein: seine letzte Geburt."*

A GLASS of bourbon and water in my hand, I followed Doctor Markapolous into the study where he saw his patients who happened to be his friends—also, I suspected, where he escaped from his family. To my relief, he didn't settle behind the desk, instead chose an immense reclining chair, motioned me into another one. "Still smoking those things?" he said as I lit a cigarette.

"The problem with a pipe," I said, "is all the junk you end up carting around with you."

"No," he said, "for you the problem with a pipe is that you can't commit suicide with it."

Like many of his pronouncements, this one left me nothing to say. I surveyed him over the top of my glass. It was odd to find Cassandra's direct grey eyes in that middle-aged man's face, set above those fleshy pouches. Odd too, seeing Zoë's delicate cupid's bow mouth adorning the abrupt jaw of a bulldog. But neither of his daughters had inherited his blunt powerful hands. He was stuffing his pipe with a finger as broad as a sausage. "How's your mother taking it?"

"I can't tell."

He drew fire into the bowl, said through clenched teeth: "Well, how are you taking it?"

"I can't tell."

"For Christ's sake, John."

He's in one of his tigerish moods, I thought uneasily. I preferred to see him separated from me, infinitely, by his age, but he never stayed in that role for very long. "I *can't* tell," I snapped back at him. I thought that maybe I could defeat him with a bit of righteous anger; after all, it was *my* father laid out in Raysburg General like a gaffed catfish. "I was never very close to him. I don't know what I feel about it. Maybe I'll know what I feel in a month."

He nodded, apparently satisfied. "So how's it going for you this term?"

"Probably get mostly A's again. WVU's not the most demanding school in the world."

"I know that. So stay in and let them give you their degree." He smiled. "Just so you can put it on the dust jacket of your first book . . . BA." That was the sort of thing he'd been telling me as long as I'd known him.

"That's no reason," I said.

"I know it isn't. Seriously, John, it doesn't have a damn thing to do with education, but it's the certification . . . the ticket. In this world that counts for a lot."

"I'm not sure I want to compromise with this world."

"You're just like Cassy," he said, laughing, "so damn self-righteous. If you don't want to compromise, you're going to have a hell of a hard life. As you get older, you see that you can't change it all, so you change what you can. It's as simple as that."

I was feeling again, as I generally did with him, that we saw things from such radically different viewpoints that even though we used the same words, we would never be able to understand each other. "It's not the world I want to change," I said, "it's me."

"Oh? What's wrong with you?"

"I can't live purely enough."

"What the hell's that mean?"

"There are moments of absolute clarity . . . I don't know how else to say it . . . that show me the way I could be all the time. But I can't seem to be there very much."

"We're none of us there except rarely. That's just the way it is."

"No, some people are there all the time."

"Who, for instance?"

"The Buddha."

"For Christ's sake, John, come back down to earth, will you?"

"Cohen's there more than I am."

"Bill Cohen's a very sweet and very bright guy. I'm very fond of him. But I'd also have to give him some kind of award for being the most astonishingly naïve kid who's ever walked through the door of this house."

"Don't you see the saintliness of him?"

"I see the youth of him. If Bill Cohen comes around here in ten years and he's still saintly, then I'll believe it." He relit his pipe. "We don't need any more saints, anyway, John."

He was smiling with that wicked edge I was used to seeing from Cassandra. "You got yourself a girl yet? What about that grad student you were telling me about?"

"I'm not sure that's going anywhere."

As we'd been talking, I'd felt the earlier gloom of the day sneaking back into me. I lay in the huge leather chair and stared at the ceiling. Education, marriage, family: that's what he always recommended. He talked about sex as though it were nothing more than an essential element in any rational young man's program of hygiene. I didn't realize it at the time, but, as the father of two daughters, he must have been walking a fairly difficult tightrope. Somehow, without saying it, he always made it perfectly clear to me that whatever he was recommending, it most certainly was not that I lose my virginity with Cassandra.

"You sound just like my father," I said. "You know the only serious question he's asked me for the last five years? 'Well, son, you getting any?'"

"Well, are you?"

"No."

"Why not?"

I had asked myself the same thing about a million times and had never found the answer. "The important thing is what happens between people," I said, quoting Cohen verbatim. "If I get close to a girl, sex will happen of its own accord."

"That's true, of course, but it's also a nice, pat little rationalization."

"What the hell do you want from me, doctor?"

"It's not what I want. It's what you want. I just don't like to see you getting in your own way. You're too bright for that. I'd hate to see you waste your brains and your talent."

"They're mine to waste."

"Yes, of course they are."

We looked at each other silently across the room. "I guess that's the thing that bothers me about my father," I said. "It seems like such a goddamned waste."

"It's pretty well over for him, John. Live your own life. Make something of that. You really are a lot like Cassy. You're so bright you tie yourself up. There's too many things you could do, too many choices."

"It doesn't matter to me that I'm bright. I always wanted to be something more than that. I wanted excellence the way the Greeks meant it . . . *arete*."

"That's a matter of work."

"Some days," I said. "I'm so goddamned depressed I can't even think of a reason to get out of bed."

"You get out of bed because that's what you do the first thing in the morning."

"I'm not sure that's enough."

With a light tap at the door, Mrs. Markapolous was announcing dinner. "Right away," the doctor said, standing. And to me: "It damned well *better* be enough."

I followed him into the dining room, Mrs. Markapolous was calling: "Zoë, right now."

"I'm coming, mother."

"Good God, Zo!" her father said. While we'd been talking, she'd found time to put on bright shiny red lipstick—and mascara, eyeliner, and even pale blue eye shadow. She was wearing nylons and a black dress with a white scoop collar, a dress that had once, I suppose, looked childish and prim, but she'd cinched in her waist with a broad patent belt. She was wearing a pair of Cassandra's heels; they were too high for her skirt. As gauche as the effect was, she had managed to achieve an iridescent Lolita sexiness. She ignored her father. "I guess I'll sit next to you, John," she said, flicking her curled eyelashes at me. I was both flattered and appalled. I held the chair for her.

The doctor appeared to have been seized by a fit of coughing. He pushed his pipe stem between his teeth, fired the tobacco, and walked into the kitchen. Mrs. Markapolous was staring openly at her daughter. "Are you going somewhere, Zo?" she said.

"Yes, I thought I'd go to the hop . . . you know, at Gerry's Inn."

"Is that still happening?" I said.

"Every Friday and Saturday," Zoë said brightly. "Are you going to be in town long, John?"

"I'm probably going back tomorrow."

"Oh, that's too bad."

I shrugged. "I've got a lot of work to do."

We settled down around the table. The doctor began to carve the roast. "Zoë, dear," her mother said, "perhaps we could have a little conference after dinner."

Zoë completely ignored her parents. "Are you enjoying school this year?" she asked me.

I was squirming inwardly; this was too close to home. Zoë, I thought, you're a doll, but there's just no way I can get around it: *thirteen* is toö young.

"School's all right," I said. "You don't enjoy it. You just get through it."

"That's the way I feel too." She gave me a radiant smile. "I suppose you already have plans for the evening?"

The good doctor's eyes met mine across the table. "John's promised me a chess game tonight," he said. (I hadn't.) "I think I'm going to hold him to it."

"Oh," Zoë said, looking into her plate as though she could already read her fate there.

Zoë did go to the dance, wearing different clothes, accompanied by a girl friend and chauffeured by her mother. The doctor and I did play chess, and I was still there at midnight when Cassandra came home. I left her to chat with her dad, went into the kitchen to get another beer. After a moment, I heard her heels following me. "Where's George?" I asked her.

"I'm not sure I'll be seeing much of him."

She poured herself a glass of milk and studied the German words I'd written on the blackboard. "What happened?" I asked her.

"Just exactly what I told you would happen, except that it was boring. I guess I don't make a very good tease. The trouble with being an X person is that a lot of the time we don't like ourselves very much."

Our eyes met. We had never played games with each other. When I was with her, I didn't have to be watchful, careful, on guard—didn't have to pretend anything. I'd never realized before how rare that was, how enormously much she meant to me. How odd, I thought, that she should be a girl.

"Dad told me what little sister did to you," she was saying. "You must have been pleased."

"I was and I wasn't. She's awfully cute, but . . ."

"Sure she's cute. And she's in the eighth grade."

"I know, I know."

"What happened to your older woman?"

"Who? Carol? Christ, that's going nowhere . . . X people. Damn it, Cassandra, it's no joke. What are we supposed to do? Go on play-acting until we get really good at it . . . so good we convince everybody we're ordinary?"

"Good question. I don't know. It's hard work, isn't it?" She did look tired. "I guess we'll never be King and Queen of the Hop, will we, John?" *Why won't you let me be in love with you?* I thought. *Why the hell not?* And then, just as I had meant her to, she pointed to the blackboard and asked, "What does that mean?"

It was too late for the punch line, but still I managed to smile as I translated it for her: "Consider: the Hero sustains himself; even his downfall was an excuse for his continuing existence, his final birth."

I MADE it from Raysburg to Morgantown in one ride, less than two hours. A fraternity boy, scraped to the nerve with hangover, saw my WVU sign and stopped for me. He was feeling horrible, he said with grim satisfaction; he'd done nothing in

Raysburg all weekend but party. As soon as he got back to the KA House, Christ, was he going to sleep! And then he was going to pull an all-nighter because he had a goddamned test Monday morning first thing and he hadn't cracked a book—and squinting at the rain, muttering about "the pain in my left eyeball," he took those twisting roads like a racing driver. It was all much too fast. My knapsack beside me, cowboy hat pulled down to my eyes, I sat not ten yards from where he'd dropped me off, the first place I'd found, on the steps of the armory. It had begun to rain the night before, had been raining ever since. The snow was gone; the paths of the campus were as muddy as hog wallows. And here I was at eleven in the morning, Sunday morning, back in Morgantown, in the steady, monotonous, undistinguished winter rain.

Cohen had left; that must be the reason it felt so particularly hideous for me to be back. Revington was still around; I wasn't ready to see him. I wasn't sure why, but I knew I'd feel even worse after *he* left. I didn't want to go back to my apartment. I didn't want to go anywhere. To get out of the rain, I went into Johnny's and bought myself a cheeseburger. I sat drinking coffee, stared at the steamed windows. I fished a pencil and my notebook out of my knapsack. There was the poem I'd begun impossibly long ago, only a few hours ago, sometime around dawn, still in bed in Raysburg, scratching down the first few words of it in the dark. Maybe I could finish it.

I wrote out several drafts easily, adding a little to each; then I got stuck. The last version in my notebook still has no ending:

For Bill Cohen

Gusty dawn-shine slides the mountains:
time of cold apprenticeship.

148

The sky, none too soon, turns toward driving
the night about imperceptibly.
So let night whiten, movement break
stark against our boots: single
greyness caught about for miles.
Well, our apprenticeship flows, breaks,
and dawn is thick, wheeling down,
running out the sides, replacing
the pall of that before. Now
we   can   talk   well.
Is the ice clear in the dark or barely . . .
Things rise irrevocably:
a house now up, invisible bird.
In a hundred nights

Parting just outside her front door last night, Cassy and I
had held a single kiss for something on the order of twenty minutes, and I was left with the taste of her now, Cassandra in the
bleak Morgantown winter rain. Waking to a dream of summer—*Lord, it is time!*—drifting down the river road in my
father's car, singing along to "Sheila" on the radio, shimmering
white solarized images of the park with the trees in full leaf, the
hot summer sun of Raysburg. "Hello, John Dupre." Cassandra
on the glider, her hair wound onto rollers as it had been that first
night when I'd met her. Cassandra in camp shorts, her long thin
legs burnished from the sun, the beautiful filthy soles of her feet.
Cassandra in a blue dress at the Louis Armstrong concert in the
park, the first time I'd ever seen her in heels. Cassandra's mouth
pressed against mine as we're sitting on the dark back porch at
her house, hiding out there, sweating, mosquito-bitten, bathed
in the dismal whir of locusts. And I dreamed of her night after
night the summer she was fifteen; in my dream she was never

quite there, not quite in the car when I reached for her, and not quite in the bed, and not quite at the end of the street when I got there, and then I wasn't dreaming at all; we were stretched out together on a blanket at Waverly Park just as we had been night after night the summer she was fifteen, but in the dream she was gone and I was really awake—or was I?—and there was a faint trace of Cassandra fading away, like an afterimage, like the perfume on the hairband she'd left in my car, that I'd saved, that I'd kept under my pillow for the scent of her. She was floating, her hair streaming out behind her longer than in life, and I was alone in my bed in Raysburg.

And now I was alone in Johnny's diner in Morgantown, West Virginia, staring out at the cold steady rain. On the page next to the last draft of my poem, I wrote: It seems to me that any time that I don't spend in bed with a girl is time wasted.

What an absolutely adolescent idiotic commonplace of a sentence, I thought. That's not what it's about at all. I turned the page.

Cassandra. *The summer was so full.* I wrote:

Dear Cassandra. Sweet Cassandra. Oh, Christ, Cassy, I keep thinking of you . . . (Can't you be more poetic than that?) Your somber grey eyes have haunted me the entire . . . (Scratch that.) Oh, beautiful sweet lovely heart-breaking incredible . . . (Scratch that.) My dearest friend, Cassandra. It's raining in Morgantown. The usual steady awful unceasing winter rain. I'm filled up with greyness. I'm flattened out and blotted. I'm nothing . . . (Oh Jesus, Dupre!) Dear Cassandra, I want you so much I think I might die from it. The incredible sweetness and sadness of life seems perfectly epitomized in your eyes, grey as . . . (Come on, Dupre.) Cassy, I miss you already. Cassy, I miss you. Cassy. (Shit.)

I wrote her name several times—Cassandra Elizabeth

Markapolous—then: I love you, Cassandra. I wrote that over and over to the bottom of the page, then scratched it all out.

Cassandra had saved me after I'd split up with Linda, but I didn't think that she was going to be able to save me much longer. In my mental movie theater, I kept rerunning the scene of her getting dressed up for George—but no, not for George at all, for practice, to prove something to herself. No matter how hard it might be for her or how many bitter jokes she might make about it, she was getting better at the dating game and was going to be successful at it, and that left me stuck with the koan she'd given me so long ago: I wasn't allowed to be *in love* with her, and that made me—what? Her brother? *That* again? A bit of an incestuous brother, but yeah, maybe it was true: we were two X people who recognized each other in the wilderness, but never boyfriend and girlfriend. What was it that Revington was always saying? "All we need is one who'll stick with us." On a fresh page I wrote:

> Linda Edmonds
> Cassandra Markapolous
> Natalie Hewitt
> Carol Rabinowitz

I stared at the names as though the letters themselves might reveal something; then I added: Zoë Markapolous. What the fuck was I doing, making a catalogue?

I turned to another fresh page. Choosing my words carefully, I wrote:

> Dear Natalie,
> I'm sorry we're so far out of touch, and it's largely my fault, but I want you to know that I

think about you all the time. Whenever I walk on the same streets where we walked together, I feel a terrible pang of missing you. Several nights when I couldn't sleep, I walked over to your house and stood across the street wishing that you were still living there. I wish that you could have been a junior when I met you, or even a sophomore, so that we could have gone on being together in Morgantown. I really want to see you. When we do see each other again, I want us to speak clearly and simply from the heart. You never said that you loved me, but I felt that you did, and I only said "I love you" once, but

Oh, God, I thought. I knew that I would never mail that letter, not in a million years. I sat for a long time staring at the steamed windows. Why did I always think I needed a girl to save me? I turned to yet another fresh page and wrote:

Sunday morning, back in Morgantown. My father had a stroke.

I CLOSED my notebook and shoved it into my knapsack. Now I was thinking about Carol, and thinking about Carol left me nowhere at all, but somehow I was on my feet and walking. Living alone, I thought, had been the biggest mistake I'd ever made in my life. What had I imagined I was going to do? Play the guitar more? Write more poetry? Study more? Get more sleep? Drink less? Find a girl who'd spend the night with me?

At the end of my alley, I leaned against the wall outside my apartment and stared at the thick rainy sky. Cohen's right, I thought. If it's going to happen, it'll happen of its own accord.

I've got to forget about girls. Maybe I can use living alone as a spiritual discipline. Maybe I can quit smoking, start working out again, run in the spring, try fasting, learn to meditate. I worked my key into the lock and turned it, stepped inside. My glasses fogged instantly so I couldn't see anything but a grey haze. It was like walking into a steam room. I shed my knapsack and coat, took off my glasses. "Christ," I said out loud, expecting Revington to answer me, "it's ninety degrees in here."

No one answered me. The lights were off in my apartment; the blinds were drawn, and no daylight was getting in. Dense clouds of steam lit by a sulfurous golden light were roiling out from around the edges of the partially closed bathroom door— a blurry image that struck me, at least for one panicky moment, as exactly like a furnace in a steel mill glimpsed at night while driving down the River Road. I could hear water running, mur- muring voices—Revington's edgy drawl, Marge's laugh. I wiped my glasses on a towel, put them back on. Saw clothes on the floor of my bedroom—Revington's shirt and t-shirt, jockey shorts, chinos, socks, and loafers; Marge's black dress, black slip, panties, garter belt, nylons, and plain black high-heels.

I sank down onto my ratty Chevy seat. I looked up at the pic- tures of young girls taped to the wall above my bookcase, looked away. It's too bad, I thought, that Cohen hadn't left his throwing knives behind . . . but no, an ordinary kitchen knife would do it. My mind, off on its own, began writing a newspaper article. COUPLE FOUND SLAIN IN STUDENT APARTMENT. November Something-or-other, 1962. William Revington, 20, an unemployed youth from Raysburg, and Margery Levine, 21, a senior at West Virginia University, were found murdered Sunday night in a student apartment in Morgantown. A spokesman for the police department told reporters that the double killing was the most bizarre in the history of the city. Each had been stabbed through the heart, apparently as they had stepped out of the bathroom. The apartment where the bodies of the slain couple were found had been rented to a John Dupre, also a student at WVU. Dupre could not be located. A statewide search is on, with roadblocks at . . .

"Ciao, Marcello," Revington said. His naked body was steaming. He walked past me, picked his clothes off the floor, and began to dress.

"Revington," I said.

"How goes it?" He gave me a glance that I supposed was meant to be sympathetic.

"It goes."

"We didn't expect you quite so soon. Is there something Marge can . . . ?"

"Look in the closet. There's a bathrobe in there somewhere." I levered myself to my feet. It seemed important, though I didn't know why, that I should be standing up. "How goes it with you, ace?" I said to him.

"Oh, it goes. Struggling with the ennui."

Seeing Marge was a shock. She was lost in my bathrobe, engulfed; on me it was too short, on her it nearly touched the floor. Her hair was skinned back, hanging wetly. Her face looked scrubbed and unfocused; it might have belonged to an earnest little girl.

On impulse, I bent and kissed her on the top of her head. Her smile, just the barest hint of one, could have meant anything at all. Then she gave me a quick hug. I could feel the ribs, the hard angles of her, beneath the robe.

"You're tiny, Levine," I said. "I don't think I've ever seen you without heels on."

"Not even five-two," she said, shrugging. "How's your dad?"

"I don't know. Not very good. Fucking laid out."

"I'm sorry."

"Thanks," I said. We stood looking at each other. An uneasiness was growing between us; I could feel it as my body tensed, could see it happening in her too. Soon we would be standing stiffly as statues. Confused, I looked past her. Revington was leaning against the wall, smoking. He'd raised the blind and was staring out the window. "Jesus, man, the rain," he said, "look at it. Like an analogy for life . . . persistent fucker." He turned to look at us. He gave Marge a nod—detached, nearly formal. "Well, children," he said, "we'll kill off the rest of the day, and then all that will be left to kill will be the night."

Part Two

6.

THAT CHRISTMAS was the first year we didn't have a tree. I don't remember the earliest ones, but the pictures in the family album show me tiny trees, small enough for my mother to carry alone, austerely decorated with all-white ornaments. The presents were wrapped in white too, tied with identical ribbons, and I was displayed next to them to be frozen by the flash bulb. Those photos, which my father must have received while he was sweating it out on his tin can in the Pacific, look as though they were designed by my mother to capture all the mythic symbols of home: tree and presents white as Christmas snow, infant son arranged against a backdrop of safety, the familiar corner of our dining room. I'm staring straight at the camera (at my mother) with huge eyes; I appear to be dazzled by the light.

But the Christmas trees I'll never forget are the ones after my father came home from the war. We'd hear him stumbling up the stairs, helped by a pal or two, under the load of something not quite as big as a redwood. I'd hide behind a chair and watch them heave and groan and laugh, threaten the panes of the bay window, while my mother waved her arms frantically and clucked like a hen. Those enormous trees persisted well into my teens, long enough for me to have my chance to join in the rite: the interminable whiskey-lubricated conference with the man in the lot about which one was really the biggest and best, the Laurel and Hardy fight up the stairs with it, and then decorating the damned thing, beginning with deliberations as formal and complex as a UN debate but ending close to riot, me as drunk as my father, both of us wildly pitching tinsel from across the room. It was my mother who always placed the angel on the top just before we went to bed.

I stood in our bay window that year and felt the absence of

a tree far more keenly than I had expected. I'd been telling myself that I no longer cared about the ancient rituals of Christmas, that I no longer cared about my family—that I was a self-ultimating artist with my own problems a million miles from anything that people like my parents could understand—but it wasn't working, and every day I felt myself sinking deeper into a sticky nostalgic melancholy.

At Christmas everything was forgiven. My father no longer had to hide his bottles but could bring them in by the case, as triumphant and grinning as a baron, because, after all, we had to have something in the house for the holiday. And, as people dropped in for Christmas cheer, the cold war between my mother's and father's families was temporarily suspended.

My mother's uncle, Ron McNair, our candidate for Scrooge, had a good paying job on the B&O line, bought so much stock in AT&T that we used to joke that he personally owned all of the wall phones in the state of West Virginia, and was as tight as a tomcat's asshole. (He'd refused to lend my mother ten bucks once when my father was "out of town" and she and I were living on macaroni and baked beans. "It's not the money," he'd told her, "it's the *principle* of the thing.") But Christmas touched even him, and he always managed to come up with small presents for everyone, even for my father's uncle, O. E. Dupre, who'd never held a regular job in his life and popped in and out of the state loony bin at Weston like a cuckoo in a clock.

I remembered Christmas dinners with so many people that my mother had to unfold all of her bridge tables and disguise them with white linen. Christmas was her one chance a year to use everything—the crystal, china, and silver that had come down to her from the various lines of our family. Even before I'd turned eighteen, my father had begun to include among my presents one that was always the same: a case of beer tied with red ribbon. And when I'd been dating Linda, she'd joined us for dinner the day after Christmas, and I'd given her those gifts my mother always warned me were "too personal" (an amethyst pendant on a gold chain, matching gloves and purse). For days our house would feel too small, jammed with friends and neighbors and relatives, an aunt or uncle sleeping in the guest room, or some friend of my father's, who would have known better than to darken our door at any other time of the year, passed out on the couch.

This year our house felt too big, hollow, about as much like home as the Raysburg bus terminal at four in the morning. My father had been out of the hospital only a few weeks. The stroke had blasted his entire right side into immobility. He lay in bed with the shades half drawn, the television set going constantly with the volume on low. From midmorning until sign-off time, I heard the distant murmur of game shows and soap operas, thrillers and domestic comedies, news and talk shows. With his mobile left hand he was teaching himself to smoke cigarettes again, but my mother had to feed him. He was learning how to talk, could now manage a few strained nouns that were always instructions: "the light," "the blinds," "water," "bathroom."

I forced myself to sit in his room for at least an hour every day. I couldn't tell if he wanted me there or not. It was hard to connect that destroyed figure on the bed with anyone I knew. Was this really the same man who'd slid around town on the fat social oil of scores of pals and drinking buddies, the midnight poker player and Vitalis-slicked tomcat I remembered wearing wing-tipped shoes and pleated pants as he'd spun out yards of fabulous bullshit, glib lies, and tall tales in front of his silent and suspicious son, the man who'd always worn an air of *noblesse oblige* pungent as his expensive men's cologne even when he'd pissed away his last nickel?

My mother kept talking about his stroke, telling me the same story. She knew she'd told it to me before, but she seemed compelled to tell me again—and again and again. He'd complained of heartburn at dinner, she said. He hadn't gone out. She'd felt funny about it. She should have known he was really sick; except for holidays or bouts of the flu, he hadn't stayed home a night in the last ten years. She'd been in her bedroom reading. She'd heard him get up, start down the stairs. She'd heard him call her name, then heard him fall. "He called for me," she said as though she couldn't quite believe it, and that was the only point in the story when she cried. She'd found him at the bottom of the stairs, had known immediately that something was wrong with him more serious than the fall.

My mother didn't play the piano anymore. She had always taken pride in her appearance, but now she didn't seem to care. She'd begun to look like a younger version of *her* mother. Her only concessions toward Christmas had been the holly wreath on the front door and the Christmas cards displayed on the mantel. I'd given her perfume, bath salts, and powder in her standard scent, and she'd given me an envelope with a check in it. "I know it isn't much, honey, but I just couldn't shop this year." I hadn't been able to think of a damn thing to give my father. Finally, in despair, I'd bought him a new lighter. He seemed to like it. He practiced with it, lighting it over and over with his left hand, scaring my mother who was sure he was going to set the bedclothes on fire.

COHEN AND Revington had gone to New York, and I felt like the worst kind of fool for not going with them. Cohen had said, "Chanukah's not a big deal for us," and Revington thought he'd more than done his seasonal duty. He'd been home for Christmas dinner, hadn't he? He'd given everyone in his family a present, hadn't he? "It's nothing but the hair and nails growing from the corpse of Christianity anyway," he'd said. "Come on, ace, let's get the fuck out of here." He had friends in Greenwich Village where we could stay. It'd give me a chance to try marijuana, which he called "tea." We'd have a blast, and after New Year's we could deliver Cohen to Harvard and then he'd drive me back down to Morgantown. Every instinct in me had told me to go, and I'd been just at the point of going, but somehow, at the last minute, I hadn't gone. I couldn't desert my mother so soon after my dad's stroke, I'd told them, and besides I had a paper to write. Within hours of their leaving, I knew I'd made a horrible mistake. Without Cohen and Revington in town, Raysburg felt truly desolate.

I kept trying to force myself to work on the paper. "A Theory of Perception Implicit in Wordsworth's Poetry" was a topic I'd chosen myself, but now I realized that I didn't know enough, and didn't want to know enough, to do it justice. My schoolbooks and notes remained arranged neatly on my desk, unused, while I lay on my bed leafing through *Seventeen* and *Harper's Bazaar* and *Vogue*. They were to me, as I knew perfectly well, exactly what *Playboy* was to a fraternity boy. Down the hall the TV was talking quietly in my father's room; I could smell my mother's cooking—one of her bland, unseasoned spaghettis—and, in a sudden twist of disgusting insight, I saw myself as the same wretched little boy I'd always been. It used to be *Galaxy* and *Fantasy & Science Fiction* and plastic ray guns; now it was folk music and Zen Buddhism and pretending I could read Rilke in the original, but what, after all, was the difference? At fourteen I'd sat here, on this same damned bed, poring over weight-height charts for teenage girls and painting my nails with clear polish, but now I was twenty, and yes, things had certainly changed. I no longer had to sneak into the library to stare at the pretty girls in *Seventeen;* now I could buy my own copy and bring it home with me. And here I was stuck in my childhood bedroom at Christmas with my fashion magazines and my own appalling mind, and there was simply no exit. Sartre's hell at least had a certain bleak dignity to it; mine had none at all. Mine was a sick kitschy child-ish hell painted by Norman Rockwell.

I lit a cigarette and stepped out onto my little balcony that overlooked Front Street. Poisonous white snow was sifting down in the streetlights. I thought of all the times I'd stood in exactly that spot feeling bored or restless or confused or sad or just obscurely miserable and wondered how many million more times I would stand there feeling just as bad or worse. I apologized to my mother for missing dinner, grabbed my guitar, borrowed the car, and took off.

I DROVE to the highest point above the city—the historical marker on Highlight Road—and parked. Below me I could see the lights of Raysburg and the olive drab curve of the river catch-ing the last of the murky sunset. The industrial haze smeared the view into soft focus like Vaseline on a camera lens. I rolled down the car window to feel the chill and for one mad moment saw myself driving away—that's right, if I went like a bat out of hell, I could make New York by dawn. The thought of it felt as elec-tric as a kick of adrenaline: yes, *moving*—up the winding road through Halleys Rise, through broad fat Pennsylvania with its sleeping farmhouses, leaving the sorry Ohio Valley behind, out-running the last of Christmas, catching up with Revington and Cohen in Greenwich Village. But by the end of my cigarette, I was back down to earth. I didn't even have the money for gas. And I finally admitted to myself the real reason I was stuck in Raysburg. *Girls.*

I had written to Natalie the last week in November—a short letter nothing like the one I'd started in my notebook. I'd read her answer so many times I'd practically memorized it:

Hi, John—

Don't feel bad about not writing. I hate writing letters too!!! College is so much harder than high school, why didn't anybody tell me? I wasn't sure I liked it here but now I think I do. Boy have I learned a lot of math! My roommates are really nice. I went ice skating & thought of you. I don't get to play the guitar as much as I want to. I saw Joan Baez!!! Dad is picking me up on Dec. 16. We'll be coming back here on Jan. 6. In between I'll be at home. Yes, come down any time. I'd love to see you.

Your pal, Nat

I didn't want to go back to Morgantown too early (to my claustrophobic apartment and a deserted campus) even to see my pal, Nat, and so I was left with my other compelling reason for not going to New York. As I'd done hundreds of times before, I walked in without knocking and set my guitar case down in the hallway. There was another guitar case there ahead of mine. I followed the sound of voices into the dining room. They were finishing dinner. Dr. Markapolous gave me his usual wave and a yell: "Come on, John. Always something left for you."

Sitting at the head of the table was David Anderson. Just what I need, I thought: the guy who dated Linda after we split up, the guy who took Cassy to his senior prom and, the last I'd heard, was still in love with her. Cassandra and I had time to exchange a quick meeting of eyes before David rose to take my hand. He still looked too good to be true—this tall, blonde, obviously fit, genuinely pleasant out-the-Pike boy. His grip was the old give-'em-hell masculinity ritual of the locker room. "Well, bless my soul," he said, "John Dupre. It's been too long."

"Yeah, it has," I said. "How are you, David?"

"Just great. Never been better. How about you? Still running?"

"Only in my mind." I was wondering how quickly I could get out of that house without looking ridiculous. But Cassandra, with an explicit grey stare, was already passing me a plate with turkey casserole on it; her mother was already asking me how my father was doing. And the good doctor was taking up the conversation where I must have interrupted it: nuclear testing was criminal, insane. But the country has to be strong, David argued back; we have to have a deterrent. "Where'd he come from?" I said to Cassandra under my breath.

She didn't answer, but mimed exasperation, eyes cast at the ceiling. Zoë, on my other side, answered me in a whisper: "He's been here all day." Then, focusing the full intensity of her exquisite blue eyes on me, she said, "Oh, I love Christmas. Don't you, John? It's so exciting. I never want it to end." I gave up. Despite David Anderson, I knew I'd stay till the drinks ran out.

Doctor Markapolous lit his pipe, pushed back his chair. I could see him expanding, see what he was seeing: a couple hours of delicious argument, every opinion welcome, and the devil take the hindmost. "What do you think, John? Should we test those damn bombs?" I'd been here before; I'd be here again. It was all too familiar, all too cheerful, like that most idiotic of Christmas tunes: "always merry and bright." I hadn't known before just how sad I was, how deep it went, down to the bone where nothing could touch it.

The front door opened and closed—another regular visitor who didn't have to knock. "In time for coffee," the doctor yelled. It was George Murray, Cassy's on-again, off-again high-school boyfriend. He saw David Anderson first, then me. He stopped just outside the dining room archway with misery written all over his face.

"Oh good grief!" Cassandra whispered.

"I didn't know you had company," he said to her.

"I don't have company. People just seem to appear out of nowhere."

"Perhaps we could take our coffee in the living room," Cassandra's mother said.

I passed up the coffee, instead poured myself a glass of Cassy's mom's famous eggnog. Everyone filed dutifully into the living room and sat down as though a play was about to begin. The tension in the room couldn't have been any higher if George had brought with him, instead of his banjo, a live cobra. Clearly some repellent blunder was in the works.

Only the doctor appeared to be at ease; he stretched out in his vast leather recliner and kept right on going: "The problem with Kennedy is that the left has nowhere else to go, and he knows it. He still looks like a liberal and talks like a liberal, but he's been swinging right ever since he hit the White House."

Cassandra had arranged herself in the center of the couch with one knee drawn up, the other leg extended, as though she'd chosen intentionally to put herself on display. George and David flanked her like two dummies. This mathematical game of permutations and combinations had paired me with Zoë; we were sitting on two chairs, side by side, back in a corner where we could watch the show. Grinning, the doctor kept hammering away at David. "The Bay of Pigs. Now would you call that a model of international diplomacy?"

David knew he had to stay in the game. It must have felt to him like nothing more than a hard tennis match; he couldn't keep the laughter out of his voice. "Come on, Doctor, how can you possibly say that? Be serious. Can we really tolerate a Russian satellite down there? What about the missile crisis?" But George didn't look amused in the least. He wasn't saying a word.

I knew the doctor would get to him in a moment.

Out of the line of fire, I tuned out the voices, tried to locate myself in the social geography. The three women were as dressed up as if they were going out later to sip champagne at the country club. George and David were both wearing suits. They'd taken their jackets off but left their vests on; it was probably some young men's fashion trend that had passed me right on by. "What's going on?" I asked Zoë.

She glanced around to make sure no one was paying any attention to her, then said quickly, "David gave Cassy his fraternity pin."

"Oh?" I felt a rush of anger at Cassandra. What kind of game was she playing?

"George probably figured out that David was here. That's why he came over."

"How would he have figured that out?"

"I heard Cassy tell him on the phone it wasn't a good night to come over. But he came over anyway. He knows about David. Everybody knows about David. He just had to put two and two together."

Right, Zoë, I thought, and you're pretty good at that yourself. And George obviously could see nothing funny in the situation; he was snapping back at Cassy's father. "I'd rather die on my feet than live on my knees."

"Oh, good God!" the doctor roared at him. "Is that the kind of sententious crap they're teaching at Canden High these days?" I could see that he knew exactly what was going on too. There were certain disadvantages to having a father that observant; after everyone went home, he'd probably tease Cassandra half to death. Yes, it was an amusing situation, but I wasn't amused any more than George was.

Cassandra did look stunning. She'd recently begun to try out her own version of the French street urchin look that Jeanne Moreau had created in *Jules et Jim*. It was an image for New York, not Raysburg, but it did suit her. She was handy with a sewing machine, and she must have made the tweed jerkin and knickerbockers herself; no store in Raysburg or even Pittsburgh would have been selling anything that stylish and extreme. She wore black tights with the outfit, lace-up shoes sleek and flat as dance slippers, white lipstick, and feathery black mascara with the mandatory zombie-pale makeup. I felt (not for the first time) that I was gifted with a mysterious prescience about fashion. Cassandra had adopted an image much like the one I'd imagined for Natalie in her pedal pushers: she looked like a beautiful boy who wanted to dress like a girl but could only allow himself to go part way. A visual pun, I thought—a girl looking like a boy looking like a girl, on forever, receding down a hall of mirrors—and I was sure that no one in the room could appreciate it as much as I could.

Zoë, on the other hand, did not look even remotely like a boy. She'd inherited a style her sister had already discarded; in fact, both the blue full-skirted dress and the matching heels were Cassandra's. With her hair teased and her lips painted shocking pink, Zoë was radiating her nascent sexuality with as much agitation as the gas in a neon tube.

"Come on boys," Doctor Markapolous was saying, "there're enough instruments in this house for a whole string band. Let's have some music."

George looked relieved. He was off the hook. He began to unpack his banjo. Music was fine with me too; I could hide behind a guitar even more effectively than I could sitting far back in a corner. But I'd be damned if I'd go first.

George and David sang "Five Hundred Miles." I didn't join them. They were both playing quite well and had learned to sing in sweet innocuous Peter and Paul voices with Cassandra making a pretty good Mary above them, but I knew I'd get them when my turn came. This is not what folk music should be, I thought, this watered-down mellifluous crap crooned by earnest young men in vests. It should be raw and fierce and mean something.

When my turn came, I chose a Scots ballad, one that had struck me to the heart. Above the drive of my steel strings, I gave it my most rough-edged authentic voice:

> I am a rover, and that's well known.
> I am bound for to leave my home.
> Leaving my friends and my dear to mourn.
> My bonnie lass for me don't mourn.

I didn't know why the thought of leaving girls behind, leaving a home behind, should feel both so tragic and so satisfying, but it did (my West Virginia boy's version of the Great Renunciation). I did know that I could never be like David or George, could never follow such safe paths. Yes, one of these days I would be gone—and, of course, it wasn't that simple. After the journey, you have to come back, as Cohen always said, "like the sage down from the mountains," and then what? Could I ever live an ordinary life and not be trapped by it? What were X people supposed to do? So these lines were for Cassandra. I loaded them with meaning—double, triple, quadruple meaning. I saw by her eyes that she got every level.

> Am I bound or am I free?
> Am I bound for to marry thee?

That was all I had to say to her in this song. When I sang the next verse to Zoë, I didn't mean anything by it. I had to sing to somebody, and she was a beautiful young girl.

> I took the pen for to write a song.
> I wrote it broad and I wrote it long.
> At every line I cried, "My dear!"
> At every word I shed a tear.

I knew immediately that I shouldn't have done it. I saw a shock pass through her, a shiver down her back. I felt an ugly sensation as though my heart had suddenly decided to pound its way through my rib cage. I hated to sing to no one at all, to a blank spot on the wall, but that's what I did, contracting back into myself. On sheer force of habit I got through to the end, struck the last chord and let it ring.

"Hey, all right," David said. "Great to hear you sing again. The original funky voice. Do something else."

"Where'd you find that one?" George was asking me. "Is it a Child ballad?"

I'd gone too far, but I didn't know exactly how or what to do about it. I thought of singing "pretty little Susie just half grown, jumps on a man like a dog on a bone," maybe even changing "Susie" into "Zoë." That would have brought things back to normal, made everyone laugh, but it would have been cruel, and I couldn't do it.

"You guys sing something," I said. "I need a drink." What I really wanted was to get the hell out of there, but I laid my guitar back into its case and walked into the kitchen. I didn't look at either Cassandra or Zoë.

I never got stage fright; singing in public always made me feel keyed-up and alive, but now I seemed to be frightened of something, although I couldn't imagine what it might be. I was sweating as badly as if it had been the steamiest night of the summer. I was even a bit dizzy—a nasty buzz at the base of my neck. I jerked open the fridge and reached for a beer. I heard Zoë's heels on the linoleum, turned around and met her eyes; they were so blue the word itself wasn't blue enough.

She was trembling. For a moment, neither of us spoke.

"Do you know where you are, John?" she said.

I shook my head. That was the one thing I certainly didn't know. I honestly expected her to tell me. "Under the mistletoe," she said.

I looked up and saw it thumbtacked to the ceiling directly in front of the refrigerator door: that ancient pagan symbol. Then Zoë and I were kissing. Not in fun or even affection, but open-mouthed and hungry. We were hanging onto each other like the only survivors of a disaster.

"Zo," Cassandra said. Her voice was low but penetrating. She had stopped just inside the kitchen door with a tray of empty coffee cups in her hands. "Mom's coming."

Zoë stepped back, unbalanced in her big sister's heels. She caught herself on the kitchen counter. I picked up the beer bottle. Mrs. Markapolous followed Cassandra into the kitchen. She was talking, but I couldn't manage to turn her words into anything that made sense. Cassandra had me by the elbow. She was aiming me away from her mother. She was saying something about somebody-or-other's last record. I couldn't get it clear. But her one whispered sentence cut through the fog in my mind: "Get that lipstick off your face."

In the bathroom mirror I saw a young man I knew slightly. He looked badly frightened, and his mouth was stained with a sloppy smear of brilliant pink. I washed my face, sat on the floor with my head between my knees. Somebody was knocking at the door. I knew it had to be Cassandra. She walked in before I could say anything. "Get up, John. We're going to the corner for more beer." I pushed myself to my feet. "Good grief! Hurry up. We've got to get out of the house before George and David see us."

She caught my hand, dragged me down the stairs, through the kitchen, and out the back door. She didn't even let me stop to get my coat. The coldness of the night instantly brought me back to the ordinary world. My teeth began to chatter. "She's in the eighth grade, *you ass!*" Cassandra said. She'd reined her voice in, hard, but it was fighting back.

We stopped under a streetlight and stared at each other. I'd always suspected that she was capable of fury, but I'd never expected anything quite like this. She didn't explode; she controlled it, fired at me in short bursts. "Thirteen . . . You ass, she's *thirteen* . . . She's not thirteen going on fourteen . . . She turned thirteen in August."

"I know she's thirteen. I'm sorry. I'm drunk." Although I wasn't.

"I don't give a damn if you are drunk. Now listen to me, John Dupre. This time you're not going to get away with it. It was bad enough with me. Dad and Mom fought about it the whole time. She thought it was terrible. He kept saying I was old enough to know what I was doing. But Zoë . . . John, she's just a little kid. You were eighteen, and I was fourteen. But now you're twenty. Twenty! And Dad always let me do what I wanted anyway, but Zoë . . . He doesn't trust Zoë to blow her own nose." I laughed.

"It's not funny. If Mom had caught you . . . Good grief, do you have any idea what she can be like? You wouldn't be allowed in our house again. Zoë'd be grounded for a year. Even Dad wouldn't think it was funny, and he thinks everything's funny. I don't give a damn what you do, but . . ."

"Oh, don't you?"

"You can make love to her in the middle of the kitchen floor for all I care . . . But she's playing, and I don't know what you're doing. What the hell *are* you doing?"

"What are you doing with George and David?"

"What's that got to do with it?"

"I don't know what I'm playing. *But you're playing too.*"

I'd stopped her. We looked at each other. "What was I supposed to do?" The anger was gone from her voice. "David gave me his fraternity pin."

"Why did you take it?"

"I don't know why I took it. He says he's in love with me."

"Are you in love with him?"

She was firing at me again. "Yes, I'm in love with him. Damn it, it's none of your business. Boy, am I mad! Just do me a favor, will you? Just one favor. Stop playing junior philosopher. Grow up, damn it. Stop lusting after little girls. Is that what I was for you? Just another little girl? Is that all I meant to you? Well, I don't know if I've grown up yet, but if I haven't, I never will. I'm sixteen. Maybe that's not supposed to be an adult, but I feel like an adult. I have adult feelings. I love David, and it's none of your goddamned business what I do. Stop faking, John. Be real. Leave Zoë alone. Leave your goddamned Buddhism alone. You're a fraud. Stop being such a phony. Oh, Goddamn it."

I'd never seen Cassandra cry before, and it would be years before I would see her cry again. "Cassy," I said and tried to put my hand on her arm.

"Don't touch me."

I didn't say a word. I waited.

"Of course I don't love him," she said, "but what was I supposed to do?"

"You could have said, 'Thanks, David, but no thanks.' If I'm a fraud, Cassandra, so are you. What are you doing with your *Vogue* outfit and your white lipstick? What are you doing playing around with those guys?"

"What were you doing with your tongue down Zoë's throat?"

"I don't know, and that's the honest to God truth. We were under the mistletoe . . ."

"Sure. And now she's flattered to death. And she's got a great story to tell all her little friends. And that's all. That goddamn well better be all."

"That's all. Believe me, that's all. But just between the two of us, two X people out here on a street corner . . . with me freezing to death . . . tell me what you're doing."

"I don't know what I'm doing. David says he loves me. George says he loves me . . ."

"I love you."

"I don't believe you."

I T W A S not late when I got home, at least not late for me, but my mother had already shut the house down. I slipped off my boots and padded into the kitchen. While I'd been gone, she'd made ginger cookies. I drank milk and ate at least a dozen of the damned things until I felt a disgusting pudding-thick lump in my stomach. I wasn't ready to face my childhood bedroom so I sat in the bay window where there wasn't any Christmas tree. I'd been right: the sadness in me *was* so deep that nothing could touch it, and I couldn't even dream up a plausible distraction. It wasn't as though I had no friends in Raysburg—I knew every bar in town where my old buddies from the Academy hung out—but as for finding somebody I could talk to, as Cohen would have said, "at the level of soul," I seemed to have run out. Cassandra was so furious with me I wasn't sure she'd ever speak to me again.

Why had I allowed myself to kiss Zoë like that? It had felt like something entirely outside my conscious volition. A sense of balance, proportion, must have slipped away from me while my attention had been elsewhere. I went over the events—the chain of causality—and each step was innocuous right up to the moment of the kiss itself, and then? What was I supposed to do, look into her eyes and recite: "Equally empty, equally awake, equally a coming Buddha?"

The enormity of what I'd done was finally hitting me: kissing Zoë was not the point; Cassandra was the point. I was sick with regret. I went over everything we'd said to each other, and I couldn't find any way to fix things.

I SAT there for a good hour so miserable I couldn't move—not even enough to light a cigarette—and then I became aware that I was looking at, had been looking at for some time, the old-fashioned roll-top desk in the corner of the living room. My mother stuffed everything in the world into that thing: documents like birth certificates and report cards, newspaper clippings, letters from relatives, souvenir menus, the best of my grade-school artwork, and old photographs, the ones that had not merited inclusion in any of the family albums. I began going through the desk methodically, taking my time. My mother, I discovered, had imposed her own screwy order on this junk, and I found in the back of the left-hand bottom drawer all of the earliest photographs with me in them.

There it was: the glossy black-and-white eight-by-ten of the Jefferson Second Grade Class, 1949–50. I was a skinny little boy in the front row, wearing a solemn expression and a plaid shirt, looking as though he'd been systematically starved. (According to my mother, I'd been the world's pickiest eater.) And I hadn't invented her, nor had my memory falsified her in the least; she was standing right next to me: Nancy Clark. She really was a very pretty little girl. She really did have Shirley Temple curls. She really was wearing a party dress with a short full skirt and classic little-girl white socks with black patent Mary Janes. And yes, right there in front of God and everybody, caught and preserved on film for posterity—I didn't even have to strain to see it—we were holding hands.

I set the picture aside to take back to Morgantown with me. Nancy was my age, so she'd be twenty now. I wondered where she was, what she was doing, what kind of girl she'd turned out to be. It'd be easy enough to find out. The old-time residents of the Island seldom moved; her parents were probably in the phone book. And then I closed my eyes and tried to remember her. I had an image in my mind as clear as a film clip: Nancy on a stage, tap dancing. Of the two of us together, all that came readily back was the warmth of her hand in mine and the tickly sensation of her breath in my ear as she whispered something. I couldn't remember anything we'd done together beyond walking around the school yard holding hands and announcing to our teacher that we were going to get married someday—but then there was something more, something floating just beyond the edge of conscious memory, and the *feeling* of it, bitter-sweet and infinitely precious. All these years I'd been wrong to think that Linda Edmonds had been my first love.

I kept on digging through the drawer until I found the other photograph I was looking for, and there *was* only one. Back in those days film was expensive, processing was expensive, so if you wanted a picture of something, that's exactly what you took: *a* picture. Seeing it was a shock. I hadn't remembered it clearly: Halloween, 1949. Did I look expectant, excited, nervous, apprehensive? No. Did I look pleased with myself as though I'd just put something over on the adult world? No. My faced showed not much of anything, or at any rate no *strong* emotion. I'd been sure that I'd struck a girlish pose, or tried to, a curtsey or something like that, but again, no. I hadn't been playing to the dress at all;

I'd just stood there in it. I looked like an ordinary seven-year-old girl dressed up as Alice in Wonderland, showing just the first hint of impatience as her mother fumbles with the old box camera.

A voice in my mind was telling me, as it usually did, that I didn't need to think about any of *that stuff*. It was years ago, lost in my childhood. It didn't have anything to do with *me now*. But of course it did. Sometimes when I was looking through *Seventeen*, I did imagine making love to those lovely, iconic, beautiful young women, but at other times I imagined that I was one of them.

I WAS so agitated that all I could think to do was walk endlessly in circles around the Island just as I had so many times before—but I didn't want to do that. Maybe there was some way out. It wasn't even midnight yet. Natalie wouldn't be in bed. I still remembered her number. I was reaching for the phone when I had second thoughts. When you're in your first year of college and you come home for Christmas, your old high-school buddies are really important to you. She was probably out somewhere with "the gang." And when we'd been dating, I'd never brought her home this early. If I called now, the person I'd most likely get was Natalie's mother, dead drunk.

OK, I didn't need to talk to Natalie. I was definitely going to see her, and I could take off for Morgantown any time I wanted, maybe even tomorrow, but, in the meantime, I needed some way to make it through the night, someone to talk to *right now*—someone whose mind might be just as hopelessly complex, convoluted, and bizarre as mine.

I called information and got the number for the only Rabinowitz in Huntington. If I heard anybody else's voice but Carol's, I was going to hang up, but she answered on the second ring. "Hi," I said, "it's me."

"John! Of course it's you. You're the only person I know who'd call me at this hour."

"I'm sorry. Is it too late?"

"Oh, no. I'm glad you called. I'm bored silly. How *are* you?"

"I'm OK . . . Well, no, I'm not. I'm having a lousy time."

"I'm sorry. Is your father worse?"

"No, no, it's not that. It's . . . you know, everything. His stroke. Being home. The whole damn works."

It made me absurdly happy to hear her voice. It was exactly what I needed: a reminder that there was another world outside the sickening circles of my own mind. We compared notes on how hard it was to be immersed, once again, in the problematical bosoms of our families, on how boring and oppressive and downright stupid our hometowns were. She told me that she'd seen a bit of her old boyfriend Stephen. "How was that?" I asked her.

"Oh, painful. But I think I had to do it . . . so I'd know it was really over. I feel free now. All that morbid brooding, all the what-ifs and maybes . . . I think I'm free of all that now."

I didn't believe her. "That's good," I said.

"How's your little schoolgirl?" she asked me.

Little schoolgirl was so far from how I thought of Cassandra, it took me a moment to get it. "Oh. Cassy. She's the queen of the hop. She's doing just fine."

"But not fine *with you?*"

I couldn't understand how she could have picked that up from my voice, and for a moment I was so annoyed I couldn't answer. "Well, no," I said.

"That's too bad . . . Look, John, I'm bored and you're bored, and I've missed you. Why don't you come down?"

"Do you mean it?"

"Of course I mean it. It'd be great to see you. We could cheer each other up. Dan's gone back to New York, so we have a spare bedroom, and I've had boys here before . . . It's no big deal. And you'd get to see my mother throw the world's most ostentatious New Year's Eve party."

Tomorrow night was New Year's Eve. I'd forgotten all about it. "I'd love to," I said, "are you sure . . .?"

"When can I expect you?" she said, laughing.

"I'll hitchhike. It'll take me as long as it takes."

"Oh, isn't this fun! I'm really looking forward to seeing you. Oh, and John . . . you do own a suit and tie, don't you?"

IT WAS great to be back on the road. As I walked across the Bridgeport Bridge to Ohio under a pink mackerel sky, my exhilaration kept growing. I loved the bite of the cold, the steam of my breath, the rhythmic swing of my legs—loved being up, and out, and moving. This was exactly what I needed. I should have remembered that my nighttime thoughts were often melodramatic, overblown, even, on some fundamental level, unreal (in the Buddhist sense of illusion); in order to disperse them, all I had to do was encounter the solid and surprising edges of the world as it is. I felt graced by luck and made Huntington in three rides.

As Carol had told me to do, I called her once I got into town. She picked me up in a blue Buick and swept me up immediately into the strange, somewhat unnerving effervescence she was radiating. "Oh, John, hello!" in her phony, faintly British accent, leaning over to give me a quick peck on the cheek. "Thank you so much for coming. You've saved me from the ultimate depths of despair," driving away before I had the door quite shut, tailgating the guy in front of her. "The moment we're home, all of us resume our appointed roles in the ancient family drama . . . Oh, damn!" slamming on the brakes. "I'm considered hopelessly impractical, the silly little sister who studies poetry," turning to look at me, her eyes sparkling. "My parents treat me like a twelve-year-old, and I can laugh about it when I'm away," aiming the car continually uphill, away from the river, onto broad shady streets where the houses were starting to look like mansions, "but when I'm in the midst of it . . . Well, I've been going simply *mad*. It's incredible to see you. How *are* you?"

We wound our way into a neighborhood that looked down over a park. Lots of money, I thought. Carol didn't use the garage, slid the Buick to a stop directly below the front door. I followed her up the steps and inside where I was astonished to see, hanging above our heads, a *thing* made of a million pieces of cut crystal; of course I knew that "chandelier" was the name for it, but the term seemed too modest for such an elaborate, infinitely convoluted contraption of hard-edged glitter. Carol caught me looking up, laughed. "How do you like the Jewish Baroque? My dad had it shipped over from Italy. Every single piece of it came individually wrapped in tissue paper."

Carol was walking quickly, her pleated skirt swinging, the leather heels of her loafers banging down hard on the parquet floor. A very pretty girl, a Negro (as we would have said then), stepped aside to let us go by. "Hi, Becky," Carol said. "This is John Dupre . . . This is Becky. She helps us out."

I guessed Becky to be in her twenties. She wasn't exactly in uniform—wasn't wearing an apron—but her navy blue dress was so severely prim and utilitarian that she was defined by it. I didn't know anybody whose family had a maid (even the Revingtons didn't; they had a Polish cleaning lady, but that was a whole other matter), and I felt hopelessly out of my depth.

I followed Carol upstairs. I was staying, I gathered, in a room that belonged to one of her brothers—a strangely impersonal space that looked as though it had been designed for boys in general but not for any boy in particular: paintings of sailing ships and an ornamental barometer, a massive oak desk and an equally massive bed with an oak headboard, everything done in shades of brown and beige. "You did bring a suit?"

"Sure," I said, fishing it out of my knapsack.

"Oh, you're pathetic . . . Give it to me. Yes, the shirt too."

"Look, you don't . . ."

"Shhh." She pressed her fingers against my lips, took my hand, and pulled me along, back downstairs again, talking the whole way. I'd seen her like this before—Carol at her most vivacious, bright-eyed, charming, and phony. She usually reserved this performance for Andrew, her Englishman, and I suppose I should have been flattered that she was doing it for me, but it set my teeth on edge. I kept wanting to say, "Hey, it's just me, OK? Stop it."

I heard a murmur of voices in distant parts of the house, smelled something cooking that was rich and meaty. Someone was running a vacuum cleaner. I'd been imagining that Mrs. Rabinowitz would be like Bill Cohen's mother—short, round, warm, and funny—but she wasn't. She was a tall, cool, handsome woman who didn't crack a smile. "It's so nice to meet you," she said, and I saw an unmistakable ripple of distaste pass over her face; then her eyes moved away from me, back to the arrangement of silver on the mahogany sideboard. Becky was doing the arranging. Carol thrust my suit and shirt into Becky's arms. "Could you iron these, please? No hurry, just some time before tonight. Thank you so much." Mrs. Rabinowitz shot Carol an exasperated look. "It's going to be a great party, Mom," Carol said.

Her mother shrugged—an eloquent gesture—and turned her back on us. Carol grabbed my hand and whisked me out of there, back outside and into the Buick. "Your mother doesn't like me," I said.

"Don't take it personally. The main person she doesn't like right now is me."

We were rushing to Carol's hair appointment. I'd never been inside a beauty salon in my life. "Maybe I'll go for a walk," I said, but Carol was already towing me through the door where I was confronted by a dozen women and girls. The youngest looked to be about twelve, the oldest seventy; all of them were eyeing me suspiciously. There was not a male anywhere to be seen.

I was thankful to be hidden away inside a small pink cubicle. A fat lady with a blurry downstate accent washed Carol's hair and set it on enormous rollers, lowered a huge silver sci-fi dryer over

Carol's head, and I had nothing to do but flip uneasily through last year's issues of *Glamour*. Eventually Carol emerged; the fat lady unwound the rollers, leaving Carol's head decorated with a precise arrangement of stiff black cylinders, and began to brush them out. The manicure girl arrived with her cart and began to work on Carol's nails. "This party's a big deal," Carol was saying to me. "It rotates around year to year, and when it's your turn, you're supposed to outdo everybody else, absolutely *kill* them with excess . . . just like something out of Veblen. Oh, boy, am I ever going to be on display! Just wait till you see my dress. Oh, just wait till you see my *shoes*. You're going to drop dead, I promise. Do you want me in a color?" holding up a hand.

"I don't know. Do you want a color?"

"Here's your chance, John. Do with me what you will."

All three women were laughing. I wasn't sure if they were laughing at *me*, but I certainly felt very much left out of the joke. I stared at the cute little bottles of nail polish, chose one that was as red as holly berries. "Of course that's what you'd like," Carol said.

Waving her newly painted nails in the air, Carol had me open her purse, pay the bill for her, and then drive her home. "I bet you like your girls helpless, don't you, John?"

Returning to her brother's room, I found my suit and shirt pressed and laid out neatly on the bed. I hadn't worn that outfit since last spring when I'd taken Natalie to her grad parties, and, remembering her, I wished that I'd gone to Morgantown—as I very well could have. I paced up and down, smoking, feeling increasingly jumpy, waiting. Then, with a light tap at the door, there was Carol in a classic cocktail dress, an iridescent taffeta that threw back flickers of a second color, aquamarine flaring off the deep green. She entered with a feminine authority that dispelled in an instant any thought of Natalie in her pedal pushers—swept into the room, bringing with her the tangy scent of her floral perfume. She must have spent hours on her make-up. She smiled and executed a slow-motion pirouette, making her skirt swing. "Well, do you like it?"

"Like it? I love it."

She hadn't put her shoes on yet. Her nylons were sheer as smoke. "And don't you look nice," she said.

Laughing, she led me down the hall, the taffeta rustling with every step. Entering her bedroom, I had again the sense of an oddly impersonal space, one designed, not for Carol specifically, but for *a young lady*: framed Watteau prints, a canopied bed, an elaborate vanity table, and, of course, the mandatory full-length mirror, everything in gold, sky blue, and creamy white. The clothes Carol had been wearing in the afternoon—even her bra and panties—were scattered all over the floor; I had to step over them. "Here," she said, handing me a pearl necklace, and bent her head forward, gently cupping the back of her pageboy with both hands. "If you mess up my hair, I'll kill you."

The skin at the nape of her neck felt warm, smelt flowery. Her red nails gleamed beautifully against the black of her hair. I fastened the necklace. "Thank you," she said, and turned to face me. She handed me a shoebox from her dresser. I held it a moment, unsure what she wanted. Then I took off the lid, folded back the tissue paper, and found a pair of black patent heels. Very high heels. "Do you want to put them on me?" she said in a low purring voice.

I don't know what my face showed, but whatever it was, it made her laugh. "Oh, you don't *have to*. But I thought you might *want to* . . . You'll probably need a shoehorn. There's one over in that middle drawer."

I had to paw through scarves and belts to find it. My mouth had gone dry. Carol stepped to the end of her bed and took hold of one of the posts supporting the canopy—to steady herself, I supposed. I knelt at her feet, lifted the shoes out of the box. They were, like everything else she owned, of the very best quality. When they had been resting in their innocent white tissue paper, they'd looked as brilliantly hard as mirrors, but running my fingertips over one of them, I felt a shiny black surface that curved, that gave, that offered a sleek resistance.

I took her foot, felt the warmth of it through the silky film of her stocking, guided her toes in, slipped the shoehorn into the back of the shoe, pressed her heel in. She wiggled her foot, stepped down. I heard that small conclusive sound of her heel sliding home into the tight leather pocket. I took the other shoe out of its box and went through the process again.

"My God, are these ever high!" she said. "I'm practically *en pointe.*" She was exaggerating. Kneeling at her feet, I could see that she had a long way to go before she would have been *en pointe*, but still they were extremely high heels, probably the highest heels you could ordinarily buy—that is, without resorting to the little ads at the back of men's magazines.

I stood up slowly. I was suffering, as I had sometimes with Linda, a sexual intensity that went far beyond something as simple as mere arousal. She was giving me an amused, knowing smile. "Hi, shorty," she said.

"I'm still taller than you are," I said in a hoarse voice I could barely recognize.

"Yes, but just nicely. Now I'm the right height to kiss."

Although I wasn't aware of having done it, I must have stepped toward her. "Oh, but not now," she said, alarmed, making a gesture to stop me. "You can kiss me later. After midnight. I promise."

She walked away in quick tiny steps, did a pirouette and walked back. "Oh, John, you're so easy to please. If we were going together, I'd have to throw away all my flats and wear nothing but spikes."

I didn't think I was that easy to please, but she was so perfectly a figure out of my fantasies that I might as well have created her. I was appalled, both at her and at myself. She was playing a role for all she was worth, and I could see exactly how she was playing it, but I was falling for it nonetheless: that parody of a perfumed, painted, powdered, pampered little tease was exactly what I wanted all the way down to the finest detail.

"What's it feel like?" I asked her. It wasn't something I'd planned to say, and I'd surprised myself, but I had to keep going. "You know, to get all dressed up like that and then put yourself on display?"

I could see the beginning of some smartass Noël Coward line forming in her mind, but then she stopped. She looked puzzled. "You really want to know, don't you?" As suddenly as if she'd just lowered a mask, she'd been transformed into someone I knew and liked. "You're such a strange boy," she said. "Sometime I'll try to tell you . . ." She laughed. "Oh, come on, sweetie, it's New Year's Eve. Let's go have *fun!*"

FUN? DRINKING a bubbly brown fluid with a celery stick in it, talking nonstop, laughing, even giggling, her eyes turned up to full blast, Carol shoved me into an uproarious sea of relatives: "This is John Dupre, my friend from WVU." (I imagined every one of them thinking: *Dupre? Is he Jewish?*) Uncle Max, Uncle Sol, and Uncle Jake who lifted a squealing Carol into the air by her Scarlett O'Hara waist: "This is the college girl? You gotta be kidding. She should be in movies." Uncle Izzy, Uncle Joey, Uncle Art. ("He's not really my uncle," she said about half of them.) Aunt Ruth, Aunt Maggie, Aunt Essie. (Carol waved her fingers in their faces: "Look at my nails! Aren't you proud of me?")

Brother Michael who seemed like a nice guy. (At any rate, he spent a full minute talking to me: "English, huh? I bet that's why you get along with Carol. What do you plan to do, teach?") Her father, short and wiry with inky black eyebrows, who shook my hand and then dismissed me just as quickly as his wife had done. Guzzling the superb imported beer ("Pilsner from Pilsen!" brother Michael had said, pouring me a huge mug of it), I decided that Carol's parents could go to hell. I was feeling that old reliable buzz coming on.

Grinning like a cretin, I followed Carol into a surging tangle of cousins, and boyfriends and girlfriends of cousins, and more kids our age who looked like cousins but weren't really cousins— the whole lot of them whooping their way toward midnight. Handsome dark-haired boys in Ivy League suits and polished Florsheims seized my hand with the grip of death. Girls met girls, shrieked, hugged, and then yelled at each other over the din: "Oh, Carol, I hate you. You've lost so much weight."

"It's an optical illusion. You wouldn't believe the waspie I'm wearing." We wormed our way into the living room where middle-aged couples were dancing to a stack of LPs. (Every record sounded like Glenn Miller, and I despised Glenn Miller). The children were supposed to be down in the rec room, but they kept exploding back upstairs: rampaging little boys with noisemakers shoved into their mouths, screaming little girls with their petticoats flying, playing hide-and-seek, using the adults for cover. Fat old geezers were collapsed into overstuffed chairs (a couple of them had fired up cigars). A strident cluster of cute teenage girls pushed past us, giggling, every one of them as dressed up as Carol: "Come on, Michael, play some rock 'n roll. Please. Pretty please."

We worked our way through the crowd and on into the dining room to contemplate the main event: roast beef with silver tureens of red horseradish, fat shiny yellow braided loaves ("Chullah," Carol said as she walked me along the sideboard), bagels and lox, pickled herring, gefilte fish, chicken baked to a moist umber in a liquor of garlic and onions—and blintzes, knishes, and verenikes, a strange orange goo called tzimmes, kugel (it looked to me like an exotic macaroni and cheese, but it turned out to be a dessert), and chocolate cake, cheesecake, apple cake, poppyseed cake, plates of cookies (and scattered throughout all of the rooms on the first floor: silver bowls of nuts, chips, crackers, pretzels, and hard candy in case you might be threatened with starvation before you got to the sideboard). But I didn't want to eat. Not yet. Eating would kill the buzz, and by now, the Pilsner from Pilsen was hitting me with a good wallop as the blare and clangor of the party beat my head in. I'd long ago lost track of which cousin was a cousin I'd met, and yet more people were pouring through the door, raising the ante on the whole damn works, pushing it toward fortissimo. "I'll be right back," Carol said, patting my hand.

She was rushing over to greet a boy—an astonishingly good-looking boy wearing a midnight-blue tuxedo. She gave him a hug and one of her bizarre kisses that never quite landed (if they had, half the males at the party would have been branded with her scarlet lip prints). I couldn't hear his laughter over the racket, but I could see it—and the big, self-assured, delighted smile that went with it. If I were a girl, I'd drop dead for a smile like that. I felt a stab of jealousy and then, on some other level, a vicarious pleasure as though I'd just watched my best friend score a hard point in a tennis match.

The boy was leading her away. The little bitch didn't even cast a backward glance in my direction. Oh, but it wasn't really *away*— just over to meet a friend, another damnably good-looking boy—no, *several* boys. Now Carol was surrounded by boys. They seemed to be a clique. Maybe they all went to Marshall. Even at that distance, I could feel the full power of her performance. There were four of them—no, five. One of them offered her a cigarette; she took it, and I imagined the rest of the scene playing out exactly like something I'd seen in a musical comedy: in a moment all of the boys would, simultaneously, whip out their lighters, light them, and surround her with fire. They didn't do that, of course, but she was surrounded with fire nonetheless.

I threaded my way back to the kitchen and refilled my mug with Pilsner from Pilsen. When I came back, Carol was still scintillating for her wolf pack. Seeing her like that dispelled any of my screwy conceits that I might have created her to fit my fantasies; no, she was herself, absolutely independent of me, and did what she did for her own reasons (the world, as Wittgenstein had told me, is everything that is the case), but if I hadn't *created* her, I'd certainly *chosen* her. I'd always thought of falling in love as a fantastic event like being hit by a meteorite, something that had nothing to do with volition, but I'd been wrong; it had *everything* to do with volition. That rainy morning in the Lair when I'd first seen her, I must have, in a flash, gathered innumerable tiny clues: the girlish raincoat, the preppy skirt, the nylons instead of socks, the prissy pageboy, the coy voice and even the first words I heard her say with it: "I don't know what I'm going to *do!* I'm so used to having *a boyfriend* . . . with his own *car* and *apartment*," and I must have added it all up and decided that she was perfect—because you choose something that matches what's already in your mind.

I looked around, found an empty space on a wall and backed myself into it, taking myself out of the traffic. I didn't want anyone to see me standing alone and try to talk to me. Oh, dear God, I thought, how many more times am I destined to stand at the back of some crowded room, getting pissed, my mind racing?

Having, more than once, been on the receiving end of Carol's glitter, I could easily jump into the mind of that tall boy in his beautiful tuxedo—feel his feelings, think his thoughts. Smiling and smiling at Carol: hey, you exquisite little creampuff, I'd love to fuck the living daylights out of you. But, strangely enough, I could also jump into Carol's mind, feel myself the center of all that wolfish attention, feel myself perched on gleaming spike heels, my waist cinched in, crinolines swirling around my thighs, waving my scarlet nails in the air, perfumed, powdered, painted, smiling, turning up the signal to a million watts of clear power: come on, come on, come on!

Come on to *what*? Did this show have a conclusion, or was it stuck forever in the middle of the act? Playing the boy in the tuxedo, I took Carol into my arms none too gently, thrust my tongue between her painted lips, unzipped her dress, stripped it from her—kissing her, kissing her—stripped off her bra, her crinolines, her wisp of lace panties, and what I had left was a men's magazine image melting backward onto the bed—passive, eager, compliant—her legs open: *come on!* And then? *Click*: an obscure switch in my mind flipped over, and I was Carol. The boy's tongue was in my mouth, and I was the one melting backward onto the bed. Hey, wait a minute . . . Then, just as quickly, I was the boy again. Wanting her. But, not twelve feet away from me, a real boy was smiling at a real Carol who was a creature of pure reflected light: ultramarine flickering from her green taffeta, a shudder of brilliance from the curve of her heels.

I felt a ghastly lurch of Sartrean nausea, but I was fascinated too, and I couldn't stop looking. I kept trying to hold either position, the boy's or the girl's, and I couldn't do it—couldn't take either of them to its natural conclusion. In each position, the thought of the other ultimately undermined me. Each side corrupted the other. But no, that metaphor wasn't right. It was like two lights: when one winked on, the other winked off. But no, that still wasn't right. The two sides made a whole, a puzzle, a demonic construction that was unstable, irresolvable. Which meant that *I* was unstable, irresolvable—or maybe just drunk at somebody else's New Year's Eve party, out of place as always, doomed to be the eternal outsider, the only boy in the beauty salon, the only Gentile in the house, as alien as any visitor from outer space that Cohen might have invented for himself to play.

Wir sindt nicht einig, I thought. Rilke's words. Absolutely true—about me, at any rate. It's so nicely compact in German; in English, you have to scramble a bit to get at it: *we're not all of a piece, not all one thing, not single-minded.* I don't know how long I would have stood there, propping up the wall, running around in frantic circles in my mind, but I heard a girl's voice saying, "Boy, do you look uncomfortable."

I jumped as if something had stung me, heard a wry laugh, saw a skinny girl I didn't know. Was she speaking to me? But then the world tumbled back into place, and the stranger turned into Marge Levine. Oh, I thought, that's right, of course she'd be here: she's *Carol's cousin.* "My God," I said, "you're wearing a cocktail dress."

"My God," she said in an absolutely deadpan voice, "and you're wearing a suit and tie."

Her dress wasn't an extravagantly showy one like Carol's—was muted, a soft fabric in one of her funereal colors, a charcoal just off black; she'd toned down her Egyptian eyes almost to normalcy. I'd never seen her bare shoulders before; they looked bony and adolescent. "So what are you doing here, buddy?" she was saying. "Not that I'm not delighted to see you . . . because I am."

"Carol invited me."

"Oh, did she?"

Carol might have *invited* me, but, at the moment, she was

certainly not *with* me—as was obvious to the naked eye. I made a hapless, shrugging gesture. Marge followed my gaze to the center of the wolf pack and laughed. "You ever heard of a Jewish American Princess?" she said. "Well, you're looking at one."

I must have needed to laugh, because that one damn near killed me. Marge rewarded me with her new-moon smile. "Come on, Dupre, let's get loaded."

"You bet." We slipped around the edges of the wall and on into the kitchen. "Try the Pilsner from Pilsen," I said.

"Speaking of phonies," she said, "I've been meaning to ask you . . . You know your pal, William Revington? Is there anybody in there? You know, behind all the poses?"

The question startled me, although, after a moment's reflection, I didn't know why it should have. "Sure there is, but you have to get through the poses. I think maybe you have to be another male to get through the poses."

"That's what I thought," she said. "Unfortunately, he's just great in bed." In spite of myself, I was shocked.

"I didn't think we were Romeo and Juliet," she said. "I didn't think we were much of anything, to tell you the truth, but . . . well, maybe a phone call? Or even a postcard?"

"No," I said, "you won't hear from him. He'll just turn up sometime." She'd never let it show, I thought, but he's hurt her. Damn him.

The teenagers must have convinced brother Michael to switch to rock 'n roll; we heard Buddy Holly suddenly blasting out of the living room. "You want to dance?" I asked her.

"I'm not much good at it, but what the hell."

We made our way toward the music. People were packed around the walls, leaving the space in front of the hi-fi open for the dancers. Carol was jitterbugging with the boy in the midnight-blue tuxedo. "Who is that son of a bitch?" I said.

"That's Larry Klein. Don't worry about him. He went to school with Carol's brother . . . you know, Dan, the older one. Carol's been driving him nuts since she was about twelve. It's just one of the silly little games she likes to play."

"Yeah?" I said, "so how about *her?* Is there anybody in there . . . behind all the poses?"

I hadn't meant the question seriously, had only asked it because I'd thought it would make Marge laugh, but she said, "OK, buddy, you really want to know?"

"Sure."

"All right. Here goes, and don't say I didn't warn you . . . She's spent most of the Christmas break chasing the elusive Stephen, but he's got her number, so that's nowhere. She's bored out of her skull, so she invites you down. Stephen's sure to hear about it, so maybe she can make him jealous . . . It's not going to work, but she doesn't know that, and in the meantime you're good enough to amuse her for a couple days, but believe me, buddy, don't think for a minute she means a damn thing by it. When she gets back to Morgantown, she'll drop you like a hot potato and start chasing Andrew again. She always falls for men who could care less about her. And of course they can't be Jewish. Jewish guys aren't classy enough for her."

Yes, I'd asked for it, but I was horrified nonetheless. "You really don't like her at all, do you?"

She didn't answer for a moment. Then she smiled. "Oh, we'll make it till spring."

I WOKE to one of those bleak blinding hangovers in which you can see with searing clarity everything that's wrong with you but you feel so ghastly you don't give a damn. Happy New Year, asshole, I thought. Welcome to 1963. I hadn't been merely loaded, I'd been pissed to the gills. I'd danced with Marge and

Carol and most of the other pretty girls at the party. I remembered, God help me, jitterbugging with a cousin of Carol's and falling on my ass, and I remembered Carol and Marge laughing at me. I remembered staggering upstairs with Carol at two or maybe three in the morning, both of us so hammered we had to hold each other up. In her bedroom, she'd said, "Now you can kiss my lipstick off," and I'd done just that. It had taken me a while. I remembered her saying, "I think you left a little bit over here," touching the corner of her mouth; "Maybe you better try again." And I remembered her shoving me out the door to stagger stupidly down the hall not quite sure which room was mine. It had never crossed my mind to worry about her parents or where their bedroom might be.

That I was conducting this post-mortem in Carol's brother's bed was an irony that was not lost on me. I lay there as long as I could stand it; then I took a shower, put on my ordinary clothes, went looking for Carol—found her in the downstairs room they called "the study": TV set, big leather chairs, wall to wall books that looked as though they'd been bought by the yard rather than by the title. She was simply sitting there, staring out the window. "Good morning," I said.

"Oh. God. I feel like hell." She was in one of her blouse and skirt outfits. There was nothing left of the glittering doll of the night before but her shiny red fingernails. She hadn't put on any make-up, not even lipstick. "Did you sleep all right?" she said.

"Yeah. I suppose. Passed out is more like it."

I sat down, and then we both sat there, saying nothing.

"I can't stand this," she said, "I really can't. Let's get out of here."

"Where?"

"Lunch or something. Just *out*. Does it matter?"

I grabbed my jacket, followed her to the car. She pulled out too fast, sent us careening down the driveway. It had started to snow. Nobody else seemed to be on the road. It couldn't have been later than noon, but already an iron-grey twilight was closing us down. "We could go see Marge," I said.

"If you want to see Marge, take a cab."

"Hey, wait a minute. We didn't seem to be going anywhere in particular, and I was just . . ."

"Oh, hell . . . I'm sorry, John. I've got a miserable hangover, and I'm in a rotten mood."

The closer we got to downtown Huntington, the more snow was coming down. Carol was a sloppy driver, heavy on the gas and inattentive; she depended too much on her brakes, jammed them on at the last minute, and she wasn't making any allowance for the snow. I could feel in my bones that she was going to screw up, but there didn't seem to be anything I could do about it. She whipped the Buick into a left turn and we went into a skid; then we were sliding—not horribly fast but fast enough to be alarming—into an oncoming Ford. Carol made exactly the wrong moves: spun the wheel to the right, away from the skid, and kicked down the brakes.

I knew that we were going to hit the other car. I grabbed the wheel, spun it to the left, and yelled, "Get your foot off the goddamn brake." We missed the Ford by a couple of feet, slithered to a stop. The driver was a fat, bald, middle-aged man. He rolled down his window, motioned for Carol to roll down hers. She did it. He didn't yell, but we could hear every word nonetheless: "You goddamned dumb broad, you should tear up your driver's license."

He rolled up his window and drove away. I'd never in my life seen anyone blush the way she did then: her entire face, even her neck, turned a spectacular scarlet. She looked hot enough to burn me if I touched her. She lowered her eyes, dropped her chin as though trying to hide behind her bangs; her lips were frozen into a painful, mortified, sickly smile. "Please," she said in a tiny strangled voice, "will you drive?"

I got out, walked around the car. She slid across to the passenger's side. "Where are we going?" I said.

"Just take me home."

I drove around the block and started back the way we'd come. Suddenly Carol exploded into a fury of motion, began to kick the floor of the car and hammer the dashboard with her fists. I pulled over to the curb. A thin, finely drawn wail was pouring out of her. I'd thought she was crying, but she wasn't. "Stop it," I said. "You're going to hurt yourself."

She was really hammering the shit out of that car; God knows what she was doing to herself. I grabbed one of her wrists, then the other, held them as she thrashed back and forth and fought me, struggled to get free. I had to use all my strength to hold her. Then she went limp, fell back in the seat panting. Slowly she raised her chin until she was staring directly into my eyes. I kept on holding her wrists merely because I was already holding them. For one long eerie moment it felt as though the universe were teetering on a pinpoint; something truly significant was happening, but I didn't have a clue what it might be. This is crazy, I thought.

I let go of her wrists, lit two cigarettes, gave her one. She took it and dragged, rolled down her window, stared out into the snow, her face turned away from me. "I ought to be spanked for that stunt," she said.

I agreed with her but didn't think that it was a good idea to say so. I couldn't find a damned thing to say. Finally, I tried, "What's the matter?"

"What's the matter?" she yelled at me. "What a moronic question! What the hell do you think's the matter? I just came within half an inch of smashing up my father's car, that's what's the matter."

She smoked the rest of her cigarette, snapped it out the window. "I'm sorry," she said. "I simply loathe New Year's. It always reminds me that there's another year down the drain, and I've got nothing to show for it."

"You're one year closer to your Master's degree." I felt as though I were humoring a difficult child.

"Yeah. Big deal."

She bent forward and pressed the heels of her hands against her forehead, kept on pressing, hard. She began to sob, gulping air. "God," she said. "Oh, please, just take me home, will you?"

I pulled out carefully onto the snowy street. She stopped crying just as suddenly as she'd started. "I could go to Ireland for a year, couldn't I?" she said in a small dead voice. "With my grades, I could even go to Trinity for a year, couldn't I?"

It was the first I'd heard of it. "Sure you could," I said, "if you wanted to. Why don't you check into it?"

"Do you think they really have bee-loud glades?"

"I'm sure they have bee-loud glades."

I put my hand on her shoulder in a gesture I meant to be comforting. She shrugged it away. "Don't. Please."

BACK AT the house, she walked straight upstairs and into her bedroom; the sound of her door slamming was like a rifle shot. Hungry, my head pounding, I shut myself into her brother's room, threw myself onto his bed. I never traveled without a book. The one I had was *The Hui Neng Doctrine on the Transmission of the Mind*, and I tried to read the damned thing. I had to go slowly, one difficult sentence at a time. It seemed to be a text expressly designed to destroy anything you'd ever thought about anything. Eventually I gave up and watched the fat snowflakes float past the window. That's all I needed. Snowed in. No exit.

I couldn't stop thinking about what Marge had told me. I'd always believed that the two girls really were, just as Carol had always said, like sisters—that they might bitch and complain about each other, say catty things and get into fights, but underneath it all, they were joined by a deep and unshakable bond. But I'd been wrong; they thoroughly despised each other. I found that revelation unnerving. I trusted Marge Levine and liked the way she looked at the world; she was a girl who always said exactly what was on her mind, and I liked that too. I considered her a good friend. But I wasn't sure I trusted her when she was talking about Carol. There'd been so much vitriol in what she'd said that it couldn't possibly *all* be true, could it? But what if *some of it* was true?

They surely ran buses between Huntington and Morgantown. But it was crazy to be even thinking about it. I had to go back home to get my Martin and my books, and besides, there was something pathetic about running frantically from girl to girl: Cassandra to Carol to Natalie. Oh, and I shouldn't forget Zoë. I hadn't thought of it before, but Zoë had mysteriously set off this whole fabulous chain of events. If I went over it step by step in my mind, I could see, however improbable it was, that I was stuck in a snowstorm in Huntington on the first day of the new year with the worst hangover of my life because, two days before, I'd kissed Zoë under the mistletoe in her kitchen in Raysburg. But, be that as it may, if I didn't get some food into me, I was going to die.

The house was humming with muted sounds: someone moving furniture, someone vacuuming. Yep, I thought, the hired help was cleaning up. I wandered into the kitchen. Becky was washing crystal wine glasses, dozens of them. Carol's mother was rinsing and drying them; that she was actually doing something made me prepared to like her if she ever gave me the chance. She hadn't said ten words to me since I'd arrived, but now she said, "Oh, you poor boy, come in here. You're probably starving."

She made me a roast beef sandwich. When I sat down at the kitchen table to eat it, she let her hand rest momentarily on my shoulder. "Don't mind Carol," she said. "She's always been a moody girl."

I stumbled back upstairs and made another futile attempt to read Hui Neng. Eventually I laid the book aside and fell asleep.

"KNOCK, KNOCK." Carol was standing next to my bed. "Wake up, you naughty thing. It's nearly five." My entire body felt unraveled.

With the familiarity of someone who's done it often before, she reached over and turned on the bedside lamp. I liked that small gesture. "I went back to sleep too," she said. "Oh, my God, we tied on a good one last night, didn't we?"

She looked rested. She'd redone her make-up. She sat down on the edge of the bed, took my hand and held it. "I should have had the good manners to say it at the time, but I'll say it now. Thank you. You really saved me."

I shrugged. "It's OK."

"No, really, John. I had no business driving anywhere the way I was feeling, and you really did save me. My God, if I'd hit that car . . . Thank you."

Everybody had gone out for the night, she said; we had the house to ourselves. We could go out too if I wanted, but she wouldn't mind staying home and watching TV. That was fine with me. I liked lying there on her brother's bed in the circle of yellow light that made such a comforting contrast to the blue-black chill of the window. I liked her sitting next to me holding my hand. Despite all the times she'd called me her brother, I'd hardly ever experienced her as a sister, but I did now, and I decided not to trust anything that Marge had told me.

Carol asked me what I was reading, and I handed her the book. "Oh, you and your Zen Buddhism."

I'd never told her much about Zen; she'd never seemed particularly interested. Now I gave her a thumbnail sketch of Cohen's satori experience. "If it can happen to him," I said, "it's real. If he can do it, then any of the rest of us can do it."

"Oh, come on, John. Bill Cohen's a really sweet boy, but an enlightened being? Do you really see him that way? He just seems . . . like a brilliant, charming, precocious twelve-year-old."

"That's because you don't know him."

"Maybe . . . Does he have a girlfriend?"

I laughed. "He hasn't even had a date."

"Oh," she said, raising her eyebrows.

I was suddenly, inexplicably angry. "What's that mean? That 'Oh'?"

"Let's not get in a fight. I didn't mean anything. It's not important . . . Come on, get up. I'm starving."

She took my hands and pulled me to my feet. I followed her downstairs. There were a million leftovers from the party. We ate baked chicken, blintzes, knishes, holishkes, kugel, and cheesecake. "When we get back to Morgantown," she said, "it's going to be nothing for me but cottage cheese and stones."

Groggy with food, we collapsed in the basement rec room in front of the TV. I put my arm around her. She snuggled into me, and we watched whatever was on. "It's good to have you here," she said.

After a while she began talking about Stephen. "I'm really glad I saw him again. It was painful . . . but all the ambiguity's gone now. It's really over." She sighed.

"My parents have never forgiven me, you know. All the time we were going out together, all I heard was, 'Carol, he's not

Jewish.' My mother was so happy when we broke up it was sickening. I wanted to kill her. If she's been cool to you, that's the reason. Oh, I know exactly what she's thinking . . . *oy vey, another one.* I told her you were a good friend, not a boyfriend. She doesn't think girls can have friends who are boys . . . I don't know, maybe they can't. I always thought you were a friend."

"I am your friend." I hesitated, then spoke the rest of the sentence I'd already written in my mind: "but I always wanted to be more than that."

"Oh, I know." She gave me what I read as an affectionate smile. "But we'd be terrible together. You're *years* too young for me . . . I know I tease you about it, but you're absolutely right to go out with high-school girls. You need a much younger girl who's going to look up to you and admire you, and I need a man at least ten years older than I am."

"Oh, for Christ's sake."

"Come on, John, it'd never work. You know that. I probably shouldn't admit it to you, but I have thought about it . . ."

My heart jumped. "You're really sweet," she said, "and I like you a whole lot. And you've helped get me through a rough time, and we do have fun together . . . Oh, I could wear high heels and frilly dresses and play the pretty little miss for you, and I'd rather enjoy it. But when anything got too serious, we'd just . . . Can you even imagine being a father, for instance? And if you're going to go on and get a PhD in something . . . which you should, by the way . . . But if you do that, you're going to be in school for a million years, so you won't be in any position to start a family. And I need someone who can take care of me . . . and give me babies. And you know all of that as well as I do."

I was devastated. Everything she'd said—delivered in such a calm, friendly, rational way—was absolutely true. "Oh, honey, don't look so hurt," she said. "We'll always be friends."

We settled back to pretending to watch TV. It really had been a mistake to come to Huntington, I thought. All I wanted now was to get out of Carol's house, but it was too late at night and I was stuck.

She snuggled into me again. Annoyed, I looked down at her. She let her lower lip drop slightly, a signal that was unmistakable. I bent forward to brush her lips with mine. It was the last thing I'd expected, but we were immediately locked into a long serious kiss. Oh, I thought, so friends get to make out, do they?

To my surprise, she took my hand and guided it under her sweater. I felt the stiff, shiny fabric of her bra. As she seemed to be inviting me to do, I massaged her breasts. She reached behind her and undid her bra, made a shrugging motion, drew the bra out from under her sweater, and let it fall onto the floor. She stood up momentarily—I couldn't imagine what she was doing—raised her skirt and sat down on my lap with her back to me. I had to bring my legs together to make a seat for her. She arched her back against me, turned her head so we could kiss. I reached under her sweater and took a breast into each hand. They were far bigger than I'd expected, and heavier—powdery smooth and deliciously warm. She made a low, resonant sound in the back of her throat. "Oh, your hands are so soft."

Her bottom, protected by nothing but her panties, was pressed tightly into my crotch. She moved her pelvis in a series of small rotations and kissed me. It was delicious and excruciating and seemed to be going on forever—and there was no way in hell I could have an orgasm that way. I was almost relieved when she said, "Baby, we've got to stop this."

She slid off my lap, smoothed down her skirt, and turned to me. She gave me her "kiss me" look again. I glued my mouth onto hers. She slipped one of her legs between mine, and now, finally, I was getting exactly what I wanted. She'd suddenly acquired an itsy-bitsy voice: "Baby gets all excited, doesn't he? Baby's really persistent tonight."

I was damnably close to finishing when she said, "John! Stop it. Right now." She'd changed voices. This was the teaching assistant. "Now. I mean it."

She pushed me away. "Am I going to have to send you upstairs for a cold shower? I will, you know. I'm not kidding. Ice cold."

She retrieved her bra from where it had fallen onto the floor, slipped it under her sweater, and fastened it. She stood up and straightened her skirt. She was looking at me with that glittering mask she'd been wearing the night before. "I told you not to start anything, so why don't you ever *listen* to me? Will you get me my purse, please? It's on the counter in the kitchen . . . Oh, don't look at me like that. You know we shouldn't get too worked up. I'm sorry. I get carried away too. I'm only human."

In a daze, I walked upstairs, found her purse, and brought it to her. She took out a compact and a lipstick, redid her lips. She took out a hairbrush and began to restore her pageboy. "The TV guide's over there," she said, gesturing. "Let's see if there's something worth watching."

I handed her the TV guide and sat down in a chair at the far side of the room. "Oh, don't be silly," she said and patted the couch next to her. I walked back over and sat down next to her.

"There's some kind of special on six," she said. "Let's try that." I got up and changed the channel. When I sat down again, she snuggled into me, head on my shoulder. "Be a good boy now," she said.

We watched the TV for a few minutes. Whatever was playing made no impression on me whatsoever. Eventually I looked down at her. She was looking at me with her magnificent shining dark eyes. She tilted up her chin and opened her freshly painted lips. Oh, my God, I thought, here we go again. I bent forward and kissed her; her tongue was in my mouth at once, along with the cloying taste of her waxy lipstick. She paused to murmur in a low smoky voice, "Oh, John, I told you not to," and then she was sucking at my lips, gnawing at them.

She licked my tongue. She drew a line of tension up the leg of my jeans with her fingertips, taking her time, until she finally arrived at my crotch. Slowly she began to massage my trapped penis. It seemed impossible for me not to respond, but whenever I moved, even slightly, she'd stop. Then, after a few seconds, she'd start again. Horrified, I heard a thick, involuntary groan come out of myself. "We've got to stop soon," she murmured. "Baby gets too excited."

But she wasn't stopping. Not a single message coming from anywhere in her body was telling me that she was even remotely considering stopping. Astonished at my own boldness, I slipped my hand in between her legs, sliding her skirt up. She wasn't wearing exotic underwear; all I saw were plain white garters supporting everyday beige stockings, but that image was the sexiest thing I'd ever seen in my life. I'd never touched a girl between the legs before. I massaged her lightly, felt the small moundlike shape of her there. Her panties were warm and moist. I slipped my fingers inside the waistband, felt hair and then more moisture. She was sopping wet. I'd read about this in books.

I jerked my hand away. It was a motion as instinctive as if I'd touched an open flame. A steel fear chopped me in half, and I heard the slam of my heart and then a buzzing in my ears. My erection withered instantly. She kissed me a moment longer and then sat back abruptly, withdrawing her hand from my leg. She pushed me away. She pulled her skirt down. She said, "Give me a cigarette."

I lit two and gave her one. We smoked in silence. I kept trying to catch her eye, but she—deliberately, I thought—wouldn't look at me. I felt utterly humiliated. Everything I'd ever feared about myself had turned out to be true.

"Carol?" I said.

"Change the channel. That show's boring."

I didn't move. "John, did you hear me?"

"What channel do you want?"

"I don't care. Try anything. Try three."

I changed the channel. "Carol?"

"Don't say anything for a while. Please."

I sat down in a chair on the other side of the room. I was looking at her, and she was looking at the TV set. "Make me a rye and ginger, please," she said. "The rye's in the liquor cabinet in the dining room, and the ginger ale's in the refrigerator."

"OK," I said. "In a minute. But look, I just want to . . ."

"John, could you just keep quiet please? I really don't want to hear your voice right now."

I couldn't believe how angry that made me. "Make your own goddamn rye and ginger."

"Well, that's nice," she said. "That's just lovely."

"Carol, for Christ's sake . . ."

"Shut up," she said. "Don't say, 'Carol, for Christ's sake' to me in that hurt, whipped-dog tone. I hate that tone. I just hate it. Just keep your goddamn mouth shut, all right?"

"Carol, what on earth . . .?"

"You're talking. I just heard you. Didn't I tell you to shut up? Why am I hearing your voice?"

I stared at her. She sat primly on the couch, perfectly upright with her knees together, her eyes glistening with something that looked like pure undisguised malice. "Carol," I said slowly, "what's going on?"

"Oh, for Christ's sake, if you ask me another question, I swear I'll scream. You're like a six-year-old. Questions, questions,

questions . . . OK, go ahead and talk. I don't care. Just don't ask me any more questions . . . Come on, I said you can talk, so talk . . . What's the matter, cat got your tongue? Let's hear one of your Zen stories. Or maybe you could sing me a song. That'd be fun. Why don't you do that?"

"Carol, what's the matter with you?"

"What was that? A question? Could it possibly be a question? No, I must have heard wrong. He couldn't possibly be asking me a question, could he? Oh no, not John Dupre. Not him. He never asks questions. He's a man of action."

"Carol, for Christ's sake."

"Don't use that whiny tone on me. It won't work. I'm not one of your little schoolgirls. Why don't you go back to grade school and play spin the bottle? Or post office. Isn't that about your speed, little boy?"

I walked out. "Where the hell do you think you're going?" she yelled after me.

I WAS used to traveling light, and I'd already packed my dress shoes and my damnable suit in my knapsack. I heard Carol's heels on the stairs coming up after me, but she'd waited a few seconds too long, and I was one jump ahead of her. "John!" she called out, but I knew the layout of the house by then. Carrying my boots in my hand, I shot down the back stairs in my socks as quietly as a ghost. Once I was outside, I walked away at a good clip. I didn't feel completely safe until I was several blocks away. You're crazy, I told myself. Nobody's going to pick you up at this hour. But on another level I didn't care. I couldn't stop a soaring elation. I'd made my escape. I was back on the road.

It took me over an hour to walk down from Carol's neighborhood, through Huntington, and across the bridge to Ohio. It was a bitterly cold night and snowing lightly, but as long as I kept walking, I was warm enough. When I saw that there was no traffic whatsoever on the river road, I began to feel the first tickle of fear. I walked north. Eventually I simply couldn't keep going. I always kept cardboard signs in my knapsack; I unfolded the one that said "RAYSBURG" and paced up and down behind it, stamping my feet and blowing on my hands. I smoked several cigarettes. It was nearly one in the morning, an impossible time to get a ride. I began to wonder what frostbite was like and how I would know if I was getting it. Then I began to wonder what freezing to death was like. OK, I thought, I'll stay here a while longer, and if nothing happens, I'll walk back across the bridge and try to find an all-night restaurant or even a hotel.

Around two, I saw a semi-trailer in the distance, roaring north on that deserted road. I'd long ago run out of hope, but I stuck out my thumb automatically, and then I saw—I couldn't believe it—that the truck was slowing down. By the time the driver got it stopped, it was a hundred yards ahead of me. I grabbed my knapsack and ran to catch up. I had a horrible fear that he was just teasing me, that he'd pull away before I got there, but he didn't. "Get your ass in here, son," the driver yelled at me. "You look like you're about half froze." I scrambled on up and into the cab; it felt a hundred miles in the air. I couldn't see the man clearly in the dark, just the silhouette of a lean face with cheekbones prominent as golf balls. From the radio some Southern preacher was shrieking the name of *Jesus Jesus Jesus!* The driver began to crank the truck through its million gears, and Jesus was lost behind the bellow of the engine.

"Help yourself," the man yelled at me, pointed at a huge steel Thermos lying on the seat between us.

"Thank you," I yelled back. I unscrewed the lid, poured out something and took a sip; it was strong black coffee heavily laced with whiskey; the mixture tasted raw and delicious. "Go on, son," he yelled, "have as much as you want."

The preacher on the radio was howling about Christ coming again in all his glory: "WILL YOU BE READY?"—a voice pitched high with hysteria, on the edge of tears. Savoring the heat and the alcohol, I finally allowed myself to realize how stupidly close I'd come to disaster. I could have died of exposure out there on that road, but once again the world had conspired to save me. The horror was over, and I was beginning to get warm. I relaxed into the seat. "Be in Morgantown in no time," the driver yelled at me.

"I'm not going to Morgantown. I'm going to Raysburg."

"Change your mind, did you?"

"My sign said Raysburg."

"Aw, come on, son, you telling me I can't read?"

For a moment I was disoriented, considered the possibility that I'd set out the wrong sign. But no, I remembered it clearly; I could see it in front of my knapsack: RAYSBURG.

Now the driver was laughing. "Shit, I'm just funnin' you. But that's all right." He reached over and punched off the radio. Until that crazy preacher's voice was gone, I hadn't realized how hideously loud the radio had been. "Seen you standing out there," the driver said, "and I thought, hell, only a college boy would be crazy enough to do that. Figured maybe you was going to the university."

"Well, I do go to the university, but I live in Raysburg."

"See, what did I tell you? Hey, pass that, will you?"

I passed him the Thermos, and he drank directly from it; I could see his Adam's apple bobbing. I felt the whiskey hitting me. I got out my cigarettes, offered him one. "Yeah, sure," he said. I lit two and gave him one. "So what are you hauling?" I asked him.

"Steel rods. I'm way overweight. You seen how long it took me to stop?" He was chuckling as though telling me the funniest story he'd ever heard. "Some poor son-of-a-bitch pulls out in front of me, he's a dead man. But don't you worry, son; it's all in the hands of the Lord."

He had that distinctive southern West Virginia accent that I could recognize instantly but could never imitate. "You drink up the rest of this," he said, handing me the Thermos. "You need it worse than me."

I smoked, drank the rest of the coffee. The alcohol and the heat were wiping me away, and I began to drift in and out of sleep. The driver turned on the radio again; the cab was filled with another preacher's voice: "JESUS PAID THE PRICE, THE ULTIMATE PRICE. HE TOOK IT ALL ON HIMSELF." I fought to stay awake, but I couldn't do it; sleep was too seductive. The sound of the engine, the preacher's voice, the driver's voice—all of it kept winding itself around me like thick dark cords binding me to the seat. Every few minutes I'd wake with a start, not sure where I was, thinking, oh, God, I don't want to be here. I want to be home in bed. "HE PAID THE PRICE FOR YOU AND FOR ME, GLORY, HALLELUIAH."

The driver was saying something to me, but I didn't get it. I sat up and stared out at the road. Tiny splinters of snow were falling in the truck's headlights as far ahead as I could see. I thought he'd been telling me not to ask any more questions, but that couldn't be right. "What's that?" I said. "What did you say?"

He turned off the radio. "I just ast you what you thought of that preacher."

"I don't know. I wasn't paying attention."

"You didn't miss much. Some of them make sense and some of them don't. That one weren't worth a bucket of piss . . . Tell me, son, are you religious?"

"I guess I am . . . in my way."

He laughed. "That's a good one. You'll be standing at the

gates of Hell so close the heat'll be scorching off your eyebrows, and St. Peter will ask you, 'Son, are you religious?' and you'll say, 'In my way,' and he'll say, 'That's all well and good, boy, but what about God's way?'"

"I don't know what God's way is," I said.

He surprised me by saying, "Well, there ain't many that does, although many claim to it. Now me, I just spend all my time driving up and down in the world, going to and fro in it, and asking questions. Funny thing is, nobody hardly ever has the answers. You with me, son?"

"Yeah, I'm with you."

"I'm a worrying man, you see. Always have been. And you know one thing I worry about? Damnation. I ain't ever been real sure there is a hell, but if there is, one thing I *am* sure about, and that's I don't want to go there."

I was still groggy and I didn't want to talk to him, but I knew I should make at least a minimal effort. "I don't believe in a hell after you die," I said. "I think we make our own hell right here on earth."

"Is that right? Well, I have heard that opinion expressed, and it's always puzzled me. What kind of hell you been making for yourself, boy?"

"Standing by the side of the road freezing my ass off at two in the morning."

He liked that one. He laughed hard at that one. Something told me that I had to be far more alert than I was, but it was an effort to keep my eyes open. To try to wake up, I lit another cigarette.

"But let's say there is a hell," he said. "You know, son, I seen things that'd make you puke. I seen men shot. I seen men burnt alive. I seen a man oncet, all ripped open with his guts hanging out. Don't take much to get a man yelling, 'For Christ's sake,

Sarge, shoot me, shoot me!' But if they was in Hell, you'd have to say, 'Sorry, buddy, you're already dead. That horrible pain you got . . . that you can't bear for another second . . . well, you're stuck with it forever and ever through all eternity.'"

"Do you think God would do that to people?"

"Now that's a good question. I've ast that question myself and I never found the answer for it . . . You know, I'm really enjoying talking to you, son, I really am . . . All right, let me ask you something. Maybe you can help me out. You see, there's two more things that trouble my mind. You want to hear them?"

"Sure."

"Well, there's that story Jesus tells about the beggar who goes up to heaven and the rich man who goes to Hell. And the rich man down in Hell cries out for mercy, and you know what he gets told? 'Between us and you there is a great gulf fixed, so that they which would pass from hence to you cannot.' Now you think about that one. There's a great gulf fixed, and even if we wanted to help you out, buddy, we couldn't do it. Does that mean you can fall so low even God can't help you?"

"I don't know."

"Yeah, I didn't think you'd be much help on that one. There ain't many people is. OK, and here's the other thing that troubles me. It's the sin you can't get forgiven for. You know, the sin against the Holy Ghost. Now I been worrying I committed that sin."

"If you're worried about it, that means you haven't committed it."

"Yeah, I've heard that opinion expressed, but I ain't so sure. Let me try something on you. Suppose I told you that I took a dog out in the woods and tied him down to a tree. And suppose I told you I made me a fire and whittled some sticks and got them good and hot and burned his eyes out with them. And then suppose I told you I got out a hunting knife and went cutting away little pieces off that dog for hours at a time while he was howling and yelling. And then suppose I told you I cut his pecker off and then walked away and left him to die however long it took him. Could I get forgiven for that?"

I was suddenly wide awake. I began to sweat. "You could get forgiven for that . . . if you were really sorry."

"Suppose I told you I weren't sorry at all. Suppose I told you I just enjoyed the hell out of it. Suppose I told you I enjoyed it so much I pulled out my pecker and squirted all over that poor dog. Could I still get forgiven for that?"

Fear had knotted my stomach. I couldn't think straight, but I had to say something. To remain silent was simply not possible. I didn't know much about Christianity, but I thought I knew the central point of it: "Look," I said, "you always get another chance."

"Oh, buddy, if you believe that, you are a fool . . . OK, all that shit I told you I done to a dog, suppose I done it to a woman. Could I get forgiven for that?"

"Yes."

"Suppose I done it to a little child. Could I get forgiven for that?"

"Yes."

"I'm glad to hear you say that, son, because it's been a heavy load on my mind. Here's what gets me real turned around. If you committed the sin against the Holy Ghost, then you can't get forgiven no matter what you do. You're damned forever. So after that, what's to stop you from doing *anything?* Are you with me, son?"

I was holding my body rigidly on the seat. If I hadn't clenched my jaws, my teeth would have been chattering. "Did you do these things?" I said.

"I didn't say I done them. I said *suppose* I done them."

We were rolling through some town. Glare from the passing

street lights pulsed across the driver's face; his skin looked yellow and sick. His eyes met mine and held. The hair on the back of my neck and arms stood up. "Let me out of this truck," I said.

"Well, sure," he said. His voice had changed, had pushed up high into his nose and came out now like a whistle. "I never carry no man no farther than he cares to go . . . especially no man of action like yourself . . . but you better give me some money for gas." I reached into my jeans. "No," he said, "not your chicken-shit nickels and dimes."

I took out my wallet. He pulled over to the curb. He caught my hand. His skin was cold and wet. His grip was unbreakable. I gave him all the money I had.

I WALKED. Already I was recoiling from what had happened to me—trying to put it all behind me as though it had been nothing more than a nightmare. I was lost in some dumb Ohio river town, but I didn't know which one. Nothing looked familiar. I kept staring at buildings, but I didn't recognize any of them. On some level, I knew it was a trick—that if I could make a turn in my mind, I would be all right. Stop, I told myself. Just stop.

When I came back to myself, I was sitting on the steps of the Ohio County Public Library directly across from the Baptist church where Lyle had seen the old woman who had cursed him. It didn't make any sense. That insane trucker had been driving up the Ohio side, and I didn't remember him crossing the river. But he obviously had. And once he was on the West Virginia side, he certainly wouldn't have turned around and driven south again, would he? So how did I get to the library? Could I have walked? Why would I have done that?

I began walking up town. The streets were empty, covered with a fine layer of brilliant frost. Already the nightmare was distancing itself. I could no longer separate what that madman had said from something I might have imagined he'd said. Perhaps, if I kept moving, I would come to see the entire experience as illusion. By the time I got to Sixteenth Street and started up Market, I was bitterly cold again.

I passed the New Moon Cafe where Lyle and I used to eat fish sandwiches on Friday, cheeseburgers every other day of the week. At Twelfth, I crossed from Market down to Main, getting closer to the river, passed the Silver Stein, one of my father's favorite haunts. It was so quiet I could hear every click of the mechanism that changed the traffic lights. I saw, between the buildings, the first black flash of the river, and beyond it, a strip of sky going crystal blue at the edge. I passed the Jamboree Shop where I'd bought the cowboy boots I was wearing, where Natalie had bought her pair, and then I was at Tenth and Main where I used to meet the boys on Friday nights when I'd been at the Academy, where I'd stood and watched the girls walk by to Gerry's Inn. That time felt impossibly long ago.

Nothing was left for me to do now but turn at the corner and walk across the Suspension Bridge, but instead I stood and looked at the empty streets. I stepped inside a phone booth, took off my gloves, pawed through my pockets for change. The glass of the booth was frosted over, the phone so cold it felt hot in my hand. My breath steamed. I needed, not just someone to talk to, but someone important, a lifeline.

After a few minutes I hung up the phone, put the dime back in my pocket, walked across the bridge to the Island, and continued up Front Street. By the time I got home, I was sick with exhaustion. I lit the gas heater in the living room and huddled in front of it. My mother must have heard me come in. Wearing her slippers and bathrobe, she joined me as discreetly as a ghost. We sat for a long time together without either of us saying a word.

Finally she said, "I didn't expect you home so soon. Didn't you have a good time?"

"It was OK."

"It's been a sad Christmas. I'm sorry."

"It's not your fault, Mom."

She heated sweet rolls for me, made scrambled eggs. I ate, went back to my room, pulled off my boots, and stretched out fully dressed on my bed. I was exhausted, but I didn't think I could sleep. I must have drifted off without noticing. When I woke, it was dark.

The next afternoon I rode the Greyhound back to Morgantown. While I'd been gone, a fine layer of dust had settled over everything in my apartment. I'd left four quarts of Stroh's in my fridge, but, of course, no food. I popped a bottle, turned on the radio, found some good rock 'n roll on a distant station, turned it up loud, and started cleaning. I washed every dish and dusted every surface. I arranged my books on my desk just as though I might be a student again. By then I was ravenously hungry, half drunk, and far too depressed to call Natalie. I decided to walk over to Johnny's. I'd never seen the campus so deserted. Nobody but a damned fool would have come back from Christmas break four days early, and Johnny's, of course, was closed. I wandered around until I found an open grocery store, went back to my place, got really loaded, made spaghetti, ate it, and passed out. All of the next day, and all of the day after that, I found a million perfectly good reasons not to call Natalie.

8

I DON'T remember much of January. The only thing that kept me moving forward was force of habit, and sometimes I couldn't rely even on that. Always before I'd been able to lose myself—for an hour or two at least—in music, ideas, poetry, books, but now I couldn't. Trying to write any of the papers that were long over-due felt about as easy as crawling down a continually narrowing tunnel lined with broken glass. I could fall asleep without much trouble, but I couldn't stay asleep; I woke at four or five in the morning, my body aching with fatigue and my mind running in frantic circles. My thoughts were exhausting me, but I couldn't find any way to turn them off. I wasn't seeing anything clearly—as though a thin film, a greasy soap bubble, had been smeared between me and the world. The light seemed dead.

Some days I went to classes, some days I didn't. Some nights I got loaded, some nights I didn't. Sometimes I forgot to eat, other times I ordered Johnny's specials and wolfed them down no matter what they turned out to be—even his vile creamed mystery meat on toast. I walked a lot. Occasionally I remembered to clean my teeth or take a shower or change my clothes. I slept whenever I could, sometimes in the back of an empty classroom, sometimes in a booth at Johnny's, sometimes slumped over a table at the Mountainlair. I didn't know what was wrong with me, didn't have a clue what to do about it, and, if I wanted to continue being a university student, I certainly didn't have the time to try to figure it out. I wrote myself a note and pinned it to my bulletin board: FIND THE NEXT THING TO DO AND DO IT.

I knew I should go home—simply pick some weekend at random and go—but I couldn't stand the thought of seeing my father the way he was. I talked to my mother on the phone every day or two, or rather, I allowed her to talk to me, to go on and on as much as she wanted—about my father's condition, about life, about *anything*. Since my father's stroke, she'd been telling me the same stories over and over again. There was nothing wrong with her memory. She knew that she was repeating herself. She even apologized for it. I could sympathize with her need to go over the same damned things endlessly, endlessly, but she never arrived at anything that resembled a conclusion, and listening to her wore me out. Once I had the truly bizarre experience of falling asleep while she was talking to me.

Except for Phys Ed and ROTC, I'd never earned less than an A in anything, but I finished the term with two A's, two B's, and a C+. On one level, I felt bad about it and blamed myself for fucking up; on another level, I thought I should have been awarded a medal for sheer survival. I registered for the spring semester and kept plodding forward. I was afraid that I was turning into some version of my mother; my thoughts were just as repetitive as hers. I was struggling to arrive at some meaningful conclusion that would resolve everything—but, given that I couldn't even define what I was trying to resolve, I continued going around in circles. The closest I could come to it was this: I had to find a way to make what had happened between me and Carol in Huntington not *comprehensible* but *irrelevant*. The only sphere big enough to offer me that kind of power was that of religion; what I wanted, and needed, was a satori like Cohen's.

My ride with that demon trucker fit into nothing whatsoever in my life—that is, I could find no personal meaning in it—but it continued to haunt me. His Biblical description of Hell had struck at something in me, and I couldn't get rid of it. Although I had a dozen or more books about Buddhism, I didn't own a Bible, so I had to go to the library to find the passage he'd been citing: "Between us and you there is a great gulf fixed, so that they which would pass from hence to you cannot." I didn't, of course, believe in a literal hell, but I kept playing with the metaphor; I could make it into a version of Plato's Cave, but, beyond that, I wasn't sure what to do with it. One night I woke up even earlier than usual—three-seventeen by my alarm clock— straight out of a nightmare that already I couldn't remember. I had finally arrived at the dark center of everything. I was afraid that the *great gulf fixed* was between me and the rest of the human race.

CAROL HAD called me her first night back in Morgantown. "My God, John, are you all right? I was so worried about you."

I'd known that I was bound to have some kind of encounter with her eventually, and I'd also known that when I did, I wasn't going to enjoy it very much, but, hearing her voice, I felt a skin-crawling, instinctive revulsion so intense it took me completely by surprise—as though I'd walked into a bright, immaculately clean bathroom and come upon a gigantic black spider. "Oh, I'm really *so* sorry," she said. "I felt terrible afterwards. I looked all over the house for you. I couldn't believe you'd just walked out."

For moments like that, I always had Hemingway: "Well, you know, kid . . . when it's time to go, it's time to go."

I don't remember how many more times she called. I do remember that eventually she switched from contrite to angry: "What are you doing, John, intentionally avoiding me?"

"No. Of course not. Been really busy. I'm carrying eighteen hours, you know."

"Look, if you don't want to see me, just say so. But I think the way things are between us right now is utterly ridiculous."

I promised I'd drop over to visit her, but I had no intention of doing it. Hoping she'd get the message, I stopped answering my phone in the evenings. I wanted her out of my life, and out of my mind, but I suspected that I wasn't through with her, or she with me—or maybe, to put it more accurately, that whatever had brought us together had not yet run its course—and I was right. One afternoon early in the new semester, I ran into her walking along Beechurst. "Oh, John. Hel*lo*."

She'd changed her image slightly, was wearing a straight wool skirt instead of a tartan, a classic Burberry instead of her red raincoat. Her purse matched her gloves matched her pretty little oxfords with high Cuban heels. She looked very much the young lady.

I felt myself retreating to a concrete bunker inside myself, throwing up armor in every direction. I was babbling frantically: "Whew, is this ever going to be a hard term, although it could be fun, the second half of Contemp Lit, yeah, that should be good. How's it going for you? You look terrific, by the way. Cute shoes."

"Thank you. You're sweet . . . How *are* you, John? It's been so long . . . It's been *too* long. Oh, I've missed you so much."

Her cheeks were flushed from the cold, her eyes sparkling. What I was feeling was shamefully double-faced: that eerie spidery revulsion was skittering over me at the same time as I was appreciating, as I always had, just how goddamned beautiful she was. She asked me to have coffee with her; no, no, no, I said, I was on my way to . . . "Oh, John, don't give me that."

She took one of my cold bare hands into her gloved ones. "I know you're still holding a grudge, and I can't blame you, but . . . Look, we can't leave things the way they are, can we? We have to be mature about this, don't we? Even if we are a pair of half-baked kids. Come on, we've got to get over this."

We had coffee in Johnny's. She was enjoying her courses this year, she said. She was getting to like teaching and thought that she might have a talent for it. She was afraid that things with Andrew were still going nowhere fast. She'd switched her thesis topic to Yeats, so at least Andrew was useful for that much—said with a wry, self-depreciating smile.

She had defined the conversational space, so I joined her there. Because I'd wanted to have another go at Rilke, I told her, I was taking an upper-level German course, God help me. I loved Rilke, but I hated German grammar; my instructor, I'd decided, must be Adolph Hitler's nephew.

We chatted like old chums while I tried to figure out what I was feeling. As though I'd needed it for psychic protection, I'd left my Levi jacket on; I felt myself sweating through not only my T-shirt but my flannel shirt and right on into the jacket. I imagined that someone could have wrung me out like a sponge. I did and didn't like being there with her. I did and didn't like *her*. She had assembled herself with the meticulous fashion-plate fastidiousness that had attracted me to her in the first place, and, yes, as always, I liked her attention to detail, and, yes, as always, I was ashamed of my own attention to detail: how I couldn't help noticing every one of her carefully calculated effects. The burgundy of her lip-stick was a perfect contrast to the darker burgundy of her shoes, purse, and gloves. The thickness of her Cuban heels allowed them to be even higher than stilettos and gave her the extra height she wanted without making her look trashy.

"I'm really sorry about what happened," she told me. Her expression couldn't have been any more contrite. "It's all my fault. I should have said that before, shouldn't I?" She took my hand and squeezed it. "Please call me. Please let's start seeing each other again. I promise I'll be good." She sounded so warm and sincere I almost believed her.

I thought that I should keep Carol in my life if, for no other reason, than to be able, from time to time, to *look at her*, but I never did call her. I kept going to classes, going to sleep, waking up, eating my irregular meals, cleaning my teeth, doing it all over the next day. I still had nightmares. Nothing seemed to be getting any better. I kept telling myself that if I kept in motion, took one step after the other, I would eventually arrive *somewhere*, but I wasn't sure of that.

"HEY, HERO." A girl's voice. Sleep was gone in a flash, whipped away like a blanket. I remember my indrawn breath—remember waiting, not knowing if I was hearing a leftover filament of dream or the crunch of real gravel in the alley outside my partially open window. My heartbeat was accelerated, my body tensed for action. I listened until I felt the strain of it in every muscle. The faint haze from the distant streetlight was just enough to give me the dark shapes of ownership. Nothing out of the ordinary: my dresser, my chair, my guitar, my pile of dirty clothes. But I was locked inside a mystery. A real girl standing outside my window in Morgantown? It didn't make any sense. Again, the girl's voice: "Hey, hero."

"Cassy?"

"Yeah," she said, laughing, "it's me. Come on, John, let us in."

I leapt out of bed, pulled on jeans, and ran outside barefoot into the alley where I'd stood so many times before, searching for omens. With the night still thick against me, I saw Cassandra, and, behind her, a black stripe of new beard making his face look pale as parchment, Bill Cohen. I wrapped Cassy into my arms, smelled the minty scent of whatever she'd used to wash her hair. I hadn't planned to kiss her, but I was already tasting the warmly human sourness of her mouth. She wasn't a memory, a ghostly fantasy, a longing set to the tune of a keening rock 'n roll song on my radio in the middle of the night, but flesh and muscle and bone, salty lips, ticking hair, narrow rib cage under her ski jacket, stingingly alive. "Oh, God, Cassy, I can't believe it. I'm so glad to see you."

A step behind her, Cohen was grinning. I opened my arm to include him. The three of us embraced. "What the hell are you doing here?" I asked him. "And don't tell me that words are no damned good."

I couldn't imagine any two people I would have rather seen appearing so miraculously out of the night. It didn't seem possible. I didn't deserve it. I felt humbled by it. I led them into my apartment, put on water for tea. Instead of turning on the lights, I lit the candles on my altar to young girls and carried them to the kitchen table.

Cassandra had unraveled onto my couch. "Guess who has her driver's license? Guess who's going to be up at two in the morning, reading? With her bedroom light on so joker here can bounce a pebble off her window? With her hair up in rollers and cream all over her face? And that was the only thing I could think of . . . good grief, I can't let anybody see me like this."

Cohen had unloaded his knapsack into a corner. His eyes were shining strangely; his face looked stark and unfamiliar inside that dark beginning of a beard. "Why haven't you written to me, you bastard?" I asked him.

"That," he said, "is a good question. A crucial question. Perhaps even the central question . . . It seems that whatever clamped itself down on my pen hand has stayed clamped."

I liked the yellow wobble of the candle flames lighting their faces. I poured the boiling water into the teapot. I felt that everything I was doing had the weight of ritual. "I've dropped out of Harvard," Cohen said. "The steely-eyed double agent who was using the Dean's office as a cover called it 'officially withdrawn.'"

"Christ, Bill, what are you going to do?"

"I'm going back down to my Uncle Harry's place in Florida."

"Why?"

"It's complex." But then he laughed. "No, it's not. It's

223

simple. It's only the story that's complex."

I waited for him to tell me the complex story, but he didn't. "It took me fourteen hours to hitchhike from Boston to Pittsburgh," he said. "Can you believe that?" He sipped his tea.

"The old man will kill me if he finds out I drove the car down here." Cassandra said. She was looking at me closely, searching for something. "He sleeps late on Sundays, so maybe I can pull it off if I leave by . . . I don't know . . . six or seven."

Of course it was dangerous running off with her father's car in the middle of the night, but I could sense that something far more important was going on. She was asking something of me, sending me a message with her eyes. I knew that the key to it was Cohen.

"I was on that goddamn Pennsylvania Turnpike so long I thought I'd grow old and die there," he was saying. "Finally a trucker picked me up at the restaurant at Breezewood. He was going to Pittsburgh."

I waited. "The road was beautifully empty all the way to Morgantown." The muscles at the corners of his mouth were drawn tense, braced against fatigue; the hours on the road had smudged the margins of his eyes, but the green corneas were shining like clear water.

"Yeah, it was a beautiful drive," Cassandra said, "although I could have used some coffee." She was looking at me again, her eyes still filled with questions. "He picked me," she said.

"Your window was beckoning like a lighthouse," he said.

I poured out the tea. "When I got home," Cohen said quietly, "I couldn't go in. I walked around outside the house. It was dark, sleeping in the dark, and I could imagine, so clearly, everything inside. I could see all the furniture in the rooms just the way it's always been . . . the beds, my family asleep inside. I could *feel* them in there, quietly asleep, could sense their breathing . . .

as though the house itself was breathing, waiting for me. And I felt such a terrible love for all of them, as though I'd been set on watch so they'd be safe. Nothing could hurt them because I was outside, awake and watching.

"Oh, it wasn't that I didn't want to go through all the drama. I knew there was bound to be a big scene, everybody yelling and talking at once. I knew what they'd say. I played it through in my mind like a movie. They'd be excited to see me, and then I'd have to tell them what I was doing. My father would say, 'Well then, Bill, so you're not going to open a laundry after all,' or something like that. And I'd have to try to find some kind of explanation. I was even laughing as I thought about it, how perfectly each of them would be themselves. I could have walked into all of that, and it would have been all right. But there was something else, and I couldn't go in."

I saw that his eyes were shining with tears.

WE TALKED quietly in the candlelight, and drank our tea, and then we decided to go somewhere to watch the sun come up. We got into Cassy's dad's car, and I guided her over the creek and up Spruce Street. I wanted to get us high above the city, but I didn't know exactly how to do it. We meandered around those insanely steep streets, always looking for a way to get higher. Eventually we turned left and found a cluster of fraternity houses. "Park here," I said. It was after four in the morning, and I thought that even the hard-partying brothers of Beta Theta Pi had to sleep sometime. We walked on up to the very end of North High Street. To the right, we could see the edges of the large dark blocks of the university, to the left, on the slow curve of the river, a faint release of light that signaled the coming of dawn, and, directly below us down the hill, a wacky assemblage of night-shrouded boxes that was the city of Morgantown.

We stood without speaking, taking it all in. Then Cassandra said, "The world's a million times weirder than anybody thinks it is."

"You're absolutely right," Cohen said. "My watch has stopped too."

I'd been desperate to talk to her alone, hadn't been able to figure out how to do it, but Cohen, in a gesture of exquisite graciousness, simply smiled at us and walked away. She sank into a squat like a garage mechanic, so I did the same thing. If I stayed in that position very long, my legs would begin to cramp, but she seemed to rest easily like that, her ski pants drawn tight over her narrow hips. "Those pants are something else," I said. "What did you do, walk into the store and say, 'Give me the smallest size I can cram myself into?'"

She laughed. "Can't you think about something other than my ass?"

We were still riding the kick and the danger of it: the sleeping town laid out below us, our parents back in Raysburg sleeping, but the three of us up and out and awake as though time had been suspended—but no, that wasn't quite right. It was more that the wires which hold the world together had been released and we were in that ticklish crossover when the old world falls down and sleep is dispelled. For the moment, we'd escaped, were outside—had slipped out of bounds at the last possible moment. Soon the wires would be yanked back into place and the world reassembled, so we didn't have much time—certainly no time for bullshit—and we both knew it. "Well, have you forgiven me?" she said.

"Forgiven *you?* Have you forgiven *me?*"

"For what? Because you kissed Zoë? It doesn't matter. I said some terrible things to you. I knew you were mad at me when you just left town like that . . . and didn't even call me."

"I wasn't mad at you. I thought I'd fucked everything up. I was afraid you'd never want to see me again."

"You ass. How could you think that?" She looked at me sharply and then away. "We're stuck with each other," she said. "Can't I get mad at you for a day or two if I want?"

"Sure, you can."

"Besides, Zoë trapped you."

"It's nice of you to think of it that way, but it wasn't quite like that."

"Oh, good grief! If she didn't want your tongue down her throat, she could have kept her little mouth shut."

I laughed, but Cassandra's grave expression didn't change. "She's had a crush on you for a long time," she said. "Can you imagine how hurt she would have been if you *hadn't* kissed her?"

"Boy, are you an understanding big sister."

"No, I'm not. It doesn't have anything to do with that. It's just that Zoë's not an X person . . ."

I waited for her to go on, but she didn't. She was looking at Cohen. He was standing some twenty feet away from us. "What on earth is he doing?" she asked me.

He was facing to the left, looking toward the blue-black edge where the light was beginning. He was swinging his arms up and down in graceful arcs. It took me a moment to get it. "Oh," I said, "he's conducting the dawn."

"Hey, yeah. That's exactly what he's doing."

He was taking it in four-four, moderato. "The funny thing is," I said "he can't even sing."

"He's beautiful, isn't he?" she said. "He's one of the most beautiful boys I've ever seen in my life. But I can't imagine sleeping with him. It's not a beauty I'd want to sleep with."

The day that Cohen was conducting out of the semidarkness was going to be one of Morgantown's dull overcast days; the streets below us were emerging in a gunmetal grisaille. "I don't understand anything now," Cassandra said. "I'm kind of afraid of him now."

"He is in a strange mood, all right. I've never seen him quite like this before . . . I think he wants to go back to where it happened the first time."

"To where what happened?"

"His satori or whatever you want to call it . . . His awakening."

"Yeah, he told me about it on the way down, about how he was walking on the beach all alone, and what he'd been thinking about, and how it just . . . happened. But I couldn't understand what it was that happened . . . Dad would call it 'the storms of adolescence.' That's one of the things he says all the time. 'Oh, it's just the storms of adolescence, Cassy.' But he doesn't know everything. I used to think he did."

By now, Cohen had teased out every bird left in the West Virginia winter; with gently sweeping arms, he was coaxing them into song. "We came down here because we both really needed to see you," she said, "but . . . John, why did he come to me? I hardly know him."

"Why did you drive him down here?"

"Don't play Socrates. Give me a straight answer."

"He's linked to you. Through me."

"I knew you were going to say that. It's . . . I don't know, like being in a secret society. I'm not sure I like it."

"Cassandra, the cat who walks by herself."

"Right," she said, smiling, "I haven't taken a vow to save all sentient beings."

"Is that what he said?"

"Yeah. Oh, he wasn't talking about himself. He's too modest for that. He was talking about . . . Bodhisattvas . . . Is that what they're called?" I nodded. "But he really *was* talking about himself. He would like to take all sentient beings into Nirvana with him, but I don't know why anybody would want Nirvana to start with. I don't. Extinction." She shivered. "I don't want to die. I don't even want to get any older."

"You want to stay sixteen forever?"

"Maybe not sixteen. Could I stop before I turn twenty?"

Picking up the tempo, Cohen called for a swelling of cool light along the Monongahela, along the edges of buildings, a slow but steady crescendo of smoky blue. "I sent David's pin back," she said.

Well, that was news. Now there was enough light for me to see her clearly. She must have been able to see me just as clearly. "I could have used Mom as an excuse. She told me I had to send it back . . . 'Cassy, you're far too young to be pinned to somebody in college.' But I thought if I said that to him, it'd be . . . just, you know, chicken shit. And it wouldn't have been the truth anyway. So I wrote him, and I was completely honest. I said, 'David, I like you a lot, but I just don't want to be pinned down.' Oh, don't look so damn pleased, John Dupre. It doesn't have anything to do with you."

"No, I didn't think it did. You and I aren't . . . I don't know how to say this . . . Do you know what I mean?"

We stared at each other, trying to communicate without speaking. Then I made another attempt with the words that were no damned good: "What happens between us . . . it's not on the same level as anything with David Anderson . . . or with anybody else."

"Oh, yeah? Well, how about you and Natalie the Silent? How about your older woman?"

"That's on a different level. You said it yourself, Cassy. We're stuck with each other."

"I don't know . . . Yeah, I guess we are. I honest to God don't understand anything. We're X people, that's about all . . . When you left without seeing me, I thought, good grief, now we're playing games. We've never done that before. Each of us waiting for the other one to make the first call. So I called you, and I could never get you. Don't you ever stay home, damn it?"

"I'm sorry. I was afraid to call you."

"Oh, you ass. Never be afraid to call me."

I stood up and shook out my stiffened legs. Cassandra stood up too. I was wondering if she was seeing what I was seeing when I looked down the hill.

"Extinction," she said. "It's so weird. How could anybody want that?"

"Did he say he wanted extinction?"

"No. Nirvana. I guess that's something different, huh?"

I didn't know how to answer her. "We talked about all that stuff driving down here," she said. "When I was a little kid, I used to ask Dad what happened when you died, and he said nothing happened. It was like going to sleep. I couldn't stand the thought of it. I'd ask him, 'But don't you remember anything?' He'd say, 'No, you don't remember anything,' and I'd say, 'But don't you go to heaven?' He'd say, 'That's a myth, Cassy. People invented that myth because they're afraid of the truth.' And he'd tell me how you try to improve the world, and you leave your children behind, and that's enough, but it never felt like enough for me . . . If *that's* the truth, then it all seems like a spinning chaos, millions of mindless atoms. It scares me silly . . ." Again, her eyes directed me to Cohen. "He said he's not afraid of dying. He said death makes us human, makes everything more beautiful."

Something was coalescing in my mind—nothing built of words but a form taking shape. "Cassy," I said. I didn't know how to go on.

"When you think about . . . that someday you just won't

exist anymore . . . Oh, I just hate all the games. We just don't have *time*. If you're an X person, people just never let you . . ."

She made an explosive gesture, flinging her hands up. I guessed that she too was coming up against the limit of words. "Oh, hell," she said, "I should have been a boy. I hate high school . . . all that crap . . . the games you have to play. And it never works anyway. I hate the way boys think if they go out with you a couple times, they own you. I hate being . . ." She didn't finish her sentence.

Her passion shot through me to tingle my fingertips. I was working so hard at understanding what was lying behind her words that it felt like a physical effort—trying to separate sheets of rock with my bare hands. Anything I said would be almost beside the point. "I'm glad you're not a boy."

"Well, me too. I didn't mean it like that. No, I just want to be able to do anything a boy can do and not get shit for it. Like when I was ten."

"Cassy, the back-alley kid," I said.

"You're damned right."

"I've always loved the tomboy in you."

Both of us knew how quickly time was running out. Soon everything would be reassembled, and then it would be too late. But still, I approached it sideways: "Well, I've thought that too. About myself."

"What?"

"That I should have been a girl"—an enormous admission for me; I hadn't said anything like that to anyone since I'd been in grade school.

She looked directly into my eyes; I could see her concentration, her effort. "Oh, Dupre, you'd be an *appalling* girl."

She laughed; it was an invitation for me to laugh with her, but I couldn't do it. "You'd be worse than Linda Edmonds," she

231

said. "You'd spend all your time worrying about getting runs in your stockings."

"Yeah, that's probably true."

I was afraid she hadn't felt the full weight of it, but then she said, "I never had a best girlfriend the way girls are supposed to, so I guess you're it."

"Thank you."

"Is that what you want to be?"

"I don't know."

"Girls can be real bitches. I don't think you understand that."

"Yeah, I do."

"No, you don't. Not really. God, I hate girls sometimes. I just *hate* them. All their damned games."

"You've never played games with me."

"Yeah, I know. And I've seen you be phony with other people, but you've never been phony with me."

We had arrived at a pause, and we both felt it, but we weren't finished yet. We were in one of those gathering points I'd told Cohen about; our lives were changing right before our eyes as we stood there, awake, and watched Cohen conduct more flat rainy light into the scene—dove grey here, steel grey there. It's as though a scrim were being slowly drawn away; now the firm shapes of buildings were emerging, objects pushing back into reality, the wires tightening, the world reassembling itself. Cohen was conducting into being everything that was needed to make a world—a bit more light swelling up at the edge, the first of the traffic, windows suddenly springing into yellow, flickering sounds, bird voices, the black smears of scrub and weeds. "I believe him," she said. "He isn't afraid of dying."

"I believe him too . . . and it's because he *knows*. It's always been comforting to me . . . to know that it can really happen."

"Yeah," she said, "maybe . . . but if you have to know what

he knows before you can stop being afraid of dying, then I guess I'd better look for it too. Sometimes I'm so afraid of dying I can't sleep. When he turned up in the middle of the night like that, I thought he was crazy. But driving down here I began to think *he's* not crazy, it's the rest of us . . . Mom and Dad and Zoë, and you and me . . . and I began to think he is a saint, which is ridiculous, because I don't believe in saints."

"Maybe we need to find a new word."

"But maybe Nirvana's not extinction. He said there's no words to define it. Maybe it's beautiful. And if he's going to take all sentient beings with him . . . maybe we can come too."

I hated to admit it to myself, but I'd always felt superior to her—as *a boy*, as somebody so much older, with a life that was so much more complex, so much specifically mine—but now I knew how wrong I'd been. Her world was everything that was the case, just as mine was. She was just as empty and awake as I was.

Cohen had nearly finished his symphony; it was almost day. Cassandra smiled at me, then looked away. It was fragile, subtle, capable of infinite motion—sentient, alive, there in that grave moment, on that divide. "I believe you too, you know," she said. "We *are* linked. You're closer to me than . . ."

"Yeah. A brother."

"No, not just a brother. It's even closer than that," she said. "Until we die. Is that what it means?"

"Longer than that."

"You guys are crazy. This is the only life we've got."

"OK, then. Until we die. No matter what happens."

"It sounds like we're married."

"Closer than that."

I looked into her eyes, and we were in each other's minds. It wasn't a metaphor. We were experiencing a moment of mental telepathy as literally as if we were characters in a science-fiction story—but it was far more meaningful than science-fiction. Now I understood how the Buddha had transmitted the doctrine without saying a word.

We could only bear the intensity for a few seconds. Then we were back in our private worlds and could surprise each other again. "Oh shit," she said, "it's true, isn't it? How did it happen? I don't understand it, but that's what it means." I turned and saw that Cohen was looking at us. He wasn't doing anything. Unsmiling, he was simply there in the full grey light of day.

We know the things we know because people have told us, but we also know the things we know without knowing how we know them—the energy thin at the edge, the crackle down the spine, the tingle at the fingertips, the twinkling of the thumbs, the clarity more real, more essential, than any of their stories. What we knew then was more real than any of their stories.

It wasn't anything that could be assembled or disassembled, not cogs and flywheels. It was in the pause, the space, the breath—like a paper cut, a nick on the soft skin between thumb and index finer, a continual ache, barely visible but unforgettable. It was what Cohen had always said it would be: an emptiness when everything is simple, something you kept with you at all times, like keeping Kosher—what it means to unwind the thread out to the end and say, "Hear O Israel," or "in the name of the Father and the Son and the Holy Ghost," or "I take refuge in the Buddha and the Dharma and the Sangha," or any of the other ritual words that are only reminders of the moment when one spool has been removed from the spindle and the other not yet placed on it: to begin again, to walk down the hill, to talk well, to drive safely; it was all returning now. The flat grey light was everywhere. "Call me, yes, please," I told Cassandra. "I'll worry about you." She was gone, moving along the twisty road back to Raysburg. Cohen and I slept.

When I woke again, I felt at first as though I were merely living through another of my endless days in Morgantown—sleeping in the afternoon, waking to early evening—but then I remembered that this time was different. I opened my eyes. Cohen was sitting on the floor, his back to the wall, looking at me. He must have been watching me sleep. "What are you thinking?" I asked him.

He answered me in the Latin we'd both studied at the Academy: *"Dormia sine cura, frater."*

I asked him why he'd dropped out of Harvard, and he didn't answer. But just when I was beginning to think that he wasn't going to say anything at all, he told me. This time the story was not infinitely complex, on many levels, something that required millions of words—hours and hours of words. He spoke as if he were choosing each word carefully, as if his intention was to use as few of them as possible. He told me that when he'd gone back to Harvard, he'd felt something shifting inside himself. He finished the term with A's the way he always did. He started the new term. He knew, on one level, that he might as well be at Harvard as not be at Harvard, but, on another level, the student business was getting harder and harder to pull off. It was beginning to feel like a prison. But then he thought, no, it wasn't Harvard that was the prison. It was the human mind. "And if you live in a prison," he said, "wouldn't the most important thing to study . . . be lock picking?"

The day before he left, hitchhiking south to Florida, I took the *I Ching* out of the library, and he consulted it on my behalf. I turned off the lights in my apartment, lit my candles. I made a pot of green tea. Cohen sat on the floor with his back against the wall and meditated while I formulated the question. When I had it, I read it to him: "What is the state of my life at the moment, and what should I do about it?"

In the closed palms of my hands I shook three pennies and then cast them onto the floor. Cohen transcribed the lines of the hexagram as it was forming. When we had six lines, I poured out the tea. He looked up from the reading and laughed. "You see," he said, "Difficulty at the Beginning works supreme success."

EVERYTHING ABOUT the reading in the *I Ching* had been right. I *was* like a tiny green shoot pushing up out of the earth, encountering obstacles. I *was* in a time of chaos like a wild Ohio Valley electrical storm—the thunder rising up and the rain pouring down, creating a turbulence that could easily turn into disaster. Yes, I needed helpers, and I had them: Cohen and Cassandra—Bodhisattvas, angels of infinite light. I knew, as the reading had told me, that I had to bring order out of chaos. I loved the image the *I Ching* had used as a metaphor: sorting out silk threads from a knotted tangle and binding them into skeins.

I straightened up my apartment, showed up on time for all my classes, took thorough notes, started researching a couple papers that weren't due for weeks. Every day I made sure that I shaved, cleaned my teeth, took a shower, and changed my underwear. I collected all my dirty laundry and hauled it to the laundromat. I hadn't been playing the guitar since I'd come back after Christmas, but I settled down to learn Holcomb's "Trouble in Mind." I wrote several new poems. And then, while sorting out the papers that had piled up on my desk, I found, neatly tucked away in a file folder, the two pictures I'd brought with me from home: my second grade class photo and the one of me as Alice in Wonderland on Halloween.

Although it contained my only image of Nancy Clark, the whole of the Jefferson Second Grade Class of 1949–50 certainly did not belong on my altar to young girls, so I taped it up to one side. Then I stared at the altar. At the center were the real girls—

Natalie, Cassandra, Linda. Surrounding them were the cinema princesses, and then, at the outer margins, my latest additions—anonymous models I'd clipped from fashion magazines and the Sunday *New York Times*. I realized what I should have known all along, that those images made a pattern. Then I saw that the girls were like a hexagram in the *I Ching*, but they weren't in their proper places. I moved all the pictures outward, creating a space; I taped the picture of me as Alice in the center. That one simple change altered the entire pattern and made the lines of force radically different.

I spent hours rearranging the girls around that picture of me as Alice—trying them one way, then another. My old pattern had been rectangular; the girls had simply formed rows. Now I made a series of concentric circles with me as Alice at the center. I mixed the cinema princesses in with the real ones. Even though I couldn't have explained the force that made me put any picture in any particular spot—to move Valeria Ciangottini next to Cassandra or Sue Lyon next to Linda Edmonds—I could feel the compelling inner logic of it. When I was finished, I knew that I'd got it exactly right. The new pattern did, in some perfect but wordless way, represent my entire life.

EARLY IN February—I remember, strangely enough, that it was about a week before Valentine's day—Carol called me. After a few polite and eminently delicate feints, she said, "This is a terrible thing to ask of you, I know, but could I pull an all-nighter at your place? I've got a paper due, and Marge is driving me nuts."

I couldn't believe she had the gall. Yes, we'd had coffee together and things had gone well, but we certainly weren't back on that kind of footing *yet*. On the other hand, I'd already decided that she fit somewhere in my life, hadn't I? And what if she *was* genuinely sorry about what had happened in Huntington? I didn't want to be cruel. I was tempted to tell her—in the politest possible terms—to shove it, but I heard myself saying, "Sure."

She told me she'd be over around eight, but it was closer to nine when I heard the unmistakable sound of high heels clicking up my alley. I opened the door, and there she was, too suddenly. Primed by the sound, I looked down and saw that she was wearing those extravagant black patent pumps from New Year's Eve. I couldn't imagine why.

"This is so nice of you," she said. "You're a life-saver." In the old days, she might have given me a peck on the cheek or even brushed my lips lightly with hers; now she caught me briefly into a stiff hug. I hung up her Burberry and followed her inside. She had brought a small green suitcase. She was wearing a tight black wool sheath.

She saw me looking her over. Her voice was clipped and distant: "I told Marge I was going to a party." With a suitcase?

Balanced on her precise little heels, she did a turn around my apartment. I could sense her awareness of being watched. "Well," she said, "I'm glad to see that nothing's changed," and laughed awkwardly. "*Plus ça change*. And it's still too cold."

I laughed awkwardly too. God, I thought, we're doing just great so far. I lit the fire for her. "Are you hungry? There's some stew . . ."

"Oh, no, thanks. I've had dinner."

"Beer? Wine?"

"A cup of coffee would be lovely. Just lovely. I have work to do, you know."

She pretended to look at the new notes and pictures I'd taped to my walls. I couldn't stop staring at those goddamn sexy shoes. "Did you walk over?"

"In these? Are you kidding? No, a friend dropped me."

I'd never seen her so ill at ease. She couldn't seem to find anywhere to put herself, came to rest at the edge of my desk, let one of her hands fall onto the top of it. "I've decided to look more mature," she said as though answering the question I hadn't asked. "It's one of my New Year's resolutions actually."

Actually? "Oh?"

"I'm tired of people thinking I'm still in high school. It's so boring. Could you put some coffee on, please?"

"Oh, yeah, sure. I'd be delighted."

"And how have you *been?*" She pronounced the word to rhyme with "queen." She was really getting Andrew's accent down. If she kept at it, no one would ever have to know that she was from West Virginia.

I told her I was just dandy, couldn't have been better, in fact. I rinsed out the percolator. I was glad to have something to do. We kept trying to find things to talk about. She thought it had been a mistake to room with Marge. Cousin or no cousin, they had almost nothing in common. "She has *her comrades* over every night. If I hear another word about politics, I swear I'm going to scream."

She was saying nothing new. "Yeah," I said, "must be tough." I filled the percolator, set it on the stove.

She started to pace again. With a skirt that tight and heels that high (I thought, with considerable grim satisfaction), she had no option but to walk like a lady. She was really getting to me. She paused in front of my altar to young girls. "And what's this? A new addition?"

She bent closer. "Who's your little Alice?"

I felt an ugly sensation as though a huge murderous reptile had just licked the back of my neck. "My cousin in Parkersburg," I said quickly.

It would have been easy enough to take that goddamn picture

down. I didn't know why it hadn't even crossed my mind. Well, I thought, if I'm out on a limb, I might as well go all the way to the end of it. "You can probably see the family resemblance," I said.

She looked at me, then back at the picture. "No, I can't really."

"People were always telling us we looked alike." I could hear how defensive I sounded. Shut up, I told myself.

"No, I can't see it . . . really . . . But then I can't see resemblances between anybody, not even people in my own family. I think people just look like themselves."

"That's an old photo," I heard myself saying. "Can't you tell? She's my age. I thought it was a cute picture. Don't you think it's a cute picture?"

She gave me a long strange look. "Yes, of course it's a cute picture . . . If you like little girls dressed up like Alice in Wonderland."

"Well," I said, "so Marge is really driving you nuts, huh?"

"Oh, is she ever. I can't begin to tell you."

"What do you take in your coffee? I should remember, but I don't."

"Just black. Are you sweet on her?"

Another of her weirdly archaic phrases; it was as bad as *petted*. My armpits were stinging. "Who?" I said, although I knew perfectly well who.

"Your little Alice."

"She's my favorite cousin. We were close when we were kids. So what's your paper on?"

"Yeats and the Irish theatre. I can use your typewriter, can't I?"

"Oh, sure. Let me get some of that stuff out of your way." I cleared away my papers and books, lit the old gooseneck lamp I'd inherited from one of my father's failed businesses.

"What's her name?" she said.

"Who?"

"Who have we been taking about?" she said, laughing. "Your little playmate."

I didn't hesitate. "Nancy Clark."

"Did you play house?"

"I don't know. I don't remember."

"Oh? I'll bet you do remember. You just don't want to tell me . . . *I* remember playing house. It could be really naughty . . . And truth, dare, or consequences. Boy, could that be naughty."

"Naughty how?"

"The *consequences*, silly . . . and I'm not going to tell *you* either."

She was, of course, flirting with me—and I knew how to flirt back. I even had the next line: "Come on, Carol, I *dare* you," but I couldn't bring myself to say it. I poured her a cup of coffee.

She sat down at my desk. "I hate this," she said. "Why do I always leave things to the last minute?"

"I won't bother you," I said. "I'll read or something."

"Oh, God, it's so hard getting started . . . So what do you hear from the two Bills?"

"Two Bills? Oh . . . you mean Revington and Cohen? From Revington, nothing. He never keeps in touch. I haven't got a clue what he's doing. He'll turn up eventually . . . And Cohen was just here on his way to Florida. He's taking some time off school . . ."

"You mean he dropped out?" She sounded genuinely shocked.

"Yeah, I guess."

"You're kidding me. Out of *Harvard?*"

"Yeah, out of Harvard. That's where he was going."

"Why on earth would he do that? I thought he was on the Dean's List."

"He is on the Dean's List. It's not permanent. He's going to go back . . . I think he wants to practice Buddhism instead of just reading about it . . ."

"*Practice* Buddhism?"

"Yeah, you know . . . it's not like Christianity. In Christianity, all you have to do is believe it. In Buddhism, you have to do something."

"So what's he going to do?"

"I don't know . . . Run. Swim. Meditate."

"Oh, my God." She was furious. It didn't make any sense. Why should it have mattered to her whether Bill Cohen did or didn't go to Harvard?

"You're hopeless, all of you," she said. "When are you ever going to grow up? You call each other by your last names just like you were still in your silly prep school . . . and William's Humphrey Bogart, and Bill Cohen's a Buddhist monk, and you're . . . I don't know what . . ."

"Holden Caulfield?" I supplied for her. "Woody Guthrie?"

"Oh, it is funny, I suppose," she said, "but how much longer is it going to go on being funny? Clever clever games for bright little boys."

Now I was angry—so angry I couldn't speak. She rolled a piece of my paper into my typewriter and began to hammer away on it. "Boy, is this damned thing stiff."

I WENT for one of my long catatonic perambulations through the bleak winter landscape of Morgantown, stayed away as long as I could. When I came back, she was still pounding my typewriter. She'd kicked off her heels. She looked up at me, smiling, and sang out, "It's going really well!" just as though I'd asked. I took a quart of beer into my bedroom, threw myself onto the bed, and tried to read. The guys upstairs seemed to be enjoying themselves; I could hear them laughing, the distant sound of rock 'n roll blasting out of their hi-fi—the boring bass line.

When she'd said "an all-nighter," that, obviously, had been

exactly what she'd meant. As the night sidled by, all I could do was wait. Around four in the morning, she appeared in my open doorway saying, "Knock, knock." I thought it was odd that she would put her heels back on to walk from the living room to my bedroom—although I certainly did appreciate the gesture.

"I'm almost finished," she said, "but you don't have to stay up just because I'm up."

"Oh, I won't. I was just going to sleep."

"I'm exhausted . . . Would you mind if I stretched out with you in a little while?"

Oh, Christ, I thought. "No, I don't mind."

I knew that there wasn't the faintest possibility I could sleep, but I turned out the light anyway. Fully dressed except for my boots, I lay down under the unzipped sleeping bag I used for a quilt. After twenty minutes or so, I heard the typing stop. Like a child pretending to be asleep, I opened my eyes slightly. I saw her hesitate in my doorway. With the light behind her, she was a woman-shaped silhouette.

She stepped out of her heels and into my room. I heard her unzip her sheath. Then she crossed back across the rectangle of yellow light that was spilling in from the living room. She was still wearing her stockings. They were attached to a long black foundation garment that fit her tightly in one clean sweep from the bra on top all the way down to mid-thigh. As a *Vogue* reader, I even knew what it was called—an "all-in-one"—and it was exactly what you were *supposed* to wear under a sheath. It made her look like a sleek shiny black mermaid. She lifted the edge of the sleeping bag and slipped in next to me. "Are you awake?" she said.

I'd never been more awake in my life. I was like an owl. "Yeah," I said.

The guys upstairs must have gone to bed. There was nothing to hear but occasional traffic; a trucker somewhere was highballing it through the night. "Do you want to talk for a minute?" she said.

"Sure."

"Can you forgive me for what happened in Huntington? I mean really forgive me."

"Yeah, sure," I said, although she was right in guessing that I hadn't forgiven her. I didn't think I ever would.

"I was so worried about you. I was sure you'd gone to Marge's. I called her the next day, and then I was worried sick."

She'd already told me that, but apparently she needed to tell me again. I thought I should be helping her, making it easier for her, but I couldn't do it. I lay there and waited.

"I was so ashamed," she said. "I hate it when that happens to me. I get in a bitchy mood, and . . . I don't know . . . When I was a kid, I used to have spectacular temper tantrums. I mean, *spectacular*, absolutely legendary, you can ask my mother. I'd get started, and I couldn't stop . . . even when I wanted to. Completely out of control . . . Sometimes I'm still like that. I just hate it. I can't stop. I really can't stop. I watch myself doing it, and I can't stop."

She was saying none of this easily, and I was delighted with her discomfort. "What were you thinking?" I asked her.

"When?"

"In Huntington. Just before I left."

"Oh, God, John. I don't want to talk about it anymore. Do we have to talk about it?"

"No, I guess we don't."

"Oh, hell. Give me a cigarette, please."

I lit two cigarettes, put the ashtray between us. We lay there side by side and smoked in the dark. "Do you have an alarm clock?" she said.

"Of course I've got an alarm clock."

"Will you set it for seven, please?"

I set it for seven. I knew that she had something more to say.

"John? . . . I've been thinking. I don't . . . I guess I've never understood why you're attracted to me."

"Oh?"

"I'm not really your type."

"What's my type?"

"You know . . . You've always dated high-school girls, and . . . Well, I suppose with a girl so much younger, you can feel . . . It must be more . . . You've got their pictures all over your walls. Those young girls are so obviously what you want, and I just don't . . . You do know what I mean, don't you?"

I did know what she meant, but I'd be damned if I was going to admit it. My mouth had gone dry. I could feel an enormous rage building up in me; if I'd been able to think, it would have frightened me. When I tried to speak, I made a strange clicking sound. "No, I don't know what you mean," I said. "What do you mean?"

"Oh, John, you know perfectly well . . . I'm not . . . Oh, I know I'm no paragon of maturity, but I'm certainly no teenager, and I just don't . . . With one of your little schoolgirls you can feel manly, and . . . "

I was so angry it blotted me out. "Wait a minute." I didn't plan any of the words that were hissing out of my mouth: "I don't want to hear that crap. 'Your little schoolgirls.' Never ever say that to me again."

I was shaking with fury. She must have felt it. It took everything I had to control my voice so I wasn't screaming at her; what was coming out sounded dry, nearly inhuman: "Jesus Christ, little schoolgirls, you make it sound like there's a dozen of them. There's only been three, and none of them are *little schoolgirls* . . . "

"John, wait a minute. I'm sorry. I didn't mean . . . "

"When I dated Linda . . . we were *both of us* in high school . . . Even when she was fourteen . . . she wasn't a *little schoolgirl* . . . and Natalie and Cassandra . . . Christ, what are you . . . ? When you say, 'little schoolgirls'? Something out of *Little Women*? Jesus, none of them are *little schoolgirls*. They're bright strong independent girls . . . Goddamn it, none of them are *little schoolgirls*."

I butted out my cigarette. She butted out hers. I set the ashtray on the floor. My entire body was shaking, but she wasn't moving a muscle. Now I had enough sense to be frightened. I should, I thought, leap up and pull on my boots and walk out of there. I should walk for miles. And miles and miles. Finally she said in a small voice, "I'm sorry. Everything I say seems to come out wrong."

She reached over to take my hand. I jerked it away from her.

"We're not very good for each other anymore, are we?" she said.

"No," I said, "we're not."

I don't know whether she slept. I kept wanting to get up and walk, but some dark inertia kept me bound to the bed. Then sleep must have crept up and mugged me. When the shrill clang of my clock woke me, I was miles deep. I slapped the alarm into silence. Carol wasn't in bed with me any longer; the shower was running. Oh, thank God, I thought, soon she'll be gone.

I needed coffee. I got up. Dazed, half awake, I stumbled over Carol's damnable patent leather pumps. She'd shed them directly in the middle of my bedroom doorway. How typical of her, I thought, and felt like hurling them against the wall, but I picked them up carefully and set them on the top of my dresser where she'd be sure to see them when she came out of the shower. I put the coffee on to perk.

She burst into the living room, one towel wrapped around her body and another around her head. "Oh, my hair! Why didn't I think to bring a shower cap? Will you call me a cab, please?"

I'd never called a cab in Morgantown and wasn't sure I even knew how to do it. I looked in the phone book, found a number, and called. She shot back into the room, now in a blouse and a tight straight skirt. She was shoving books and papers into her suitcase. "Is that coffee? Oh, good." I poured her a cup. She pawed through the suitcase, pulled out her Cuban-heeled oxfords, threw them onto the floor, shoved her feet into them, sat down and laced them up. "Oh, John, this has been so good of you." Her fake British accent was quite pronounced. "You've really saved my life."

She did her makeup, brushed her hair, flung her sheath, and then that disturbingly erotic all-in-one, into her suitcase. Outside, a horn was blowing. "Oh, God!"

I helped her on with her coat, carried her suitcase out to the cab. "Take care of yourself," she said and kissed me on the cheek.

"Yeah," I said, "I will. You too."

Long after she'd gone, I continued to stand in the alley, smoking. I felt abraded and raw, exhausted beyond the point of mere fatigue, but at the same time still angry enough to drive spikes. What, in God's name, had that been all about? The longer I thought about it, the stranger and nastier it seemed. I had the sense that something obvious had been going on, something I'd been too stupid to see. One thing was certain, however: it was pointless to worry about what she might or might not have meant by anything she'd worn or said or done. I could translate "take care of yourself" easily enough. It meant "Goodbye."

I went back inside, picked up her wet towels, saw in the bathroom mirror that she'd marked my cheek with a scarlet blur in the shape of her lips. I wiped it off. I considered going back to sleep, but I had a class in an hour, so I poured myself the rest of the coffee and sat on the edge of my bed sipping it. Then I saw that Carol had forgotten her high heels. They were still on my dresser where I'd put them. Something monstrous happened in my mind; it was as though I were hearing, faintly, from very far away, a sound like cold steam at high pressure being forced through an opening no larger than a pin head. I picked up one of the shoes. It was a size 6. Inside, it said "Suzette." I couldn't tell if that was the name of the brand or of the style. The heel was thinner than a pencil and an inch longer than my index finger, the patent leather as shiny and black as the pupils of Carol's eyes.

9.

I DID not make a conscious decision to begin fasting. Within days after Carol had spent the night at my place, a terrible winter clamped itself down on Morgantown and hung on. The temperature dropped to well below freezing and stayed there. Instead of the usual flurries alternating with rain to turn the paths of the campus to mud-pie slush, the snow poured down and kept on coming—piled up, drifted, and clogged the streets until the campus looked like Siberia. Classes were cancelled, but I probably wouldn't have gone to them even if they hadn't been. Carol's visit had left me so depressed I couldn't do much of anything. That she'd forgotten her damnable high heels seemed like one of those mysterious accidents that isn't an accident at all. I kept digging into myself, looking for the tiny green shoot of hope that had sustained me after Cohen and Cassandra's visit, but I couldn't find it. My mind seemed as hopelessly contracted as the mercury in the thermometer nailed to the wall outside my door, and the snowstorm was the last straw. I'd run out of food; even worse, I'd run out of beer, but I couldn't force myself to go outside.

I searched my kitchen and the best I could come up with was half a box of stale Ritz crackers and the green tea Cohen had given me as a parting gift. I ate the crackers and drank the tea. In an attempt to escape into another world, I read Rilke. It was a mistake, I thought, to study him in a university course. I was certainly learning a lot more German grammar, but I'd lost something of the wild excitement his poetry had generated in me when I'd first discovered it, and I wanted to experience that again. I read Rilke until nearly four in the morning.

I woke far too early the next day, sick with the kind of steel-edged hunger that won't put up with any nonsense, the kind that says: DROP EVERYTHING YOU'RE DOING AND EAT SOMETHING NOW. I piled on several layers of sweaters and ventured outside. It had stopped snowing, but most of the sidewalks hadn't been cleared. I slogged up to Johnny's, but he was closed. Instead of trying to find the nearest open grocery store, I took off, driven by an obscure anger, walking quickly, sliding and nearly falling, panting, pushing myself hard, up to the elevation where Cohen and I had stood and watched the first snowfall in November. I found the sharpness of my hunger oddly satisfying, and that's when it occurred to me that maybe I was fasting.

I'd learned enough Buddhism by then to know about "the beneficence of the mind-body unity"—that what altered the body altered the mind, or, as Lyle used to say, that the purpose of training is to make the flesh match the spirit. "You've got to get light," he used to tell me, and he hadn't been talking merely about *physical* weight. I needed a major change in my life, and I was sick to death of waiting for it. I needed that change, not sometime in the constantly receding future, but *right now*. On the way back to my apartment, I bought oranges and apples. I'd read somewhere that fruit is good for you when you're fasting.

The first two days were truly unpleasant. The hunger never let up. I had sick headaches. I rationed out my oranges and apples, tried to stretch out the time between them. I drank tea and huge amounts of water. I kept coming back to Rilke and making entries in my notebook. I began to have extraordinarily vivid dreams. On the third day, I found myself seeing the world with a strange euphoric hard-edged clarity. My hunger was beginning to feel almost pleasurable—something to push my mind against like an inner knife blade. I vowed to walk in the snow for at least an hour a day no matter how bad I felt.

My mind kept making brilliant leaps, and I knew that I couldn't have achieved such speed and clarity with food weighing me down. Lines of Rilke's came burning up from the page and went sizzling straight through me. "*Du im Voraus vorlorne Geliebte, Nimmergekommene* . . . You're already lost, beloved . . . never going to get here . . ." Yes, I thought. "Ah, you were the garden. I saw you with such hope." Yes, *yes.*

The world had never looked sharper or brighter, and I understood why religious seekers have always fasted: everything was charged with meaning. I wanted to keep on going until I achieved a state that was as pure and clean and brilliantly focused as sunlight reflecting back from a mirror.

MORGANTOWN RETURNED to normal; the temperature went up, the rains came back, and the snow began to melt. Walking became easier. I had infinite energy. I walked for hours. Eating a whole orange or apple began to feel obscene; I ate either a single segment of an orange or a thin slice of apple, but never both at once, and I forced myself to wait at least an hour before allowing myself to eat again. Even though I kept the gas heater turned up high in my apartment all the time, I could never get warm enough. Taking endless showers, I used up all the hot water so often that the guys upstairs complained. I knew that Cohen was the only person who would understand what I was experiencing. I wrote him a long letter. A few days later I read it again and thought it was too extreme, too melodramatic—and too presumptuous. I'd said that I was sure I was right on the edge of a major satori. I tore the letter up and threw it away.

It never occurred to me that it might be a good idea to go back to classes. I jotted my insights into my notebook and continued to read Rilke. I copied his enormously evocative lines about childhood onto a card and taped it to my wall: "*O Stunden in der Kindheit, da hinter den Figuren mehr als nur Vergangnes war und vor uns nicht die Zukunft.*" Having spent years doing my best not to remember my childhood—putting it all behind me—I was now trying to remember every detail, trying to recreate that numinous feeling when, as Rilke says, what was behind each image was *more than merely the past* and what lay before us was *not* the future.

I kept running into huge holes in my memory and wondered what might be lost in there. Mere trivia? Or maybe something repressed but absolutely essential—something that might hold the key to my entire personality? I took the picture of me as Alice down from my altar to young girls, laid it on my desk, and shone the full light of my gooseneck lamp on it. What I wanted was impossible. I wanted to stare at that picture until I melted back into it.

I COULDN'T remember where my mother had found the dress, apron, wig, and petticoat. Maybe she'd rented them from a costume store. I clearly remembered borrowing the black patent Mary Janes from a girl named Cindy Douglas who lived two houses down from us. If our moms had been involved, I would have been too embarrassed to go through with it, but they hadn't been; I'd simply walked over to Cindy's house and asked her. She was a grade ahead of me, part of that familiar group of people called "the neighbors," and we'd known each other forever. Until I'd grown old enough to realize that boys shouldn't do things like that, Cindy and I used to spend whole afternoons playing with her dolls, and sometimes playing dress-up—which we'd both had enough sense to keep secret—so I knew her shoes fit me. She wasn't the least bit surprised to hear that I wanted to be Alice, but they were the shoes she wore to parties and church, and she was reluctant to lend them: "Promise not to get them dirty. Cross your heart and hope to die." I thought it was really nice of her to trust me, and I was careful not to get them dirty. Before I gave them back to her, I polished them, first with a damp cloth and then with a dry one, wiping away even my fingerprints.

I couldn't remember what had attracted me to *Alice in Wonderland* in the first place. I took the book out of the WVU library, brought it home and read it, found it to be witty and occasionally wildly funny. As a child, I hadn't felt that way about it at all. My mother had read it to me a chapter a night, and it had felt like an enormous saga, stretching out in all directions into infinity. It hadn't been the least bit funny then, but rather a magical journey—fascinating, bizarre, and sometimes deeply frightening. Yes, the Tenniel illustrations were the smudgy drawings I remembered, and maybe I had used them as guidelines for my costume, but I didn't feel any electricity coming from them, not a flicker of anything that would have said to me when I'd been seven: "You absolutely *have* to be Alice." But I seemed to remember another book.

All of my childhood toys and books had vanished long ago, so I couldn't simply go home to Raysburg and look on the shelf. I went back to the library, to the stacks where I'd found Alice. I could see at once that there were a number of different editions. I was prepared to look through them all, but I didn't have to do that. The third book I pulled off the shelf was the one. On the cover was a picture of Alice and her cat. The moment I saw it, the world went spinning out from under me and I had to catch the nearest shelf to steady myself.

In the earliest years of my childhood, I'd believed that some storybook characters were real people; I'd certainly thought that Alice was a real little girl. I now recognized in the Tenniel illustrations an element of caricature; when I'd been a child, I'd simply thought that whoever did those pictures couldn't draw very well. But the illustration on the cover of that other book was exactly what I'd thought the real Alice looked like. I might even have taken the painting for a photograph. The illustrator, some-one named Gwynedd M. Hudson, had moved Alice forward in time, and her Alice could easily have been one of my classmates at Jefferson Grade School—could, in fact, have been my first love, Nancy Clark.

Hudson's Alice was posed, standing just in front of her cat, exactly like a real little girl waiting to have her picture taken. Her house looked remarkably like our house. I could see, through an archway off to the right, a window seat exactly like ours. (It was a spot where I used to lie for hours and read.) Like Tenniel's Alice, Hudson's wore her long hair brushed straight back from her fore-head, but it was held with a modern hairband. When I was little, you could tell a girl's age by her skirt length; Tenniel's Alice wore a skirt that was, to my eye, far too long, but Hudson's Alice had it just right—above her knees where it ought to be—and she wasn't wearing long stockings with her patent leather shoes, but, just like any real girl I knew, little white socks. But the final touch that made her look so much like an ordinary little girl was the way she was standing: facing the viewer, her toes pointed straight ahead, one leg supporting her weight and the other bent slightly, her knees pressed together in a shy, modest, intensely girlish pose. She looked so sweetly awkward I knew she had to be real.

I laid the book with the Hudson illustration on my desk next to the picture of me. I took down my class picture from the sec-ond grade and put *that* on my desk. Now I had me as a boy hold-ing hands with Nancy Clark, Nancy Clark herself, the "real" Alice, and me as Alice. I remembered that wearing the dress, even the petticoats, hadn't felt the least bit strange but perfectly natural. Much like Hudson's Alice, I was facing the camera, but I hadn't imitated her girlish pose. I was standing with my feet about a foot apart. Looking at that picture, I realized that I hadn't been *imi-tating* a little girl, I'd *become* one. I didn't have to prove anything to anybody, didn't need to pose in an unnatural position with my knees pressed together. Because I was a girl, I could stand any way I pleased. My absolute conviction—based on an equally absolute ignorance of human anatomy—came through strongly in the picture.

As a boy, I'd been far less sure of myself. For my second-grade class picture, I was wearing a plaid flannel shirt and what appeared to be corduroy pants. My hair was neatly combed but, from the point of view of most adults at the time, far too long. I wasn't the shortest boy in the picture, but I was certainly the thinnest, so underweight I looked sickly. My face was inwardly focused, closed off, unreadable.

All of the girls in my class picture were wearing dresses, most of them nothing fancy—patterned fabrics, stripes and tartans—but a few, like Nancy, were in party dresses. Nancy's mother must have worked on her interminably to get her ready for the class photo; even in that small image, each separate ringlet was clearly visible. Nancy was already an experienced performer, accustomed to being looked at and photographed; she was staring straight into the camera lens with a pretty girl's prepared face that was just as unreadable as mine.

Neither of us was smiling. She appeared to be exactly my height. We were not trying to hide the fact that we were holding hands; we were doing just the opposite, raising our intertwined fingers toward the camera as though to make sure that everyone would notice.

I stared at those pictures, tried to put myself inside them, feel what I'd been feeling, think what I'd been thinking, but how much could I trust my own memory? I closed my eyes, searching for any evidence I could dredge up that was not merely a story I'd been telling myself over the years—not an embellishment, not an interpretation, not a falsification. What I wanted was a vivid image that would carry the weight of authenticity, and then, suddenly, I had it: my feet in black patent Mary Janes.

I'm dressed as Alice, standing at the back of the classroom, looking down at the floor. I can feel my hesitancy, confusion, embarrassment. Our class has just split into girls' activities and boys' activities, and I don't know which way to go. I look up and see Nancy Clark. She's some kind of princess: blue dress with a million petticoats, cardboard crown painted gold, rouge on her cheeks and bright red lipstick.

It's Nancy who saves me. She takes my hand. "Come on, Alice, sit by me."

Then that flicker of memory was gone, and I couldn't find much of anything else beyond what I always remembered: that I stayed with the girls and no one objected, that by the end of the day, they were all calling me Alice. My memory of walking around the schoolyard holding hands with Nancy tells me it was spring by then—trees budding, warm electric feeling in the air—but Halloween was in the fall. Could Halloween have been the magical moment when Nancy and I first connected? And if it was, did that mean she'd liked me as a girl?

A S I moved into the second week of my fast, I knew that I had to give up my orange segments and apple slices. I'd been pampering myself, trying to ease into things gradually, but all I'd done was avoid the clear burning heart of fasting. What was required was a purity as intensely focused as Bodhidharma's when—in the legend—he'd cut off his own eyelids so he wouldn't fall asleep when meditating. Suffering arises from attachment, and what was required of me was obvious, was Zen simplicity itself: *Do not eat anything.* I had only two oranges and two apples left, but I threw them into the garbage—and felt a wave of dark grief. Of course freedom was painful. What else had I expected?

Since I'd left high school, I'd been developing a little beer belly, but now it was melting away. Hollow spaces were appearing under my cheekbones; so that I could see them better, I shaved off my sideburns. I hadn't thought about losing weight, but now that it was happening to me, I was delighted. I began to spend long periods of time staring at myself in the mirror. Maybe, I thought, I would eventually become so thin that I would be able to see the sharp lines of my stomach muscles under the skin. Yes, that was possible. Anything was possible. Every object in the world radiated a fierce, nearly murderous power, and I felt myself just on the edge of being able to comprehend that power, absorb it, use it. Maybe that's what Cohen had meant when he'd said, *you're alive.*

I knew now that there had always been a great gulf fixed between myself—the thing that I called my *self*—and life. My *self* was a puzzle, a double-sided demonic construction that was irresolvable by ordinary means. I could not *think* my way out of my dilemma; I could not even *feel* my way out of it, but I could sense that there was plenty of power available in the world. If I kept on fasting, I might be able to tap into it. I now recognized my experience with Cassandra at the top of North High Street as a tiny satori, and it had been one of the most profound experiences of my life. So what would *the big one* be like? Incomprehensible. Far beyond words. A psychic lightning strike. And that was exactly what I needed. Sex is absolutely irrelevant to an enlightened being.

I WENT through my back issues of *Seventeen*, cut out more pictures of slender adolescent girls, and taped them to my walls. I thought of them as "muses." I retrieved Carol's high heels from the back of my closet and arranged them like art objects on my altar to young girls; surrounded by candles, their gleaming black surfaces reflected the light beautifully. I wrote in my notebook. I stared at my pictures. I stared at myself. Something deeply significant was about to happen. But I was also getting dizzy spells when I'd have to lie down. Walking was becoming difficult. I was running out of energy, but I didn't let that stop me. *Do not eat anything.*

I'd never had such trouble sleeping. Falling asleep was easy— I was drifting off a dozen times a day—but I couldn't stay asleep for very long. Bad dreams kept waking me up. I wandered through ominous buildings with endless corridors. I took strange trips on mysterious Greyhound buses that didn't seem to have drivers. But the dreams that really annoyed me—because I thought they were beneath me—were about food. Like a rat, I skulked into dark corners and gobbled up whatever the dream gave me: cheeseburgers, spaghetti, fried chicken. I sat down with my family at Grandmother Dupre's and ate one of her enormous Sunday dinners, the ones that had two kinds of meat, two kinds of potatoes, and both cake and pie for dessert. I ate with manic speed, shoved in the food and kept on eating. I was never satisfied, always woke up hungry, disgusted for having betrayed myself, even in my dreams. Hunger was my friend, my constant companion. *Do not eat anything.*

Some of my dreams were genuine nightmares that woke me to a racing heartbeat and an icy panic. I wrote some of them into my notebook. This was one of the most vivid ones:

I'm in Zoë's bedroom. (In real life, I've walked by her open door many times, but I've never stepped through it.) Looking at myself in a full-length mirror, it occurs to me that I should be wearing one of Zoë's dresses. It's a kind of joke. I open her closet and see the blue dress she'd been wearing the night I'd kissed her under the mistletoe. I take off my own clothes, put on the dress,

and it fits me perfectly. I'm thinking, this can't be right, nobody's
going to think it's funny, but I can't quite remember why I
shouldn't be doing it. Then I'm downstairs. There's a party going
on. It's Cassandra's living room, but it seems able to hold an infinite number of people. Everybody I've ever known in my life is
there—except for Zoë. It's important to me that I find her, and I
keep looking for her, but she's nowhere to be seen. I keep trying
to think of something I can say that will explain why I'm wearing her dress, but nobody's paying the least bit of attention to me.
I push through the screen door and step out onto the front
porch. It's like the front porch of Cassandra's house, but it's also
like the front porch of our house on the Island and the front
porch of my Allen Street apartment. I immediately feel the pressure of summer: high hot sun, smell of vegetation, trees in full
leaf, and I think: *Herr: es ist Zeit. Der Sommer war sehr gross.* It's
a line from Rilke, but in the dream it feels as though it's my own
thought, something that has just occurred to me: "Lord, it is
time. The summer was so full." Then I see that there's someone
sitting on the glider on the porch. I step tentatively forward. It
feels very quiet: the middle of an eternal afternoon of a huge
summer. I see that it's a girl. She's sitting with her feet up on the
porch railing and her head turned away from me so that I can't
see her face. All I can see is a sweep of long beautiful hair. I'm
painfully aware of wearing Zoë's dress. I hear the sound of my
own breathing, and I know that soon the girl will turn and look
at me. I'm instantly awake, sitting up in bed, my heart pounding.
Deeply frightened. Panting. Still trying to figure out what was so
frightening, still can't find words for it.

I THOUGHT that the girl in the dream might have been
Natalie, so I wrote her a long letter. It took me hours, but once I
finished it, I tore it up. I went for a long walk, came back, sorted

through my photographs, and found the two that I'd been remembering. One was of Natalie at Waverly Park; she was wearing a white dress shirt borrowed from me, jeans, and the cowboy boots she'd bought at the Jamboree Shop. She had on no make-up whatsoever. She was standing with her feet wide apart, her jeans low on her hips, her thumbs tucked into her belt just below her hip bones, facing the camera, leaning against an oak tree. "Don't smile," I'd told her. She'd tried not to, but the smile had gone to her eyes.

The other picture had been taken by a professional photographer at the prom. Natalie was wearing her baby-pink formal, her white shoulder-length gloves, and lots of make-up. I'd been standing to the left of the photographer, and Natalie was looking directly at me, giving me the kind of smile any boy would be delighted to get from a girl he liked. Each picture seemed incomplete without the other. I taped them up side by side. I was fully aware of what I was doing, what those pictures meant: Natalie as a boy, Natalie as a girl.

I'D BEEN sleeping an hour or two whenever I'd felt like it, and I'd gradually become separated from the rhythms of the ordinary world. I kept the drapes in my apartment closed all the time, so the only way I could tell whether it was day or night was to go outside and look. I began to feel as detached from my body as though it were a sullen mass of modeling clay, mucilage, and old bones. Eventually I couldn't walk for much longer than ten minutes, and my sleep began to have a nasty sick drugged quality to it. After a burst of letter writing—another one to Natalie, then one to Cassandra, and another one to Cohen—I didn't write anything. Even making notes took more energy than I could scrape up. I was, I had to admit, feeling terrible—downright ghastly, as a matter of fact—but there was only one thing I could trust, only one thing that would never fail me, and that was the tiny burning center of my own will saying: *Do not eat anything.*

The last in my series of dreams was the most frightening of all. I didn't write it down, but I remember it clearly. It began in such an ordinary way that it didn't feel like a dream at all. I woke up in the night, knew that I couldn't go back to sleep, sat up and lit the light. Everything in my room looked perfectly ordinary. I got up, put on my bathrobe, and wandered around my apartment wondering how I was going to kill the time; the only thing I could think to do was walk. Without giving it a second thought, I picked up Carol's patent leather shoes from the top of my bookcase and slipped my bare feet into them. They fit me so perfectly they could have been made for me, and I was surprised that I'd never worn them before. I put on my coat over my bathrobe, stepped outside into the night, and began walking toward campus.

It was bitterly cold, far colder than any night had a right to be in Morgantown, West Virginia. The sky was clear with the inky black of infinity; the stars appeared bigger than usual and were glittering savagely. Wearing Carol's high heels made walking a challenge, and that, I realized, was the point. It was a test. I had to walk like a girl, and, like a girl figure skater, I was being judged on my form. But, like a boy runner, I was also being timed. The text was extremely difficult because it had those two elements: a girl's grace and a boy's speed.

I walked to the hill above the stadium and back again. I knew that I had scored very well on the test, perhaps better than anyone else had ever done. Pleased with myself, I stepped into my apartment, took off Carol's shoes and put them back on my bookcase, undressed and got into bed.

I woke several hours later feeling groggy, sluggish, and sick. The dream had been so real that I had to check to see if I could really wear Carol's shoes. Of course I couldn't; I didn't even come close. All I wanted to do was take a hot shower and go back to sleep, but I knew I had to walk. I put on my coat and stepped outside. In the snow, from my door to the end of the alley and back, were footprints—delicate heart shapes from the ball of the foot, tiny puncture marks from the heels. For a moment I thought I might still be dreaming; then I knew that I wasn't. I checked Carol's shoes against the prints in the snow. They matched perfectly.

Then, with a brilliant flash of insight, I understood exactly what had happened. I'd slipped through the time continuum. It was easy enough to do; the only surprising thing was that it didn't happen to people more often. I had been the girl that Cohen and I had tracked into that cul-de-sac behind Woodburn Hall. Of course we hadn't been able to catch up to her. If I had met myself, it would have caused a cataclysmic disturbance in the continuum, an atomic explosion at the level of time rather than at the level of space—utter devastation.

I came back inside and threw myself onto my bed, still with my coat on. I couldn't tell if what I was feeling was cold or fear, but I was shaking all over. Even my teeth were chattering. As I was lying there trying to find a way out of the cul-de-sac, I fell asleep. When I woke again, I felt even worse. I was glad I was still wearing my coat. It didn't seem possible for someone to freeze to death while wearing a coat in a small apartment with the gas heater on high, but I felt as though that's what I was doing. I made tea and drank several cups. I took a hot shower, dressed, and looked outside. There were no footprints. It hadn't snowed for days.

I was truly desperate. I had to do something, but I couldn't figure out what. Then I saw my guitar standing in the corner. I hadn't played it since Carol had spent the night. That was odd. Hardly a day went by when I didn't play it for at least a few minutes.

I picked it up and tuned it. Without my conscious thought guiding them, my fingers began to pick out "The House Carpenter." The sound of it, the feeling of the strings under my fingers, was wonderful. Why hadn't I played my Martin? Where had I been? Except for a few words on the maintenance level necessary to buy something or check a book out of the library, I hadn't spoken with another human being since Carol had been there. Except for a half a box of Ritz crackers and my carefully rationed oranges and apples, I hadn't eaten anything for days—how many days I couldn't quite remember, but I knew that I was well into my second week. Maybe I'd even entered my third. I put my guitar down, stood next to the gas heater trying to get warm (I knew it was hopeless) and asked myself how I was feeling—asked the question in a clear detached way. I answered myself in exactly the same way. The best I could tell, I was feeling sick and crazy. Sartre was wrong, I thought. Hell isn't other people. Hell is the inside of your own head.

I could do *anything*. Of the many things I could do, one of them was to keep on fasting until I died. I called Marge Levine.

If Carol had answered, I would have hung up, but Marge got it on the first ring. "Hey, asshole," she said, "do you know what time it is?"

Of course I didn't know what time it was. Panicked, I stepped partway into the kitchen to look at the clock on the stove. "It's six-thirty," I said. "If you're having dinner, I'll call back."

"*Dinner?* What the hell are you talking about? I haven't even had *breakfast*."

Shit, I thought, it must be morning.

"Look, I'm sorry," I said, "but I'm kind of . . . I don't know . . . in a bad way," and then, as though someone had opened a sluice gate, words came pouring out of me: the beauty of fasting, Bodhidharma's eyelids, the sharpness and clarity of the world, on the edge of breakthrough, possibly even a satori, fantastic insights, flashbulbs going off in my mind, but weird places, *cul de sacs*, kind of scary . . .

"John, wait a minute. What do you mean, fasting?"

"You know. *Fasting.* A spiritual discipline. All over the world religious seekers have always fasted . . ."

"Shut up. Do you mean it literally? Not eating? You've gone a couple days without eating?"

"Oh, no," I said proudly, "it's been more than just a couple days. It's been at least two weeks."

"You're kidding. You're crazy."

"Oh, no, no, no. It's been great . . . It's just . . . Well, you know . . . when your dreams and your waking life get kind of mixed up . . . and you get kind of lost . . ."

"What do you mean, lost?"

Frustrated at trying to translate myself into something somebody else might understand, I yelled at her: "I've got myself into a really *weird place*. I've got to get out of this *weird place*."

She took me literally. Her sharp penetrating voice came crackling out of the telephone: "What are you talking about, John? Dropping out of school?"

"Oh, God, no," I said. "I mean a place in my mind."

"Oh, for Christ's sake." There was a long pause, and then she said, her voice lowered to a whisper, "Look, I really can't talk right now. Give me half an hour, and then meet me at Johnny's."

IT WAS not a long walk from my place to Johnny's, but I was so sick I had to keep stopping to catch my breath. Johnny's was packed with students having breakfast, but Marge had nailed down a table at the back. The first thing she said to me was, "Christ, you look like hell."

She ordered scrambled eggs, toast, and a chocolate milkshake. "I'm your Jewish mother, asshole. Now eat!" I sipped the milkshake. Within minutes I felt the sugar hitting me. It was like an electrical current I could feel throughout my entire body. I began to eat the eggs, taking small bites. Nothing in my life had ever tasted as good as those stringy overcooked eggs. "Now tell me what's going on," Marge said.

I tried again. It was hard to explain. Words really were no damned good. I heard myself wandering off into elaborate excursions: Rilke, the *I Ching*, seeing into one's own nature, intensely vivid dreams . . .

"Wait a minute," she said, interrupting me, "when did you start this craziness?"

"In the big snow. When they closed the campus. It was right after Carol pulled that all-nighter at my place and . . ."

"She did *what?*"

"You know, she had a paper to write. She came over to my place."

"She came over to your place *to write a paper?*"

Marge's eyes narrowed, and she looked out across the crowded restaurant at nothing. "Was she all dressed up?" she asked me.

"Oh, yeah. She had on a black sheath."

Marge remembered that night quite clearly, she said. Carol had told her that she was going to a party, that she was going to spend the night with Andrew. She'd left with him. None of that made any sense to me, and I said so. "Oh, my God, and she told me *a friend* dropped her."

"Seems pretty weird to me too," Marge said, "seeing as she hadn't spent the night with him before . . . and she hasn't since. So she gets him to drop her at your place, huh? My God, what on earth could she have told him? . . . It was supposed to make him jealous, of course . . . So what happened?

Did you *do* anything? You know what I mean."

I wasn't sure that it was any of her business, but I said, "Well . . . no."

"What did you do?"

I didn't answer.

"Come on, buddy," she said, "I'm just like Sergeant Friday . . . All I want's the facts."

"She wrote her paper and we talked."

"Talked? What did you talk about?"

Again I didn't answer.

"Oh, you don't have to tell me, but I bet it wasn't lots of fun, was it?"

I laughed. Then I realized that it had been a long time since I'd found anything funny. "No," I said, "it wasn't lots of fun."

I was finally getting warm. I kept eating bits of egg and toast, sipping the milkshake. Eventually I began to get downright hot. I started to sweat. I had to take off my coat. Marge had fallen silent. I could almost see the cogs turning over in her mind.

"Why have you been wasting your time on that little bitch?" she said. "Sure, she's pretty and bright, and she's also . . . Who needs it? I mean really? . . . It's too bad Natalie didn't go to school here. You seemed happy with Natalie."

"I *was* happy with Natalie." My eyes filled with tears. "Sorry," I said, "I'm kind of fucked up."

She let her hand rest on the back of mine. "Listen, John, you should have called me a long time ago . . . You've read Mills. If there's one man who can't find a job, that's a personal problem. If there's hundreds of men who can't find a job, that's a social problem. How many students do you think there are . . . all over campus . . . feeling lonely and isolated, going quietly crazy?"

I couldn't believe she was talking about C. Wright Mills. What the hell did he have to do with anything? She was asking me what would happen if all the fucked-up kids in America got together and understood that they didn't have merely *personal* problems. As I always did, I appreciated her passion—although I couldn't see how anything she was saying applied to me. I couldn't imagine any problem more personal than mine.

"If you ever get yourself in another mess like this," she said, "call me, OK? You're not alone. And I want you to promise me something. Just take it on faith for now, OK? Don't see Carol again. I mean, not for any reason at all. Not even for a Coke. Don't even talk to her on the phone. If you call our place and she answers, just ask for me and leave it at that. Do you understand what I'm telling you?"

I did understand. Far better than she might have guessed. "Yeah," I said, "I've got it."

"You've got to stop isolating yourself. Go back to classes. Come to SDS meetings. Play your guitar. Visit your friends. Find yourself another Natalie. There's a whole crop of freshman girls you haven't checked out. Come on, buddy, get with it."

I'D NEVER felt as grateful to anyone as I did to Marge Levine. She'd brought me back down to earth. But how had I allowed myself to drift so far away? I thought I'd been paying attention to the *I Ching*, but I obviously hadn't been. It had told me not to be alone. Now I was going to call Cohen and Cassandra.

I bought groceries, enough to fill two bags, and it damn near killed me to haul them back to my apartment. The moment I walked in, the heat nearly knocked me over. I'd been keeping the windows shut tight, the drapes drawn, and my gas heater on high. It must have been over eighty degrees in there. Oh, God, I thought, how am I going to pay my gas bill? I turned the heater off, opened my windows, and put the groceries away. I wasn't hungry, but I wanted to keep the nutrients coming, so I drank a glass of milk. I was yawning, my eyes watering; my mind felt thick and useless. If I didn't go to sleep soon, I might simply fall over where I was standing. I crawled into bed and was gone.

I slept nearly ten hours. It was a good sleep, a deep sleep, the best sleep I'd had in weeks. The sound of my telephone ringing woke me up sometime in the afternoon, but I couldn't think of any reason why I should answer it. I woke again to the sound of the rain falling steadily in the alley outside my open window. I loved that sound. Eventually I got up, walked out into the alley, lit a cigarette, and stared up into the rainy grey sky. I felt almost human. I knew I was going to be all right.

I heated up a can of mushroom soup and ate it slowly. It tasted so good I could have written a poem in praise of it. I looked around. Debris littered the floor in every room: scraps of paper, cut up magazines, rejected and crumpled up letters, dirty socks and underwear, jeans and shirts, damp towels. The place stunk of cigarettes, moldy tea bags, and my own misery. While I'd been fasting—while I'd been *gone*—I'd spent hours, day after day, poring through fashion magazines, clipping out pictures and taping them up. Behind my altar to young girls the images fanned out in the shape of a peacock's tail. They filled up every inch on the wall all the way to the ceiling, continued around the corner and invaded the other wall. They'd begun to appear in the kitchen and my bedroom. *Girls.* My God, I thought, the guy who's been living here was crazy as a bedbug.

The rainy wind blowing through my windows wasn't enough; I wanted a torrent of air. I opened my door. I needed to clean up the mess. I started by peeling the pictures off my walls. I was standing on a chair, stripping off a girl near the ceiling, when I heard the bang, bang, bang of hard leather heels coming down the alley. I jumped down off the chair just as Carol walked in. "You bastard," she said, "just what do you think you're doing?"

She stopped in the middle of my living room, rain streaming from the gleaming red surface of her raincoat. She was so angry she was panting. "Why the hell don't you answer your goddamned telephone?"

I felt my stomach clench into a knot. I finally understood something I should have known for a long time: I was frightened of her. "What are you doing here?" I said.

"How dare you?" she said, not yelling, but slamming the words out hard. "How *dare you* go around telling people it's all my fault?"

"Wait a minute. What are you talking about?"

"It's not my fault. How dare you say that? I tried to be your friend. I feel *utterly betrayed.*"

I could not imagine anything I might have done to betray her. All I could do was stare at her.

"Did you think I'd just let it go? Did you think you could tell any lies you pleased and get away with it? Did you think about *me* at all? Obviously not . . . It's time you faced up to yourself, John. Go over to the medical center and see a psychiatrist. That's what they're there for. But, please, in the future just leave me out of it. Do you want to know how I feel? Do you even care?"

Take a deep breath, I told myself. Go slow. Take it one step at a time. "I don't know what you're talking about. I honest to God don't. What do you think I've been saying about you?"

"You're dropping out of school, aren't you? Isn't that your latest brilliant plan? And it's supposed to be all my fault, isn't it? That's what you told Marge, isn't it? Oh, the bitch. I always knew she was jealous of me, but I didn't know she hated me that much."

"Carol, stop it. Just shut up for a minute, all right? What did Marge say?"

"She wasn't going to tell me anything. 'It's none of your business, Carol. It doesn't concern you.' Oh, the bitch. But when you called this morning, I heard her say, 'dropping out of school,' and I knew it. I've seen it coming for months. So, were you going to tell me? Or were you just going to leave town and let me find out later? After you'd told everybody that it's *all my fault*?"

It was so far-fetched, and at the same time so weirdly plausible, that I had to laugh. "I'm not dropping out of school. That's ridiculous."

She stared at me. "You don't have to lie to me."

"What on earth do you think I said to Marge? I never told Marge that anything was your fault."

I could see her hesitating. "Nobody has ever . . . How *dare* she? Nobody talks to me like that! She has an opinion on everything. 'I don't care whether you want to hear it or not, Carol, you're going to hear it.' Well, screw her. Who does she think she is?"

I was beginning to get the picture. It was all I could do not to laugh again. "How about me? What is it I'm supposed to have said?"

"Oh, for Christ's sake, John, you obviously gave her an earful. She told me to stay away from you. 'You let him alone, Carol. I mean it.' What *did* you tell her? How could you do that to me?"

"I didn't tell her anything. I know she doesn't like you. I wouldn't tell her anything about you."

She looked away from me. For a moment, her face looked oddly pinched, turned inward, and I felt a small victory. I didn't need to be afraid of her. What could she possibly do to me? "Carol," I said, "this is my place. I didn't invite you here. Would you please go home now?"

She deliberately unzipped her raincoat, slipped it off, and handed it to me. Stupidly, I took it and hung it up in the hallway. "Oh, John," she said in the voice of the teaching assistant, "whatever am I going to do with you?"

I DO not want Carol in my apartment, and, strangely enough, I'm not sure she wants to be here either. I've seen her grey suit before; it's one of her favorites. There's a pair of grey heels that goes with it, but she's wearing penny loafers instead—probably because she walked over. And I've seen her standing like this before: a peculiar stiffness in the way she holds herself, in the way she moves, as though the muscles in her lower back are contracted as tightly as door springs. Circling my living room, she studies the garbage bags, the cartons, the stacked up papers and books, the pictures and notes I've taped to my walls—and the ones I've begun to tear down. For the last half hour she's been giving me a lecture on why I shouldn't drop out of school. I've been telling her that I have no intention of dropping out of school, but she obviously doesn't believe me. "Could you close the door?" she says, "It's freezing in here."

I close the door and the windows. "Could you light the fire please?"

"No. I like it the way it is."

She sighs. "You don't have to be mean." Our eyes meet. "You're a terrible liar, you know."

"Oh, for Christ's sake."

I don't know how much longer I can put up with her, but for the moment I appear to be stuck with her. Relenting, I kneel at the gas heater and light it. I look at her and feel the same electricity I've always felt; I could never convince myself that she is anything other than beautiful. Marge was right; I shouldn't be seeing her. She shoves a stack of books off my big chair; they fall with a bang, and she sinks into it, still holding her back rigidly upright. "Carol," I say, trying it again, "I've got a lot to do, and I'd really appreciate it if you'd go home."

"Oh, God," she says, "you're impossible. Give me a cigarette, will you?"

I pound one out of my pack and light it for her. "So what do you think you're going to do with yourself?" she says.

I retreat to the far side of the room and say nothing. "Well, you must have planned *something*," she says. "I can't understand what you could possibly be thinking. The university is just made for people like you . . . You're so impractical, what on earth do you think you're going to do?"

"I'm not dropping out . . . Come on, Carol, it's true. Believe me, believe me, believe me. I'm not going anywhere."

She looks at me, smiling. Infuriatingly smug. "I don't know why you think you have to lie to me. I know you, John. This is one of your big, dramatic, romantic gestures. Utterly stupid. Utterly self-destructive. And somehow you're blaming it on me. And it's just not fair. I can't help the way things are, and neither can you."

We look at each other across the space of the room. Outside, the rain falls; inside, the gas heater hisses. There's a warning note sounding somewhere in the back of my mind; I can feel it as a tingle on my neck, my arms.

I have to find some way to get her out of here. I dump her high heels onto her lap. "Oh, my God, I've been looking for these. Where'd you get them?"

"You left them here."

"I *left* them here?" with a light tinkling laugh.

"Yes, you left them here. How the hell else do you think they got here? It was when you pulled that goddamn all-nighter . . ."

"OK, OK, don't be angry."

I'm not just angry, I'm furious. "Carol, for God's sake, just go home, will you? I really don't want you here. I can't make it any plainer than that."

A flash of anger in her eyes. Maybe she's going to blow her role as the infinitely mature older woman. She puffs on her cigarette. Eventually she butts it out. "All right, I won't *bother* you any more. But first, I want you to tell me just what the hell you think you're doing. You owe me that much."

I feel something in me snap. I'll say anything to get her out of my apartment. "Oh, for Christ's sake. I'm going to hitchhike to Florida. I'm going to tan myself dark as a buckeye. I'm going to work in a hot dog stand. I'm going to sit on my ass and play the guitar. I'm going to write the great American novel . . . All right? Now will you please just get the hell out of here?"

She sighs again, says in her most superior, big-sisterly voice: "Oh, John, it takes so terribly long to get any insight into yourself, and . . . You're not going to solve anything by running away, you know. No matter where you go, you're still going to have to face yourself."

"Look, Carol, I don't want to talk to you right now. Maybe I'll talk to you later, and maybe I won't. But will you just take your goddamn patent leather high heels and go home?"

She stands up abruptly. "I don't know what I've done to deserve this, I really don't."

"Oh, Jesus. Just get the fuck out of here."

"Please. You don't have to swear at me. I'm going. Just remember, I tried to be your friend." But she's not walking toward the door. She's walking over to my altar to young girls. She stands there studying it, then turns to me with her most glittering smile.

"You know, John," she says, "your little schoolgirls . . . they must be very convenient for you. Not only do you get to pretend to be a mature older man, but you can date them, and even fool around with them . . . but you never have to *do anything* with them . . . You *do* know exactly what I mean, don't you?"

I feel my body absorb the shock of it: something in my chest flinching away from her. I've had plenty of bleak thoughts about myself, God knows, but never that one, and she could very well be right, but that's not the most terrible thing. It's the cruelty of it.

She's still smiling. She turns back to the wall, pretends to be studying the pictures. Cassandra. Natalie. "Oh," she says, "and the other thing about little girls? They look an awful lot like little boys."

I'm one jump ahead of her: sometimes little boys look like little girls. Now I understand what's so frightening, so sickening, about what she's doing. It's not what she's said—or anything else she might find to say. It's the unmasking of her hatred. I still can't react, can't move, can't speak. Something is telling me to fight back, defend myself. Two can play this rotten game. She might know my weaknesses, but I know hers too.

"And now you're on your way to Florida," she says in a softly purring voice. "How very nice. Dropping out of school. Giving it all up. You must be deeply in love with him."

She's moving too fast for me. My voice does work, although it comes out low and harsh: "What the hell are you talking about?"

"Bill Cohen . . . Oh, John," and she laughs, "you're so obviously in love with him."

I grab the nearest thing I can get my hands on, a kitchen chair, and throw it, not at her, but at the far wall. It rebounds, skitters back, and falls. There's a smear of red haze in front of my eyes. "Listen, you bitch!" I hear myself yelling. She's looking up at me, her lips slightly parted, her face oddly shining and expectant.

I have always imagined that when the moment of revelation comes, it will require a mighty action, a heroic effort, a sprint to the finish. I have never imagined it like this. I hate her so much it's like swallowing acid, but she's just invoked Bill Cohen, and now that he's in my mind, all I do is stop. Attachment makes you slow, he'd said. See the human being in front of you. I look into her eyes and think: *equally empty, equally awake, equally a coming Buddha*. And then it's there like a beam of light. My God, I've been stupid and clumsy and slow. Why has it taken me so long to see the obvious? I've been like a sleepwalker.

I can still feel the adrenaline pounding through my body. I could easily do what she so badly wants me to do, what she's wanted me to do for months: slap that frozen smirk off her lovely frightened face.

I turn away from what I see in her eyes and walk out into the alley. It's raining hard, and I'm glad of that. I've always liked the rain. I crouch forward and cup my hands to get a cigarette lit. I stare up into the blue-black nothing of sky. It's not merely an idea in my mind; I can feel the pressure of the past, my attachment to the past, my desire for something lost in the past. But the past is not a place, and nothing will undo the chain of events that brought us here. Carol has to do exactly what she is doing. I have to do exactly what I am doing. We will continue to do exactly what we are doing, making the same mistakes over and over again without ever learning from them, and even if we change masks, put down old ones, pick up new ones, the attachment will remain the same, and the suffering will remain the same, and the process will go on forever through endless cycles of death and rebirth. It's true: the only thing worth studying is lock picking. Because Hell is not a literary conceit or a metaphor. Hell is not somewhere else. Hell is right here, and we're living in it. We should, at the very least, have compassion for each other. God help us.

I don't know what God I'm invoking, whether the Buddha in any of his incarnations or a more personal deity left over from my childhood, but I immediately feel an inner response and it's exactly what I've been seeking—a clarity that has nothing to do with choice, a power that enters me from the outside. The message is unmistakable. I've got to get out of here, and I'm already gone.

Author's Afterword

THIS, THE second volume of the *Difficulty at the Beginning* quartet, bears only a distant relationship to the version of John Dupre's story previously published as the second half of *The Knife in My Hands* (General Publishing, Toronto, 1981). The large general shape of the story is roughly the same, but nearly all the details of it have been changed. Although I incorporated some of the writing incorporated that appears in the published version, I based most of my work on earlier, unpublished drafts now housed in the archives at the University of British Columbia library. Much of the writing and all of the reorganization was done in the last two years, and I consider this book to be a new work.

I knew that if I wanted to get John Dupre's story right this time, I would have to revisit the places where the story happened, and it is only fitting that I thank a few of the many people who assisted me on my quest. Gordon Simmons helped me out so often and in so many ways that I don't have space here to list them all. Patrick Conner and Cookie Coombs shared invaluable memories of Morgantown with me. Harold Forbes, the Associate Curator of the West Virginia Regional History Collection at WVU, provided me with copies of the student handbook and university catalogues from John Dupre's years there and then went far beyond the call of duty to answer my long series of questions. Phyllis Wilson Moore, that greatest of friends to West Virginia writers, drove me around—and around and around—the city of Morgantown as I attempted to reconnect how it was then with what it is now.

John's opinions of WVU and Morgantown are, by the way, very much his own and are not those of the author. My years at WVU were quite different from John's and, in most respects, better.

The translations of Rilke that appear here and in later volumes of *Difficulty at the Beginning* are John Dupre's—that is, they were done by me in a way that I imagined John would do them. My colleague Andreas Schroeder assisted me in untangling Rilke's German. The "already lost beloved" poem is "*Du im Voraus.*" The lines "Lord, it is time (*Herr: es ist Zeit*)" and "Whoever doesn't have a house by now isn't going to be building one (*Wer jetzt kein Haus hat, baut sich keines mehr*)" are from "*Herbsttag.*" "Consider: the Hero sustains himself . . . (*Denk, es erhält sich der Held . . .*)" is from the First Elegy of the *Duino Elegies*, and Rilke's resonant comments on childhood ("*O Stunden in der Kindheit . . .*") are from the Fourth.

I want to acknowledge some of the other literary works that had a strong impact on me as I was writing this one. I am not talking about *influences*; I am talking about *dialogue*. In previously written versions of this story, Alice in Wonderland was always the figure John chose to embody on Halloween in 1949, but I doubt that I would have looked again as deeply as I did at Alice as a mythic figure if I hadn't been inspired to do so by my colleague Stephanie Bolster's brilliant book, *White Stone: The Alice Poems.* My *Bildungsroman* would not have taken exactly the shape it has if I had not been struck by the *clarity* of Meredith Sue Willis's splendid "Blair Morgan trilogy."

One cannot organize one's thoughts around concepts that have not yet been socially constructed, so it is not possible for John in the early 1960s to think in terms that we now might find useful—"gender dysphoria," for instance, or "anorexia"—and I tried to keep such contemporary concepts out of John's consciousness, but what I have written would not be what it is if I had not read Marya Hornbacher's stunning *Wasted: A Memoir of Anorexia and Bulimia*, a book I cannot praise highly enough.

Now I must make, and *mean*, the standard fiction writer's disclaimer: the people in this book are not real and should not be mistaken for any real people. John and Marge and Natalie are fictitious characters and so, of course, never sang in the basement of the Episcopal Church in Morgantown; neither did

WVU's minuscule chapter of the Student Peace Union ever meet there, and I should know because I was the president of it. But, having said that, I must also say that I have tried to make my characters, inside their fictitious world, as real as I can get them. And, finally, I must end with another standard line from authors' afterwords, one that I also stand fully behind: yes, many people helped me with this writing, but I am the one who is ultimately responsible for anything that's wrong with it.

Keith Maillard
Vancouver, October 31, 2005

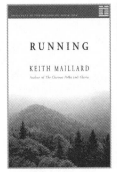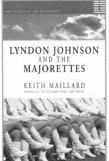

The *Difficulty at the Beginning* quartet follows John Dupre from his awkward high-school years in the late 1950s through the burgeoning counterculture movement of the early 1960s to the tumultuous and devastating late-1960s political and psychedelic underground.

Each of the four volumes is written in the style of the times. In *Running* the façade of post-WWII American optimism is just beginning to crack. *Morgantown* hums and throbs with the freewheeling energy and free-floating angst of youth pushing against the boundaries of social acceptability. *Lyndon Johnson and the Majorettes* situates the anxiety of the years following Kennedy's assassination and the impending threat of the Vietnam draft in the oppressive heat of a West Virginia summer. In the final volume, *Looking Good*, all the currents of the high sixties draw together in an explosive climax.

By any measure, *Difficulty at the Beginning* is a major addition to American and Canadian literature, a brilliant and supremely readable social chronicle that ranks with the best of North American fiction.

RUNNING • 1-897142-06-4 • SEPTEMBER 2005
MORGANTOWN • 1-897142-07-2 • FEBRUARY 2006
LYNDON JOHNSON AND THE MAJORETTES • 1-897142-08-0 • APRIL 2006
LOOKING GOOD • 1-897142-09-9 • SEPTEMBER 2006

BOOKS BY KEITH MAILLARD

Novels
Two Strand River (1976)
Alex Driving South (1980)
The Knife in My Hands (1981)
Cutting Through (1982)
Motet (1989)
Light in the Company of Women (1993)
Hazard Zones (1995)
Gloria (1999)
The Clarinet Polka (2002)
Difficulty at the Beginning
    Book 1: *Running* (2005)
    Book 2: *Morgantown* (2006)
    Book 3: *Lyndon Johnson and the Majorettes* (2006)
    Book 4: *Looking Good* (2006)

Poetry
Dementia Americana (1995)